THE MAN

WHO WOULD BE

KING

ADDISON J. CHAPPLE

WITH VINCENT LONGOBARDI

This book is printed on acid-free paper.

Published by:
Level 4 Press, Inc.
13518 Jamul Drive
Jamul, CA 91935
www.level4press.com

Library of Congress Control Number: 2019943923

ISBN: 978-1-933769-74-5

Printed in the USA

Other books by

ADDISON J. CHAPPLE

UNDER COVER

DESTINATION WEDDING

THE MOONBEAM SOCIETY

CON CRAZY

RAMBLING WITH REBAH

"Welch is where people would go to
die if they weren't already dead."

—An anonymous Travel Guide review

W elch, Iowa, is one of those towns that popped up after
World War II. Each house was popped out of the same
factory and plopped down on an identical quarter-acre lot.
Each house was occupied by a couple who each popped out two kids.
At least that's the way it used to be if you listen to the old-timers tell
it. Back in those halcyon days of the post-war boom, everyone wanted
to move to Welch. It showed you had a good job, good means, and a
good head on your shoulders, and that you knew how to provide for
a family. Not wanting to move to Welch during that time was tantamount to craziness.

Now?

Now is a different story, which is often how these things go. Now
all the girls leave as soon as they can for new and exciting locales.
Faraway places like New York City and Los Angeles, places where you
can make it and not get stuck married to a Mc or a Fitz who would
just wind up working at the mill or the plant. The boys stay behind to
work in the aforementioned mill and plant. They work there until the
day they drop dead. Inexplicably, that's always when they are about
fifty. No one has ever questioned it—it's just what happens. A man

is healthy one day and then the next day he croaks. It's simply the Welch way.

One such man, Benjamin Fitzgerald, or Jam, as he was nicknamed (because in Welch, a name of more than two syllables always necessitated a nickname), slipped out the front door of his house. He tugged down on his white 7-Eleven uniform as he left, trying and failing to smooth the wrinkles that consumed it. Tacked to the door were letters from the local homeowners' association, all complaints about the minor infractions that plagued the house his grandmother had let him have after she'd gone to the old folks' home: high grass, chipped paint on the fence, dirty windows.

He paid the accumulated complaints no mind, picked up his bike, and cycled into the street. He traveled past the uniform white homes, each with a uniform gray, American-model sedan in the driveway and a white picket fence. It was said that Old Man Fitzpatrick once painted his fence sky blue. If you believed the gossip, the homeowners' association had been so inflamed that a lynch mob had formed and dragged him out of town. Other, more level-headed individuals said he simply had a massive heart attack after he finished painting it and dropped dead on the spot. Either way, it led to a quick moratorium on the painting of fences any color but white.

Just like their houses with their white picket fences, his neighbors were all uniform, too. All wore khaki pants—or khaki skirts in the case of the women—paired with a neat, white button-down. They all had the same uniform names, all preceded with Mc or Fitz. An Epstein moved to Welch once, causing a small uproar, but luckily she soon married a Fitz, and the status quo was restored with a collective sigh. If there was one thing Welchers abhorred more than anything, it was a break from uniformity. They greeted each other in the same uniform manner. One would say, "How's the weather treating you?" To which the response was always, "It sure beats the snow! Ho-ho." This sometimes was accentuated with a guffaw or a slap on the knee, and the two would then proceed on their merry ways, happy to have fulfilled the

Welch social contract. This greeting even sufficed in the cold heart of winter, when snow was nearly knee deep. Conformity must be conformed to, no matter the present contradictions.

At the railroad crossing, red and yellow lights flashing, Jam came to a halt. He was in front of Mr. McCormack's house. Being that it was just past ten, McCormack was out in his khakis and button-down mowing his grass. It was a daily ritual. Every morning at ten o'clock he would come out, mow, rake, and then water. Spring, summer, fall, and winter it was always the same routine. Not even the weather stood in his way: sun, rain, and even snow. In the dead of winter, McCormack employed a system he had fine-tuned over decades. It involved the use of a snow blower, ample application of Miracle-Gro, and a series of UV lights that would be the envy of even the most prodigious pot grower.

McCormack's yard was the envy of Welch, and growing a fine set of grass of the proper shade of green and the ideal length of three-quarters of an inch (no more, no less) was known as "Growing a McCormack," an issue of much pride for those able to obtain it. That green was about the most color the whole town had.

The train flew by and the gates lifted. Jam pedaled off over the tracks and into the old commerce district. These days there wasn't much commerce going on. Strip malls lay abandoned, their signs fading and rotting away. Now they were just the relics of a past boom. The vacancies were blamed on Obama, before that on Bush, and when Jam was little, the decline of Welch was blamed on Clinton. Word had it that the homeowners' association was planning on passing the blame on to Trump just as soon as the matter was properly discussed and voted upon.

The last measure of commerce in town was the 7-Eleven, where Jam had found himself dutifully employed since his high school days. He liked to tell people that he was only working there while on break—a break from what was never explained, nor was it ever asked. He was simply on break. The 7-Eleven was a veritable hotbed of interstate commerce for Welch. It survived mostly on people who accidentally took the wrong exit on the interstate and were trying to find their way out of Welch, a town that inexplicably had a dearth of signage for its roads and surrounding highways.

Jam's best friend and fellow 7-Eleven clerk, Jim McLeod, leaned over the counter, hand perched under his chin, eyes fixed on the old cathode-ray tube television in the corner. The decades-old television's image flickered from age and several falls from the shelf. Like everything else in Welch, it was from a bygone era.

Jam walked into the store and took his place behind the counter. Jam and Jim had an important ritual at the beginning of every workday. In fact, it was the closest thing to a religious observance that either had. They checked their lotto tickets. After all, if they were winners and didn't know, they would be wasting an entire day working for no reason.

Jam was the official keeper of the tickets, and produced them from his back pocket with a flourish. In total, there were three tickets they hadn't checked yet, and he slid the first one into the lotto machine. The pair waited with bated breath at the prospect of instantly being propelled into the category of millionaires. The lack of cheery, digitized music emerging from the machine marked the ticket as a loser.

That loss did not deter the pair. Jam slid the second lotto ticket into the machine and was met with the same result. He held the final ticket in his hand and rubbed it vigorously for luck, then with closed eyes slid it into the machine's slot.

A second later a cheery tune played, announcing that they were winners. Jam snapped opened his eyes, hoping and expecting to see a sum with a vast amount of zeros attached to it. Instead, the amount was much smaller—single digits small, in fact; they had only won back the original amount they'd invested—three dollars. That always seemed to be the case with them.

With a shrug of acceptance, Jam purchased three new tickets with their winnings and resolved that those new tickets would indeed be the next jackpot winners. Eventually, their numbers would be the winning ones. After all, it was simple math.

Their morning ritual continued. If they couldn't be million-dollar lotto winners, they could at least win with scratch-offs. Both Jam and Jim produced a twenty and ripped off several scratchers. The pair was perennially broke, but somehow managed to always have twenty dollars for scratchers. Quarters in hand, they went to work, seeing if they would be able to walk away from the 7-Eleven forever that day. After several minutes of strenuous scratching, it was confirmed that they would need to keep their jobs.

The two then solemnly surrendered to another lackluster day of working behind the register.

As if on cue, a gray, American-made sedan pulled into the parking lot and a man in khakis and a neat button-down came in.

"How's the weather treating you?" the man asked as he approached the counter.

"What can I get you?" Jam said.

The customer froze, not sure how to proceed. The social order had been violated. The man's mind searched for possible explanations. The only one that dawned upon him was that the clerk behind the counter had misheard.

"How's the weather treating you?" the man attempted again.

Jam let out a long sigh. "It sure beats the snow, ho-ho."

The social order restored, the man smiled. "You know it! Can I get a pack of Lucky Strikes?"

Money was exchanged and a pack of cigarettes handed over. The man snapped his fingers, flashed a smile, and said, "You take care now, and watch out for that snow."

Jam inwardly shivered. Jim seemed to pay it no mind and kept his eyes fixed on the TV. With that same sticky smile on his face, the man loaded back into his gray sedan and pulled out of the parking lot.

"How was it this morning?" Jam asked Jim.

"Same, as always," Jim said. "Some smokes, some taquitos. Some kids buying beer."

"Did you sell them the beer?"

"Well, yeah. They had money. Why wouldn't I?"

No one ever told them they couldn't sell beer to kids. Sure, there was signage about the "recommended age" for cigarettes and alcohol, but no one explicitly told them not to do it. Meanwhile, the kids were so damn happy to get their beer that most left their change on the counter. That change quickly got used for scratch-offs that never won.

Jim flicked through the channels on the TV—*Cops*, soaps, and reality court shows—before settling on reruns of *Lifestyles of the Rich and Famous*. It was required watching whenever the two were together. It was an escape from banal life in Welch, and more importantly, it was a font of ideas: if those guys on TV could make it, what was preventing them from making it? "We're just one big deal away from 'champagne wishes and caviar dreams,'" Jam was overly fond of saying. What that "big deal" was going to be, neither of the two had the faintest clue. There had been multiple "big deals" over the years, and each ended in failure, but Jam always had a way of bouncing back.

"Would you look at that," Jim said and pointed at the TV.

The rich bastard had a swimming pool surrounded by an aquarium. You could watch the fish swim as you swam. It was a degree of opulence normally reserved for the most outlandish fictional films, but there it was in real life.

"App money," Jam grunted.

"App money," Jim agreed

App money was a sore subject. They'd had a killer idea for an app a few years back. Only problem was, neither of the two knew how to program. It was all the fault of the public schools, they decided. In order to make their champagne wishes and caviar dreams come to fruition, they'd fallen upon the logical idea of outsourcing the production of the app to an outsider. After all, isn't that what every American business does these days?

Unfortunately, for Jam and Jim, the outsourcing company was a scam job intending to steal people's money, and the pair was just another set of unwitting victims.

Fortunately, a quick-witted bank teller noticed the irregularity associated with the transaction and froze Jam's account. It was quite obvious when one considers that Jam's debit card had never been used outside of Welch, and even more obvious when previously it had only been used to buy beer and cigarettes and never to purchase the western hemisphere's largest collection of foot fetish magazines, as the scammers had attempted to do.

But that was several "big deals" ago, and none had been even remotely successful.

Aside from *Lifestyles of the Rich and Famous,* Jam had another source for ideas: the store's magazine rack. He flipped through the pages of *Fortune, Forbes,* and *Business Insider* looking for key words that would home him in on the next big thing. Mostly, he tried to find articles about people who made it big before they hit thirty and were on easy street. That was where the app idea had come from, but Jam was a diverse man and open to multiple avenues of wealth. A good businessman had to keep his eyes open to every opportunity, as long as that opportunity involved the least amount of work possible for the highest reward.

Jam's face lit up. "Check this one out. This dude started a company at twenty building cell phone towers in rural areas with no service. He already made a hundred million in the last ten years. We could totally do that—think about how shitty the service is outside of Welch."

Jim wasn't paying much attention. He simply said, "Those towers are pretty tall and I don't like heights."

That was a thought that hadn't crossed Jam's mind. "Damn, you're right," he said. That idea was quickly discarded and Jam began his search for the next big deal that would bring them their millions. He worked his way through the first two magazines in quick succession. The problem with most of the business models presented was that they all required long hours, hard work, and copious amounts of dedication. All things that Jam lacked and shunned. If he couldn't be a millionaire overnight, what was the point?

Jam's fingers drummed across the counter as he searched through the final magazine. "Here's one," he said and jabbed his finger at the article. "This guy is crowdsourcing cleaning the ocean from plastics and shit, and he has already raised a couple million dollars, and they said real investors are going to come in soon and finance the rest. We could totally do that."

Jim was deep in thought and didn't say anything.

"Plus," Jam continued, "I bet we can convince mad girls to come on the boat with us while we clean the ocean. Girls love partying on boats."

Jim stayed silent for a long moment. "What about sharks?" he then asked.

"What about them?"

"Think about it. How many movies have we seen that started out like that: bunch of guys on a boat with girls and then next thing you know they're all getting eaten by sharks."

"Shit," Jam said somberly. That was the way things went once you got out on the ocean partying—you were a goner, for sure. "This dude is done for. He is going to get eaten his first trip out."

Quickly growing bored with the unattainable dreams of the show and Jam's equally unattainable ideas, Jim sauntered over to the magazine rack and pulled out the latest issue of *Soldier of Fortune*. Leaning on the counter, he opened it to a random article, tongue sticking out as he tried to read it. His undiagnosed dyslexia made the letters a confusing jumble. With a furrowed brow, he finally deciphered most of the article. "These SEALs are crazy; they rescued some kidnapped girl down in Somalia from pirates. Jam, we should have joined the army."

"Huh?" Jam said as he looked away from the TV. "Why's that?"

"We would have been beasts in the army. Think about it, bro. Have we ever lost a match in *Call of Duty*?"

"Fuck, man. You're right. We missed our calling."

"You know how many girls those army guys get?"

Jam didn't really care. He would probably be a virgin on his wedding day. "You know what we're missing, Jim?"

Jim hadn't the faintest idea. "What's that, Jam?"

"Think about it. At the end of every level in *Call of Duty*, and in the movies, they always blow up the bad guy's base. If only we had something to blow up . . ."

All the synapses in Jim's brain fired at once. "Wait right here! I'll be back!"

Before Jam could respond, Jim was running out the back door. He ran down the street toward his house. Nothing could deter him on those rare occasions when his mind was set to something. He ignored the "How's the weather treating you?" greetings of passersby and ignored the pebble that firmly implanted itself in his shoe and then in the sole of his foot. He ignored his mother working in the front garden and stormed the garage. It was there that he found the object of his desire: a red backpack.

Barely stopping his run, he scooped it up and turned tail the way he'd come. Again he paused for no one—nor for that burdensome pebble. He had a goal that needed to be accomplished, and Jim knew if he delayed in his task, he would forget all about it.

Jam was waiting in the very spot where Jim had left him. Jam was very accustomed to these flights of fancy, though he often didn't know what they entailed until Jim returned. But for Jim to have been so motivated to take off in a run like that, Jam knew it had to be good.

Only after dropping the bag to the ground did Jim pull his sneaker off and shake out the beetle-sized pebble that had lodged itself in his foot and torn a wide hole in his sock.

It was then the big unveiling was conducted. Jim proudly ripped open the backpack. It was full of fireworks, from the smallest cherry bombs to the largest drums. The contents had been collected over the past months in preparation for Independence Day, because the best way to celebrate the birth of your country is by blowing up a small part of it.

Jam rubbed his hands together eagerly. He knew exactly what they were going to blast to smithereens. "Jim, grab the trash and drag it outside."

Behind the store, the pair cut open the firecrackers and dumped the gunpowder they contained into the giant trash can.

Back in the store, the ignored customers coming in for the lunch rush dutifully adopted the honor system. They had become accustomed to the pair going MIA, and their Midwestern sensibilities would not allow them to leave without paying for the goods they took. So, they carefully noted what they had taken on a notepad, left their money on the counter, made change from the money already left on the counter, and if that couldn't be made, they left careful notes stating that they would return later to pay the balance. Most even calculated the sales tax owed and included it. After all, it was the least they could do.

Jam and Jim were just finishing the vital task of filling a can of trash with gunpowder. Satisfied, they placed a large firecracker face down to serve as the detonator.

"Blow it, soldier," Jam ordered.

"Roger that, sir." Jim snapped a salute, produced a lighter from his pocket, and ignited the drum's charge.

The two darted behind the corner of the building and waited. Their heads peered out, Jam on top with Jim squatting below, both smiling like it was Christmas morning. This was going to be epic. It was going to go off any second now.

Any second now . . .

It just needed another second to go off.

Nothing happened.

The pair blinked in unison.

Then there was a slight pop and fizzle. *Here it comes*, they both thought and then—again—nothing.

"I don't think it took, Jam," Jim said sadly. It was the same tone a child would use if that child discovered Santa didn't exist.

"Let's light it up again," Jam answered, undeterred.

The two scurried out from their hiding spot and got within two yards of the trash can when a sudden whistle occurred. That lone whistle was soon joined by an angry orchestra of pops and whistles. Thick black smoke poured out from the can. The duo froze on the spot. Neither able to advance nor retreat, they were fixated by the burning refuse in front of them.

With one final hiss, the gunpowder caught, and a deafening roar raced over them. The can exploded in a shower of plastic and the accumulated refuse of the past week. In silent awe, Jim and Jam braved the stings of plastic shrapnel, old cardboard, apple cores, and wasted taquitos.

Covered in dirt and grime, the two turned to each other in shock. Finally, as if on cue, both jumped up and high-fived.

"Awesome!" they declared as one.

2

"Treasurer Luxury Black, the cigarette
that says 'fuck you' to cancer."

—A REJECTED AD SLOGAN

Moments after the very successful destruction of the trash can, Jam and Jim were busy counting the accumulated money on the counter left during their escapade. It was a double victory: they got to blow shit up and avoid the humdrum interactions that their fellow Welchers would have imposed upon them. Also, the counting of the money kept them away from the unenviable task of cleaning up the mess they'd created; hopefully they would be able to leave it for the next shift.

A roar louder than the exploding can reverberated through the store as a yellow Lamborghini with Massachusetts plates sped into the parking lot and, with screeching, smoking tires, came to a quick, perfect halt.

Jam and Jim pressed themselves against the glass to get a better look at a car they had only ever seen in movies and magazines. It seemed as if the car was from a sci-fi movie, because the doors opened up instead of out.

The driver was a super-rich, style-conscious, entitled-looking dude wearing a Bluetooth earpiece, a Boston Red Sox cap, Gucci aviator sunglasses, skinny jeans, and Ferragamo shoes that cost more than Jam and Jim made in a month combined.

The woman who emerged from the passenger side was a platinum-blond mannequin. It would take a team of expert surgeons just to find something still natural and original on her body. Jam was in love. She was everything he could possibly want a girl to look like, just like the girls from music videos, or from that one scrambled channel on cable back in the day. Once Jam got his champagne wishes and caviar dreams, he would be able to date a girl just like this.

The automatic doors opened with a ding as Super-Rich Ken Doll strolled in, chatting away on his Bluetooth. "Yeah. I don't know when I'll get there. The GPS fucked up and sent me through some May-fucking-berry-looking town. I'll call you in a bit."

Super-Rich Ken Doll strolled up to the counter as Platinum Barbie went to the beverage aisle. Jam and Jim stared slack-jawed at the pair. The man looked over the selection of cigarettes and sucked on his teeth in disdain. Finally, a pack held in a unique display case that was coated in the accumulated dust of years of zero sales caught his eye.

"Yeah, let me get a pack of Treasurer Luxury Black," he said.

Jim took a deep swallow, Adam's apple working up and down in disbelief. "Treasurer Luxury Blacks?"

"Treasurer Luxury Black." Super-Rich Ken Doll dragged out each syllable as he pointed at the cigarette packs that were held in the special humidor to keep them fresh.

"Those are eighty-nine bucks a pack," Jim said, more in a warning than as a statement of price.

"You don't say." The tycoon produced a money clip from his pocket. It was solid gold, with its slides encrusted in diamonds. The stack of bills in it was thicker than the length of McCormack grass. He peeled off a hundred and dropped it on the counter, then quickly added a second hundred. "Plus, whatever she wants," he said. "Babe, I'll be in the car making some calls."

Jam had a plan. With her boyfriend heading to the car, it was now time for Jam to makes his move. He didn't have much information to go on, but he knew she was from Massachusetts because of the license plate and her boyfriend's hat. All he needed to do was find common ground with her, and Jam knew exactly how to do that.

She waved coyly back at her beau and Jam wasted no time. She was taking a Lime-a-Rita from the fridge. *Whoa!* thought Jam. *She is hot to trot.*

"Hey," Jam said as he leaned against the adjoining fridge door.

She looked at him, vibrant green eyes half hidden under long curled lashes. Jam briefly wondered if such a green was naturally possible or if those eyes were store-bought, like her blond hair. "Hey." Her voice was high but throaty and her "hey" had three syllables.

Jam flicked away a piece of an old, brown apple core that was stuck to his collar. "So, you know, when I'm not working here I go to MIT."

A perfectly fake glittery nail popped the canned margarita open. "MIT?" she questioned, as she fluttered her eyelashes.

Jam let out a slight, breathless giggle but quickly recovered. "Yeah, the Massachusetts Institute of Technology."

"In Boston?" She brought the can to her lips and leaned her head back ever so slightly, neck muscles working as the sweet elixir passed down her throat. Finishing her sip, her pink tongue glided over collagen-enhanced lips.

Jam couldn't help but watch, momentarily lost in the thought of what those lips and tongue could do. "Uh. Yeah, in Boston."

She toyed with one of her hoop earrings. "What do you do there?"

"I don't know."

"Oh? Where do you hang out?"

"I don't know."

"Oh? Where do you live?"

"I don't know."

She smiled and batted her eyes in a way only a girl who'd already heard every line from much smoother players could. She read his nametag, where Benjamin was sloppily crossed out and Jam was written below it. "Well, I'll see you later, Jam from MIT."

All Jam could do was watch that specimen of perfection walk in perfect rhythm to the counter, close out her tab, and then disappear from his life forever.

"How did it go?" Jim asked sincerely.

"Pfft," Jam let out. "What the hell does that dude have that I don't?"

"It's probably app money." Jim thought for a second. "Or greenhouse money. Probably greenhouse money. Those guys make bank."

"Fucking greenhouse money," Jam grumbled.

Greenhouse money was another sore point for Jam and Jim—another "big deal" gone haywire. Things had started out pretty well for the pair, progressing further than most of their "big deals." They had managed to actually set up the initial greenhouse but had been unknowingly roped into an illegal marijuana-growing scheme. Somehow, banking on his good fame from the app scam, Jam had managed to convince the police that, again, this had all been a preplanned setup. He presented as a model citizen instrumental in the sting. This goodwill earned him another front-page article in the *Welch Watcher*, pushing the twenty-fifth annual Thanksgiving pie-baking contest off the cover.

Jam ground his teeth. Ken Doll and his picture-perfect girlfriend rubbed him in all the wrong ways. There was no way he could stick around there all day serving Slurpees, smokes, taquitos, and beers.

Jam had to get outside and clear his head. There was only one way he'd be able to get his mind off of that asshole. "I'm going to visit Grandma. You're in charge, Jim. I'll catch you at the bar later."

Ample Hills was like every other retirement home—that is, if every other retirement home shared the same name as the local cemetery and was situated directly across the street from it. If any of the residents noticed or cared, they certainly weren't talking about it. Likewise, no one talked about how the logo of Ample Hills closely resembled a woman's buttocks. It was just one of those unspoken oddities of life in Welch.

Jam knew exactly where he would find Grandma Jelly; it was the spot where she always spent the afternoons: perched on an old recliner, knitting some socks or other knickknacks that she gifted away. Everyone knew her spot and knew not to sit in it lest the supply of knickknacks dry up for whomever took her favorite chair.

Jelly wasn't her real name, truth be told. Jam didn't even know her Christian name. Nor was he entirely positive whether his nickname of Jam came about because of her nickname, or if it was the reverse—or if they came about at the same time. For as long as he remembered, back to when his parents walked out on them, she was always Grandma Jelly and he was always Jam, but to Jelly he was always and only Benjamin. If Jelly knew which name came first, she certainly wasn't telling anyone.

The halls of Ample Hills smelled of antiseptic and something subtler, a far stranger aroma for an establishment of this sort—the smell of coconut oil and baby oil lubricants. The home's bulletin board was filled with flyers advertising a crafts day for grandchildren, meeting times for the local smutty book club, a geriatric spin class, and a request that a lost or stolen purple, double-ended dildo please be returned to room 5B cleaned and sanitized.

Old ladies sat around the common area in muumuus, shifts, and housecoats. They perused books on baking and handicrafts, as well as others whose covers featured heaving bosoms and men with long, flowing hair and eight-pack stomachs. They also enjoyed magazine centerfolds of scantily clad firefighters and policemen; some even went the more risqué route and fixed their gaze on centerfolds of women many years their junior. The staff gave up long ago trying to enforce a modicum of decency and modesty and just decided to go with the flow and leave the old ladies to their own devices.

Jam found Jelly in her usual spot, in her usual flower-print dress.

Jelly looked up from her knitting, and that toothy smile spread across her face. "Oh! My sweet Benjamin! I'm so glad you came. I was just knitting you some socks. It's going to be fall soon, and you're going to need something to keep you warm." She held up the multi-colored yarn that was quickly coming together.

Jam plopped down on the couch next to her. "Thanks, Grandma Jelly," he said with a sigh.

"What's wrong, Benjamin? You don't seem yourself today."

"It's just—"

Jam didn't have time to finish his thought before Gertrude, the feistiest of the octogenarians, snuck up and slid onto the couch next to him. Her hand slipped up Jam's thigh. She coquettishly ran her tongue over her toothless gums before speaking. "Why, Jelly, isn't he a handsome one. Why don't you introduce us?"

Jam stuttered, his brain entering fight or flight mode as Gertrude's hand rapidly advanced toward his bulge, which was rapidly growing. His brain screamed for immediate flight, but his body decided petrified terror was better.

"He's my grandson, Gertrude," Jelly growled. "Leave him alone."

"Oh," Gertrude bemoaned playfully. "That's a pity. Well, if you ever want to taste my peach pie, you know where to find me. And afterwards I'll even bake you a pie." She winked and once again ran her tongue over her toothless gums.

Jelly eyed Gertrude as she went off seeking a new victim amongst the visitors at Ample Hills. With Gertrude quickly out of earshot, Jelly moaned, "Oh, Benjamin, you don't know how hard it is here for me. I've even been thinking about crossing over."

Jam hadn't the slightest clue what his grandmother was referring to. "Crossing over? You mean dying?"

"No, I'm not going anywhere. Switching teams."

"Grandma Jelly, you can't do that! The Cougars need you. You're the best shortstop they've ever had. Without you, they'll never make the playoffs."

"Oh! Sweetie, I could never leave the Cougars. I mean switching teams sexually. Lesbianism."

"Oh," was all Jam could muster.

"There are no men around for us old ladies. And you know I won't pay for it like the rest of the hussies here. There's only Al." She sighed.

Old Al was the king of Ample Hills, by virtue of being the only man in the establishment. King Al was an anomaly in Welch. He had beaten the odds by any measure of the term. Reaching the ripe old age of eighty, he had defied the Welch curse. The curse certainly wasn't idle when dealing with him, having thrown everything his way. This included several heart attacks, a stroke, massively high blood pressure, and uncontrolled diabetes. Each one King Al defeated or tolerated and carried on with. He held court in the corner of the room where the ladies fawned about him.

In the blink of an eye, the conniving, horn-dog looks of Jelly slipped back into that of the old, doting grandmother. "But what's wrong, my sweet little Benjamin?"

Jam's shoulders slumped. "I don't know, Grandma Jelly. This rich asshole came in the store today, and it just pissed me off. After all the big deals, I've got nothing to show for it." The word "deals" was stretched out with a long "eel." It was the only way Jam ever referred to any of his get-rich-quick schemes.

"Don't you worry about him. Your big deal"—Jelly said deal in the same way—"is going to pull through someday, and you're going to stick it to everyone how big of a success you are."

Jelly always seemed to have a way to uplift Jam's spirits. No matter what, she was able to put a positive spin on things. "You really think so, Grandma Jelly?"

She'd never been so sure of anything in her entire life as she patted her grandson on the knee. "Of course I do. You're my grandson. We always win in the end. It's a family tradition. Everyone said I would never be able to get your grandfather and that I should just give up and find someone in my league. And did I listen to them?"

Jam shook his head like an oversized bobble-head.

"Damn right," she continued. "I made sure to get him so drunk at the Watering Welch that he didn't know up from down. We had a magical night together and then your father was on the way and your grandpa was locked in after that. The next thirty years were the best years of my life."

Then at fifty, like a good Welch man, Jelly's husband dropped dead on the spot, but that goes without saying. "So, no one can tell you it's not going to happen. The next big deal is going to be the one."

"You're right, Grandma Jelly," Jam said, beaming. "I'm going to get out there and work on the next deal. I was just reading this thing last night about timeshares in Venezuela. I'm sure there's a fortune to be had!"

"You go get them, my sweet Benjamin!" Jelly smiled back.

Victoria, or Vic as everyone called her, was perched inside the Ample Hills pharmacy window. She was a rare case—one of the few girls who decided to come back to Welch after going away to college. She was the prototypical girl next door. Technically, she was the girl around the corner from Jam, but that would just be splitting hairs. Spotting Jam, she waved. It was more than a simple wave of the hand; it was the type of wave where each finger moved independently of each other, each giving their own little wave, starting with the pinky and working its way to the thumb. It was a wave that carried a certain warmth and affection. It was a wave that Jam was oblivious to.

"Hey, Jam," she called out and leaned over the counter.

"Hey, Vic," Jam greeted back half-heartedly. He was mid-fantasy about the Venezuelan timeshare money that would be had and the fame he would obtain as a timeshare mogul.

She bit her lower lip. "Whatcha doing?"

"Just visiting Grandma Jelly. Had to get out of the store for a while. Work was making me angry."

"Everything okay?" she asked with genuine concern.

"Yeah, I guess. This guy came in. Some highfalutin dude. What's worse is he had this smoking hot girlfriend. Vic, you had to see this girl. There's never been a girl like this before in Welch."

"Oh? Tell me more." Her voice dripped with venom.

A more astute, mature, aware, conscious person would have known to shut his trap and move on, but Jam was none of those things. "She was the type of girl that was just perfect, you know? Everything about her was perfect."

Vic rolled her eyes and, changing the subject, said, "What about *him*?"

"Him?" Jam shrugged. "Living Ken Doll?" Even as he spoke the words, there was a certain envy in his voice. "He was driving a yellow Lamborghini with doors that went up like the car from *Back to the Future*. What makes him deserve a Lamborghini? I should have a Lamborghini after all the big deals I've put together. What does he have that I don't have? This is some bullshit. I should have his money."

Vic rolled her eyes again and sighed. It was a conversation that she'd had dozens of times with Jam. "Money isn't everything."

Money isn't everything? Claiming that money wasn't everything was a foreign concept to Jam. Sure, he'd heard about the idea, but it was completely and utterly lost on him. He couldn't possibly fathom not caring about getting filthy rich. Jam stared at Vic like she was nuts.

3

"My pirate kidnappers were very professional. My cell was roomy and there was weekly laundry service offered. Netflix was provided, but Internet service was spotty at best. All in all, it was an enjoyable experience. I would get kidnapped by them again."

—Four-out-of-five-star review on Yelp for a Somali Pirate Gang

The Watering Welch had existed for as long as Welch existed. It was the premier bar in town, though this was largely due to the fact that it was the only bar in town. Like everywhere else in Welch, options were not an option. Like the rest of Welch, there was uniformity to the Watering Welch, down to the sawdust on the floor, presidential campaign posters from the last president Welchers took a liking to (Dwight Eisenhower), and the Welch-centered advertisements on the wall. If it wasn't for the pair of TVs shelved above the bar, there would have been no connection to the world outside of Welch, and that was the way every good Welcher liked it.

Like the rest of Welch, the clientele were all cut from the same cloth. It went beyond the khakis with the neat button-down; it carried over even to what the patrons of the Watering Welch drank. They each ordered a Dewar's whiskey on the rocks with a Busch Light beer backer. There were, of course, other bottles of alcohol lining the shelves, but those were all coated in a thick layer of dust and dutifully ignored. They each drank with their right hand and balanced a Lucky Strike cigarette between the index and middle fingers of their left. Word of the ban on smoking in bars had not yet reached Welch and would almost certainly be ignored when it did.

The bartender, Fitzroy, didn't give Jam and Jim the chance to order before placing the dual whiskey-beer drink in front of them, and he quickly followed it with an ashtray he set between the two. Ordering wasn't a thing at the Watering Welch. Neither was the option of not smoking, though he did hold their drinks for ransom till they answered properly to the question "How's the weather treating you?"

"I got a good feeling about this big deal," Jam said as he lit up a Lucky Strike.

Walking over to the bar, they had been discussing Jam's latest big deal that would finally earn them fame and fortune, this time through the dizzying heights of timeshare ownership. It had largely been a one-sided conversation, though, as Jam had explained how he'd come about it and Jim had just nodded along. It was through an Internet forum of like-minded get-rich-quickers that someone had posted a link to a shady website. Even amongst that gullible crew, the general consensus was that the whole operation was a straight-up scam. Jam, however, believed that it all rang true and that the others on the forum were just trying to discourage him from making money. He'd phoned the website and through a series of calls, he'd become a true believer in the idea of the fortunes to be had through timeshare ownership.

"Me, too, Jam." Jim bobbed his head eagerly. Jam was always able to come up with the best ideas, at least according to Jim. It was a damn shame that some outside trash always screwed them up. "I never heard a bad thing about Venezuela."

"Timeshares are definitely the next big thing. What's not to like? It's like a vacation that you own. You can't go wrong."

With a solemn nod exchanged between the two, they clinked their glasses and threw back the whiskey, slammed their glasses on the bar, and followed it with a sip of beer. Without needing to be asked, Fitzroy appeared and quickly topped off their rock glasses with more whiskey.

A certain look spread over Jim's face: a look that only appeared when he was deep in thought. It was similar to but different from his reading face in that his tongue did not stick out. "Jam, I got a question."

"What's that?"

"Where are we going to get the money for the timeshares?"

"From an investor, of course. Who wouldn't want to invest in a big deal like this?" Jam was utterly assured that an investor would swoop in immediately to be a part of their big deal. After all, the guys in those business magazines always seemed to have an angel investor come in—it was just the way these things went.

"Of course." The answer made perfect sense to Jim as well. Jam always had the answers for their big deals, even though they always wound up failing in the end. Another question sprang to Jim's mind. "Jam, how are we going to make money off the timeshares?"

Before Jam could answer, the two of them were pulled by a force from behind and embraced in an awkward three-way hug. "Hi, guys!" Vic said cheerfully. "What are you talking about?"

Jim opened his mouth but Jam jumped in first and said, "You know . . . things."

Vic, with her hand on her hip, tilted her head to one side. "Is it about a big deal?" She said it in the same way Jam would stretch out the "deal" into a long "eel."

Jim started, "Yeah, we got a good one now. We are going—"

"Stop! Don't tell her!" Jam interrupted.

Vic humphed and looked away in mock disdain. "Why not? Are you afraid I'm going to steal your idea and make millions instead of you?"

"It's not that, Vic. It's just when you put things out there into the universe"—Jam clenched his fists together and then opened them ex-plosively quickly—"they have a way of disappearing. We got to keep it close to the chest. That way we don't lose the momentum."

Vic laughed and picked up her Busch Light, which Fitzroy had left for her dutifully. "You guys need to learn to have fun. Live a little."

"We can have fun after we make billions."

Vic pouted in a playful way as she caressed Jam's elbow. "Oh, come on. Let's go play pool."

"We can't, Vic. We have business to discuss," Jam said in all seriousness.

Vic grabbed Jim by the arm. "Jim, come play pool with me. Maybe Jam will decide to join us."

Jim laughed a stupid laugh. "Sure thing, Vic."

Jam grabbed Jim's other arm. "We got to talk business," Jam said.

A tug of war erupted over Jim as he was pulled to and fro between the two. Jam and Vic laughed uproariously as Jim moaned, "I'm getting dizzy."

All the eyes in the Watering Welch stared at them through the cloud of smoke. Anywhere else it would have been considered a minor ruckus and ignored by the staff and other patrons, but at the Watering Welch, this was the largest ruckus seen in years. It was tantamount to when the previous owner's cat got loose and ran ramshackle through the bottles for all of five minutes. It was an event still spoken of in hushed tones as if it was said too loudly, the ghost of the long-dead cat would return to make another mess.

"Hey!" yelled Fitzroy. "Can't you read the sign?" He pointed to a sign that hung above the entrance:

BE GOOD OR BE GONE

Jam and Vic relinquished their grip on Jim. No one wanted to be kicked out of the only watering hole in town. The possibility of getting banned or even suspended from the only bar in town was a frightening prospect.

Vic fixed her hair, which had fallen over her face. "Well, I'm playing pool. If you two want to join me, you're more than welcome." With that, she disappeared into the smoke-filled back room.

Composing himself, Jam asked, "What was your question again?"

Jim stared off into the distance, his mind working to recall what, for all intents and purposes, was ancient history. Finally, after some time, it dawned on him. "Oh, how are we going to make money on the timeshares?"

Jam looked both ways to make sure no one was listening. "Do you know what hyperinflation is?"

"Uh . . . yeah . . ." Jim lied.

Jam was rather shocked by this, especially considering that he wasn't exactly sure what hyperinflation was himself, except for the fact that it could be a moneymaking scheme. "Really?"

"No," Jim admitted with a shrug.

"Well, this guy was telling me that hyperinflation is when the value of things goes up really fast. He said everything in Venezuela is doubling in price every week." Jam could tell when Jim was about to zone out and knew he needed to check back in with him. "Are you following this?"

Jim nodded.

Jam sighed. *That's the problem with being a genius*, he thought, *you always need to explain things to everyone.* "Basically, it means if we buy a timeshare this week for ten thousand it will be worth twenty thousand next week. The week after that it will be forty thousand. In ten weeks, the value will be over a million dollars."

Jim popped up when it was put in those simple terms. "That's a lot of money."

"It gets better," Jam said. "This guy said we only need to put down ten percent for each timeshare and don't have to pay the rest for six months. So if we get an investor to come with a hundred thousand, we can buy a hundred timeshares. Tell the investor he can get double his money in ten weeks, he'll be happy, and we'll walk away with over a hundred million when everyone is clamoring to buy from us." It had taken Jam multiple attempts with a calculator to come to that number, but he was certain that his math was right after triple-checking and getting the same figures.

"This is brilliant, Jam," Jim said, his head bobbing up and down. "How come no one else is doing it?"

"No one knows about it yet except some of the guys on the Internet." Jam's voice got extra low so no one would hear them. "That's why we need to get in on the ground floor before everyone comes in and starts buying. If those guys beat us to it, the prices are going to go sky high. We need to find an investor—that way we can make the big bucks."

"Jam," Jim posed another question, "where are we going to find someone with a hundred thousand?"

"I don't know."

A hundred thousand was an almost unfathomable number to the two—an almost unfathomable number to most Welchers. It was a town where ten thousand was spoken of in whispered tones, and even a thousand dollars would cause a long whistle of shock. The articles in those business magazines also never discussed just how exactly these angel investors came onto the scene in the first place. To Jam, it just seemed that they came flying in, bags of cash in hand, and dispersed money freely to those blessed with genius and dreams of big deals. Though even Jam had to admit that it probably didn't work that way and he would somehow need to reach out to an investor. That was a task he was entirely unclear how to achieve.

"Hey, turn the TV up!" a Welcher yelled from the end of the bar.

Taking the remote, Fitzroy raised the volume of the ancient TV, blasting the news report through the bar. ". . . The resident of Des Moines was released earlier today from the clutches of Somali pirates. Over the course of the last several months, his family managed to raise the necessary million-dollar ransom and deliver it in cash to the kidnappers. While the American government refuses to negotiate with terrorists, it has become more common in past years for families of kidnapped tourists and sailors to establish GoFundMe campaigns to get their relatives home. An additional five fundraisers are currently being held on that website attempting to reach million-dollar goals."

"Holy shit, bro. That's fucking nuts," Jim said, slack-jawed.

"One million dollars," Jam said. "One million dollars," he repeated, drawing out every syllable of every word.

Jim, still staring at the TV said, "You can probably get, like, five Lamborghinis with a million dollars."

That's some real money, thought Jam. *Real money that is being wasted on Somali pirates. What can you even buy in Somalia? There certainly isn't a Lamborghini dealership on every corner.* There wasn't one on any corner in Welch either, but Jam figured they'd probably be able to find one in Iowa easier than they would in Somalia.

"Treasurer Luxury Black cigarettes," Jim said.

"Here we are busting our asses in and out every day and can barely buy the things we need, and these Somali pirates just get a million dollars for holding some guy for a few weeks—a million bucks they can't use because they're in Somalia. It just isn't right."

"Just isn't right," Jim parroted.

"Man, if only we could get those Somalis to invest in our big deal. We'd have all the money we need for the timeshares. But they're all the way over in Somalia and no damn help for us. This sucks, man."

It was with a slight fit of anger and jealousy that they slammed down their whiskey. Fitzroy appeared again with a bottle in hand, all too ready to fill their glasses back up. "Those Somali pirates are something," the bartender said.

"You know about the Somalis?" Jam said.

"Of course I know about the Somalis. I did twenty years in the navy with the Fifth Fleet. A month didn't go by where we didn't have to deal with some shit that Somali pirates stirred up."

Jam leaned in close. "What did you guys do with them?"

Fitzroy poured himself a shot of Dewar's. He raised the shot, Jam and Jim followed suit, and they clinked their glasses together before bringing them down to tap the bar and then downing the shots. "Only thing you could do. We would find their camps with drones and then drop a bunch of bombs on them. It was the only thing they respected."

Jam and Jim nodded along.

"Or," Fitzroy continued, "if it got really bad, we would send in the SEALs. They would send the Somalis running. Those pirate fucks were terrified of them. Otherwise though, those pirates were bad motherfuckers. I'm glad not to be dealing with them anymore."

Maybe it's a good thing that the Somali pirates are all the way over in Somalia and we're in Iowa, Jam thought. *Plus, they probably wouldn't be interested in Venezuelan timeshares anyway.*

Sweat poured down Jam's face as he strained terribly. One hand clutched tight around the bathroom vanity, the other on the bathtub. Those taquitos had done hell to his bowels, but they were so good the gastronomical stress was worth it. With deep breaths, he pushed and pushed. If one were to watch from afar, it would almost appear as if Jam were in labor.

That sweet release was almost upon him, and then the phone rang. It wasn't his iPhone, which sat on the bathroom vanity next to him, that rang—it was a relic of the past that clung to the wall in the kitchen: the house phone he had inherited from Grandma Jelly. The very same house phone that had received weekly calls from teachers, guidance counselors, deans, and principals regarding Jam's academic abilities. Those calls all used phrases such as "needs improvement" or "promotion in doubt," or they advised his grandmother that Jam should be forbidden from hanging out with Jim, as the two were bad influences on each other.

Jam was going to have to drag himself to the kitchen.

Pants around his ankles, Jam waddled into the kitchen, his butt cheeks clenched so he didn't let one slip accidently on the linoleum floor.

"Hello," he said, exasperated as he grabbed the corded phone.

"Yes, yes, hello," a thick African-accented voice answered. "This is General Fonzi."

Jam twisted and pulled at the corded phone, stretching the coiled wire to its limit, as he tried to navigate back to the bathroom using the same penguin-like waddle. "Hello? Who? Who?"

"Yes, hello, this is General Fonzi."

Jam could barely keep the phone to his ear as he twisted and turned around walls and furniture. The cord caught on a cabinet handle and only relented after a hard tug from Jam, which also nearly dislodged the phone fixture from the wall. "I can't hear you. Who are you? Did you say Genius Fox?"

"No! This is General Fonzi!" the man said with exasperation.

"Fonzi from *Happy Days*?" Jam pulled the cord over the bathroom vanity. It was stretched to the breaking point, its wall mount teetering and the connector clip at the base of the handset holding on with the tenacity that only 1970s American engineering could obtain.

"Happy days?" Fonzi was getting impatient. "I am General Fonzi of Somalia."

Jam perched himself precariously over the toilet. It was more of a squat than a sit, as he was at an angle and only one cheek was firmly planted on the porcelain throne. "General Fonzi?"

"Yes, yes, this is General Fonzi of Somalia." The man sincerely hoped he was finally getting through to the confused American. After all, this call was costing him nearly a dollar a minute. "I have thirty million dollars in gold that I need to get to United States. I need your help."

"Did you say thirty million in gold?"

"Yes, yes, thirty million in gold and I need help." Fonzi sped up. A confused mark was an easy mark. "First, you must go to Western Union and wire five separate wires for one thousand American then—"

"Wait, you're General Fonzi from Somalia? Are you with the pirates? Is this the ransom money?"

"What? Yes! This is General Fonzi of Somalia! I have Somali

treasure! You need to wire money to purchase the rights for the treasure, then I need money for document stamps for government authorization—"

Jam twisted around on the toilet, desperately trying to make sure his legs didn't cramp and that he didn't drop a deuce on the seat or the floor. "So is this treasure buried somewhere?"

"Yes! Yes!" Finally, progress. "The treasure is buried. I need fifty thousand to get it out of Somalia. You need to—"

Jam had heard somewhere that if something was meant to be it would happen, and after the talk the night before about Somali pirate investors, Jam was certain that this was something that was meant to be. "So is this treasure just gold? Or are there gems and diamonds and stuff?"

Fonzi gritted his teeth. "Just gold! No diamonds! We split it fifty-fifty, but first I need authorization forms and fees from you."

"Okay. So it's just gold. You said it was buried, right? Do you have a map so you can find it?"

"Yes, gold! Yes, map! Listen, I need authorization fees, passport documents, stamps, fifty thousand dollar cost. You send to me with Western Union and pre-paid debit cards. Send to—"

"Okay, I got that, but how long is this going to take? I have time-shares in Venezuela I need to buy."

"What? No. Fifty thousand first. You send me—"

The phone, reaching its cord's breaking point, finally gave out with a snap and the phone shot from Jam's hands, careened across the vanity, and slid across the floor all the way back to the kitchen.

"Fuck," Jam said solemnly. *There goes my Somali investor.*

General Fonzi, real name Mohahmed Okafo, of Lagos, Nigeria, and possessing no military rank, jabbed his cigarette out. That was a complete waste of time. He wasn't entirely sure if that last American was too dumb for the scam or far too smart for the scam. Either way, the phone call had cost him five dollars for the trouble. Not only that, but he was also behind on his quota for successful scams, and if he didn't pick up the slack, he would have to try his hand at more unsavory careers. The very thought of peddling old, faulty Hondas where the buyers could come back to find him sent a chill through his bones.

All around him, the other callers in the cubicle farm were chatting away on their own calls, each working similar but different scams. Every one of them seemed to be reaching profitable results except for him.

Perhaps he would have luck with his next call. His finger scrolled down the old, beat-up paper to the next name on his calling list and he prepared his General Fonzi pitch again.

Jam scooped up his phone, not the corded affair that lay broken on the kitchen floor, but the iPhone that sat next to him on the bathroom vanity. He tapped at the most contacted contact and waited for Jim to pick up.

"Hello," Jim answered.

"Jim, you home? I got big news," Jam said, pants still around his ankles and perched on the porcelain throne, the business of taking care of business completely forgotten.

"Nah, bro. I'm at the 7-Eleven."

"You're at the 7-Eleven? Isn't the new guy, Keith, supposed to be working today?"

Jim grunted in disdain. "The boss fired him. The fucking idiot broke the storage room door and didn't even tell him."

"Really? What a dick. Who does something like that and doesn't own up?" Jam agreed, forgetting that it was the two of them who had broken the door. "But anyway, I got big news. Don't leave the store. I'll be there in a few minutes."

Jim was just finishing up selling a pack of Lucky Strikes and a six-pack of Busch Light to a recent middle-school graduate when Jam came bursting in, barely avoiding clipping the slow-opening automatic doors.

Out of breath and already midsentence, Jam wheezed, "—wasn't . . . a million . . . it was thirty million."

Jim scratched at his head just as the middle-school grad lit up his first cigarette and cracked open his first can of Busch Light. "Hey!" Jim yelled. "You can't smoke in here. You want me to lose my job or something?" The kid shrugged and took his smokes and beers out to the parking lot. "What an idiot. Who doesn't know you're supposed to wait till you're outside to light up?"

Jam was bent over, hands on his knees and wheezing heavily. Years of smoking and couch surfing had clearly taken its toll on his over-worked lungs after the run over. He shouldn't have run the entire way, but he couldn't find his bike, and news like this had to be delivered in person in case anyone was listening in on the phone and about to steal a big deal right out from under them. "Thirty . . . million . . ."

"Thirty million what?" Jim asked.

Jam took big gasps of air between each word. "Thirty. Million. Dollars. Pirates. Somalia."

Jim had that distant look in his eyes, a look only present in soldiers coming back from war and in completely confused dimwits. "Bro, I don't know what you're talking about."

"Remember on the news? The ransom the pirates got? The news screwed it all up. It was *fake fucking news*. It wasn't a million dollars, it was thirty million! And it wasn't in cash, it was in gold!"

Jim's mouth worked itself in an O of recognition. "That's nuts, Jam. How did you find out?"

Jam was finally able to catch his breath and explain coherently what had transpired, at least as coherently as possible for someone who was as excited as a kid on Christmas morning. "I got a call from Somalia. It was this guy General Fonzi and—"

"*Happy Days* Fonzi?" Jim interrupted.

"No, it was General Fonzi of Somalia, not *Happy Days* Fonzi. You got to keep up. He called me from Somalia about the treasure. It has to be the ransom! They're trying to get it out of Somalia and he called me for help."

"He called you?" Jim interrupted again.

"Jim." Jam grabbed Jim by the face, not in a violent way, but more in the way that a mother grabs a toddler by the cheeks when she wants to explain something slowly and carefully. "Yeah, he called me. But that's not important. They're looking to get the treasure out of Somalia, and they need help to do it. They're willing to split it fifty-fifty if we help them. We got to move fast on this before someone else gets all that gold. Do you understand now?"

Jim, face all scrunched up by Jam's hands, nodded slowly.

"Okay, good." Jam released his hold on Jim. "So we need to figure out a plan. They need fifty thousand dollars in order to get it out of the country."

"When do they need it by?" Jim asked.

"I don't know."

"Where do we send the money?"

"I don't know. The phone disconnected before he was able to tell me that."

"But, Jam, if we don't have his number, how are we supposed to get in touch with General Fonzi to get the treasure?"

The gears in Jam's head came to a grinding halt as he considered the implications of it all. But Jam wasn't a quitter. He was an improviser, even if those improvisations were dangerous or poorly thought out. Those very same gears that came to a grinding halt began to turn again as a plan formulated in his head. A plan that was, at least according to Jam, pure genius and unable to fail.

It had taken the Welch Public Library several days to track down the White and Yellow Pages of Somalia. It was also by far the oddest request the library had received in some time. This is, of course, if you disregarded the regular and often large-in-volume requests that came from Ample Hills for all sorts of erotica and sexual manuals.

It was far less odd that such an odd request came from the likes of Jam. He was a frequent sight at the library and checked out myriad books. At this point, these requests hardly caused an eyebrow to be raised. The last time an eyebrow had even so much as twitched was when he'd asked for resources on exotic animal training and trading, and that incident was already nearly half a decade in the past.

It was considered all well and good, though, as, despite Jam's many faults, he normally returned the books on time, and even on the occasion that he didn't, he would gladly pay the late fee in order to check out new books.

The pair sat in Jam's cluttered living room with the Somali Yellow and White Pages laid out in front of them. The pages provided quite a conundrum. Under the White Pages there were no names listed for Fonzi. Jam had concluded that there must be a different spelling for Fonzi in Somalia or that it was some nickname that the general was using in order to get the gold out of the country so he wouldn't be caught doing so. After all, if he was a general, he probably wasn't supposed to be working with the pirates. They encountered the same issue with the Yellow Pages; while there were some "General" offices present in the book, none referenced a General Fonzi or even a department that a General Fonzi would be a part of.

It was quickly decided that the logical course of action was to go through each individual entry for F in the White Pages and every entry for General in the Yellow Pages until they happened upon General Fonzi and were able to obtain more information about getting the treasure. The express course of action was then quickly decided upon. Jim would handle all entries for General and Jam would handle entries for F. It was a tactical decision on Jam's part—calling government offices always necessitated a long hold time, and Jam didn't want to get stuck listening to the equivalent of Somali elevator music.

Do they even have elevators in Somalia? Jam momentarily mused.

Jim went to dial the first number from the Generals when Jam stopped him. "Wait. It is international, this is going to cost us a fortune trying to find General Fonzi. We should call collect. After all, Fonzi has millions in gold, he can afford the charges."

Many hours and many collect calls later, they were no closer to finding General Fonzi than when they'd begun. They were met with rejected calls, confused officials speaking in halting English, as well as many who could not speak any English. They were cursed at by Somalis they woke up because they forgot to account for the difference in time zones, something they continued to ignore even after being advised of the time.

Jam did manage to connect with a nice Somali grandmother. She spoke surprisingly good English, with a slight British accent. She didn't know of this General Fonzi but was very intrigued about the gold. She promised him that she would ask the other old ladies in her town if any of them had a son or grandson who went by the name General Fonzi and she would get back to him. Jim told her all about their plans and big ideas, which she found all to be fascinating while lamenting that her own grandson was a layabout who was content with his mere engineering job that kept him working on an oil rig far away from home all year. Either way, she dutifully took his number down and said she would call him even if it was to just check in on him and his ventures.

Several hours passed, and the floor of Jam's cluttered living room was further cluttered with several new pizza boxes and Busch Light tallboys. Jim had already given up on the endeavor and was now playing *Call of Duty*, a half-extinguished cigarette hanging from his lips.

Occasionally, he mumbled around the cigarette to curse at the TV or trash talk his prepubescent opponents.

Jam persisted until he got to the end of the phone book. It was at that point he finally realized they were never going to be able to find General Fonzi this way. It also dawned on him that even if they found someone who knew General Fonzi, that person wouldn't trust Jam just on his word that he was the one the general had reached out to. It was, after all, a hush-hush operation.

Still, Jam knew this was a multimillion-dollar idea, quite literally, and his focus on it saved him from losing money on the Venezuelan timeshares, which, of course, turned out to be a scam. There had to be a way for him to get back in touch with General Fonzi. Champagne wishes and caviar dreams were just one phone call away.

"This isn't going to work," Jam said.

Jim wasn't really paying attention to what Jam was saying. His focus rested entirely on the game. "Guess we need to do something different," Jim said almost as an afterthought.

Something different—that's exactly what we need to do, thought Jam. The only question was what exactly it was that they needed to do. He ruminated on it, the blare of *Call of Duty* and Jim's mumbled cursing creeping into his mind. A plan of action began to form in his head. There was only one way to get in touch with General Fonzi. "Jim, we need to go to Somalia," Jam said.

Jim looked at Jam and the cigarette fell from his lips.

4

"In the scramble for Africa, Somalia was Italy's
participation trophy."

—The Hitchhiker's Guide to World History

The histories of Somalia and Italy are intricately linked. For nearly fifty years, Somalia was part of the small Italian Empire. It was only with the end of World War II, in which Italy had settled on the wrong side, that the end of Italian involvement in the region would be seen. Even with the departure of Italy so many years before, there were still many things left over by the Italians, and the history of Somalia was thus shaped by the Italian occupation. There is even a story that when Italy deployed troops to Somalia in the early 1990s, an old Somali man approached the Italian camp dressed in the uniform of a colonial soldier. Dutifully, the man would show up every morning when they raised the flag and each morning would shout, "*Viva Re! Viva Duce! Viva Italia!*" all of this to the dismay of the Italian soldiers, who no longer had a king or a dictator.

It is in this history of Somalia that the settlement of Villaggio di Mussolini (literally, the village of Mussolini) was formed along the Somali coast. Built in the Mediterranean style, this small coastal village was set up to convince Italians to move to the colony. The little village was heavily militarized, with a string of bunkers around it, and was designed to serve as a line of defense against any possible British invasions from the British-held part of Somalia. When that day came, the Italian defenders decided that they very much preferred the idea of cooking pasta in a British prisoner-of-war camp than fighting and following in the Italian war-making tradition. They promptly surrendered their leader's namesake village without a shot being fired. Now the settlement is known as Tuulada Mussolini (literally, again, Village of Mussolini). The Italians left, but the name stuck despite all the implications.

Despite the previous militarization of the town, it was quite idyllic, being of that serene Mediterranean style and situated on the coastline. It was the type of town that would usually attract tourists. These tourists would visit the sites and listen in on talks about the dangers of the past, the brutal reign of dictators, and why people must remain vigilant and ever on the alert for signs of oppression. These tourists would then depart feeling good about themselves, believing that by simply hearing the talks they would now be a bulwark against authoritarianism. This type of town would also attract another kind of visitor: neo-fascist pilgrims, who would flock to the spot trying to revel in a historic era when their Italian leader wasn't openly considered a comedic buffoon, second fiddle to a genocidal madman in a much wider war. Inevitably, these different types of visitors would clash, and the resulting fights, batteries, and arsons would be a small news segment, or perhaps even the focus of an indie documentary.

But this particular village didn't attract either of those types of visitors, for a very simple fact: the whole village served as a base for a notoriously violent pirate gang. They were so notoriously violent that they'd been expelled from a larger pirate gang for being too violent. This was considered quite a feat, considering the gang they were expelled from had been the very same gang that was responsible for kidnapping Captain Richard Phillips. The split, which came only three months before that incident, is the very reason that the gang managed to enjoy a continued existence and continued to terrorize the high seas.

Faarax, the current pirate leader, held court at the village's old church. The church was the ideal location to run the affairs of the gang and the village. It was not only the center of town, as any church should be according to the original designers, it was also the largest and most lavish structure present. A palace fit for a corrupt parish priest or even the leader of a pirate band.

Business over the past few months had been slow, and Faarax and the rest of his crew were growing restless. The art of piracy, and indeed it was an art form, was very much feast or famine. Aside from their one big score, they were not able to find any new targets they could pick off. The area had become too hot after a series of kidnappings by other gangs, much to the dismay of Faarax, who preferred good old-fashioned theft to kidnapping. Theft was far more profitable and far less attention-grabbing, a fact that many of his fellow pirates chose to ignore in exchange for the glamour and headlines of armed abductions. These high-profile kidnappings all drew the unwanted, but expected, attention of the United States Navy and forced Faarax to lie low for now. His men were increasingly growing agitated over the lack of work, and there was talk that many were planning on leaving for greener pastures. Even though the job market was grim, the last man to leave came back after the only job he could find was that of a used car salesman. It was common knowledge that pirating was a far more honest way to make a living.

It wasn't often that he was afforded such downtime, and Faarax was taking the lull in stride, spending it the only way he knew how: by catching up on the latest in American television—at least the latest in American television that Somalia had to offer. He eagerly popped season four of *The Sopranos* into the portable DVD player and was ready to watch the fascinating exploits of the New Jersey crime family.

Tony Soprano would have to wait, however, as the doors of the old church burst open and Ali, Faarax's top lieutenant, came in dragging another member of the gang at gunpoint. Those assembled in the church looked up from their dominos and card games at the interruption.

"Boss," Ali said, "I caught this man attempting to break into the bunker and steal the treasure."

Faarax leaned forward in his chair and pushed aviator sunglasses away from his eyes so he could look the thief in the eye. "What do you have to say for yourself?"

The thief struggled in Ali's grasp. "This is not right, Faarax. You have no right to hold the treasure all to yourself. You need to give us our shares."

The other pirate gang members in the church took notice. There had been some talk of when they would get their share of the treasure. Talk was becoming much more common within the camp. Despite Faarax's position as leader of the gang, piracy was a rather democratic affair. They were entitled to payouts for their hauls and the right to discuss whether they wanted in on a particular job or not. There was a precarious balance of Faarax's power and the rights of the pirates beneath him, thus it was important for Faarax to assert his authority heavily when needed. And this was one of those situations. Faarax needed to put a quick end to any talk that could diminish his authority in the eyes of those he ruled over.

"I am the boss here," Faarax said. "You will get your treasure, but I decide when our treasure is dispersed." *Did Tony Soprano have these kinds of problems?* he wondered.

"It has been a month already! We want our treasure!" the thief said, trying to appeal to the crowd.

There were some murmurs in the crowd as private conversations and arguments sprang up on whether any codes of conduct were violated by the delay in distributing the treasure to the men.

Faarax rose from his seat, picked up his AK-47, and rested it in the crook of his crossed arms. His presence dominated the room. "No! I cannot have you go around flaunting the treasure to everyone. The United States Navy is just looking for targets, and you taking the treasure and showing off will only lead them to us. We must wait!"

The pirates in the crowd nodded along to Faarax. He was right, he hadn't led them astray in the years he had been their boss, and in this line of work a year might as well be a decade. Those pirates who were old enough knew that there had been some close calls with the previous administration—close calls that led the way to Faarax coming to power.

"What should I do with him?" Ali asked.

Faarax knew he had to make an example of the thief. If he let the thief go, more of this gang would try to subvert his authority and attempt to steal the treasure—or worse yet, try to overtake his rule. "Take care of him."

That was all Ali needed to hear. He threw the thief to the ground and cocked the bolt of his AK.

"Please, Faarax," the thief cried. "Mercy! I beg you for mercy!"

From the side of the church's nave, a young woman hurried to the altar where Faarax held court. "Brother," said Shadya, Faarax's sister. "Don't do this."

Faarax looked at her with a nonplussed gaze. He really hated this part of the job.

"Drive him to the desert, way out, and tie him to a tree. If you cannot find a tree, stake him to the ground." Faarax addressed the man, holding his chin roughly. "If the birds don't peck your eyes out and the hyenas don't eat you, maybe we will see you again. Take him away." Faarax returned to his seat.

Ali dragged the still-begging man out of the church.

The treasure would remain safe for now, and for a long while no one would dare to question Faarax's rule.

"I don't know, Jam," said Jim as he was stocking the cigarette shelf. "Somalia is pretty dangerous. I saw *Black Hawk Down*."

"It's not *that* dangerous," Jam tried to assure him. It was the same argument they had been having for the past two days. The two had been stuck in an exchange of circular logic on the merits of going to Somalia. Jam was aware of the danger, to a degree, but felt that the dangers were of course overblown and overhyped by people who would lead them astray and get the gold for themselves. Jim was, at least according to Jam, far too cautious in all endeavors.

"You saw the article in *Soldier of Fortune* and the thing on the news. They got pirates there kidnapping people. That sounds pretty dangerous to me."

That's the problem with Jim sometimes, thought Jam. *He doesn't always see the big picture. Dangerous was good.* "That's what makes it a great plan. No one else is going to go to Somalia to find General Fonzi. We got this, bro."

Jim shifted uncomfortably on his feet as he continued to stack up the packs of Lucky Strike cigarettes. There seemed to be an infinite supply of them. No matter how many packs they sold, there was always another carton ready to be cracked opened and divvied out. "I get that, but what is preventing them from kidnapping *us?* We don't have a million dollars to pay for ransom."

This was something Jam hadn't prepared for. The thought of pirates kidnapping them had never crossed his mind; the idea of thirty million in gold far outweighed any sense of danger or even obstacles that could be in their way. "I—" he began, but was interrupted by the dinging of the automatic doors, buying him much needed time to come up with an answer for Jim.

"How's the weather treating you?" the khaki-clad customer greeted.

"It sure beats the snow, ho-ho," the duo answered in monotone.

Jam and Jim fell silent. They couldn't keep talking about Somalia with the khaki-clad customer in the store. Too many big deals were lost by simply being overheard and having someone else beat them to the punch. This was, according to Jam, a common occurrence. It was also a way of explaining their continuing lack of success. The thought that perhaps the idea wasn't that good—or was, in fact, already invented and implemented—or they simply did not have the time, resources, acumen, or skills to see it to fruition never once crossed Jam's mind.

The khaki-clad customer picked out his case of Busch Light, then mulled over the hot food display. His mouth silently worded out the different taquitos as he leaned in close to examine them. "Hmmm . . . hmmm . . ." he considered.

Jam drummed his fingers along the countertop. He had just figured out the means by which they could assure their safety in Somalia. The answer seemed so obvious now. But they had to wait till this Welcher decided what taquito he wanted. There was thirty million in gold at stake and them getting it or losing the opportunity to someone else now rested entirely on what dollar snack this guy wanted.

"Which taquito would you recommend?" the khaki-clad customer asked.

"I don't know, they're all pretty good," Jam said as Jim nodded along absentmindedly. It was perhaps the most truthful answer he could have given considering he loved them all and ate multiple of each per day.

"They sure look it." He went back to his hemming and hawing at the display case in search of the perfect taquito.

Jam drummed his fingers more rapidly and harder across the counter. Either the indecisive man wasn't taking the hint to hurry up or he was simply ignoring it. Either way it wasn't working, and Jam kept on drumming, trying to get things to move along.

After a few long moments, the khaki-clad customer declared, "Well, shucks, I just can't choose. Let me get one of each. Also a pack of Lucky Strikes."

Four taquitos were hastily put in wrappers, and soon the man was on his way.

As soon as the automatic doors clanged shut, Jam was already back in planning mode. He wasted no time in saying, "I know how we are going to stay safe in Somalia."

"How's that?" Jim said.

"Remember what Fitzroy said at the bar?"

"Uh, yeah," is what Jim's mouth said, but his tone and demeanor said: *I have no idea what you are talking about.*

Jam prompted: "About the Navy SEALs?"

"Uh-huh." Jim was still clueless.

Jam was getting more and more excited as the plan began to formulate in his head. It didn't even matter that Jim was barely paying attention. Jam generated his own excitement from the simple act of planning. It was turning out to be the best plan he'd had, at least since the last one, and he was sure that this was the one that was going to make them rich. "He said that Somali pirates were terrified of Navy SEALs!"

Jim nodded along again.

"So that's what we are going to do!" Jam said with the plan now completely formulated.

Jim still wasn't entirely sure what Jam was up to. "Do what, Jam?"

"We need to hire Navy SEALs to protect us!"

It was after much discussion, a mostly one-sided discussion that was rather typical during the plotting phase between Jam and Jim, that they realized there was only one possible way for them to hire Navy SEALs, and that was through *Soldier of Fortune*. *Soldier of Fortune* had ads for everything and anything military related. More importantly, being quite a poor seller in a town inhabited by largely risk-averse people who rarely left or sought any form of adventure and excitement, they had easy access to the magazine, with their 7-Eleven having over a year of back issues. Now all they would need to do was go through the magazines, find SEALs looking for contract work, and work out a payment plan. Jim thought that a fifty-fifty break was fair, but Jam knew the SEALs would most likely do it for fun and would be willing to take only ten percent. With that number in mind, they began their search.

Unbeknownst to them, *Soldier of Fortune* had stopped publishing ads for hired guns after a series of high-profile murder cases. Now the ads in the magazine were strictly relegated to military paraphernalia for those looking to play weekend soldier and also the occasional neo-Nazi looking to buy old iron crosses and SS uniforms to terrorize their elderly neighbors with.

They attempted to call the magazine about placing their own ad and were told by multiple customer service representatives, each more agitated than the last, that they could not place an ad for hired guns. Their repeated attempts to claim that they weren't for hired guns—that they would simply be there to offer protection if needed—fell on deaf ears.

"I guess that's that," a defeated Jim said.

Jam's mind was already in top gear going over the possibilities. He was ecstatic. "This is great. Think about it!"

Jim tilted his head at the statement. It was a look very reminiscent of a dog confused by what its owner was saying.

"There's a good reason why they pulled those ads from the magazine. What was stopping the SEALs from robbing us after we got to the treasure? Nothing," Jam said. "They're the guys with the guns and would have just taken the gold and left us with nothing. This means we will be able to get all the gold for ourselves."

"But, Jam, what is stopping us from being robbed by pirates? We need someone to protect us."

Jam had already worked it all out. "Bro, we can protect ourselves. Think about it. You said it yourself the other day. We should have joined the army. We know all the lingo from *Call of Duty*. We can protect ourselves in Somalia."

Jim stared at him, blank and confused. "But we aren't in the military."

Jam knew that Jim wasn't getting the big picture and it would all need to be explained in the most minute of details. "It doesn't matter. We just have to make everyone *think* that we are in the military."

"So we are going to pretend to be in the army?"

"No!" Jam jumped to his feet. "We are going to pretend to be Navy SEALs!"

As could be imagined, trying to impersonate SEALs was much harder in reality than both Jam and Jim could conceive. A trip to the local army-navy store yielded no surplus Navy SEAL uniforms, and the proprietor said in no uncertain terms that he couldn't get them authentic SEAL uniforms. They couldn't even try to buy the uniforms from the military, as the nearest military base was over three hours away and even they realized that they probably wouldn't be allowed on base without some sort of official ID. They were stuck.

Jam handed off the Xbox controller to Jim. He hadn't the head for *Call of Duty* right now and had bombed his last three matches. His mind kept going over and over just how they were going to impersonate Navy SEALs and get to Somalia. There had to be a way for them to get those uniforms. It was a topic that was quickly becoming all-consuming. Once they had the uniforms, everything else would just fall into place. Jam knew this one was going to be their big break and would lead to fame and fortune.

It was underneath the discarded pizza boxes, old Busch Light cans, and abandoned taquito wrappers that Jam spotted an issue of *Soldier of Fortune*. How had he not thought of it before? He realized that it was all so very simple. It was so simple that he was amazed that his brilliant mind (a self-proclaimed brilliance) hadn't come to this conclusion sooner. *Soldier of Fortune* was filled with ads for military surplus.

He dove for the magazine, sending pizza boxes and beer cans flying, and scoured the magazine looking for just the right ad. He found it at the back, a small ad that read:

STOLEN VALOR WARE
WE SELL ALL UNIFORMS, ALL BRANCHES, ALL UNITS
ALL ACCESSORIES, COMMENDATIONS, AWARDS
VISIT US TODAY AT STOLENVALORWARE.COM

"Jim!" Jam shouted. "I found it! I found it!"

Startled, Jim dropped the Xbox controller as Jam shoved the ad in his face, his dyslexic eyes struggling to bring the text into focus.

"All uniforms, all branches," Jam continued. "We can get the SEAL uniforms."

There was no time to waste for Jim to process the information and respond. Every moment that slipped by let someone else get closer to the treasure. Jam pulled his phone out and hastily typed in the website. He was met with a blank white page and black text that read, "Yuor Devize is not compatble. Pleaze uZe a computer. Thx."

Jam scrambled up the flight of stairs that led to his room. Jam's room resembled the rest of the house and could accurately be described as another location in which a small bomb had gone off. He began rummaging through the mess of his bedroom, searching for his laptop. It wasn't on his desk or on his bed, where on multiple occasions it had previously resided. He tossed clothes from his closet on the floor and tossed clothes from the floor into the closet and searched under the bed. It was there, buried beneath even more clothes and old blankets, that he finally found his laptop.

He raced back to the living room and fired it up. Jim was still sitting where Jam had left him and was still attempting to process the current course of events.

It seemed to take forever for the old Toshiba to load Windows 7 and for Jam to log in. Pulling up Internet Explorer, he typed in the website again.

They were met with a garish display. To say it was poorly designed would be an insult to poorly designed websites. Brightly colored GIFs in Chinese and broken English rolled across the screen. Flaming text was everywhere, advertising the site's features. To the average person it was hardly the type of website that would inspire confidence in the products being real or that the owners of the site wouldn't be stealing your credit card information. But Jam wasn't the average person. He was a man on a mission to find a treasure.

Jam clicked through the confusing interface, facing several broken links. In any other situation, he would have given up five dead links before, but he was motivated—more motivated than he had ever been in his life. This was finally their chance. This was going to be the big deal that got them their champagne wishes and caviar dreams.

Finally, he managed to find the page they needed for SEAL uniforms. Clicking through, they had to choose their ranks. It was obvious to Jam that he should be the leader because the idea was all his, and he selected lieutenant for himself. He let Jim select his own rank as long as it was lower than lieutenant, and Jim picked out the rank of petty officer first class.

A quick input of Jam's credit card, and their order was placed. All they had to do now was wait the two to three weeks for the uniforms to be delivered.

It would be the longest three weeks of their lives.

5

"Stolenvalorware.com is the worst supplier ever. The Medal of Honor sent to me was from the wrong branch of service; I requested a navy medal but was sent an army medal. It had the wrong number of stars on it, and on top of that, the certificate of presentation and ID card had my name spelled wrong. When I wore it out I was laughed out of the bar."

—Forum post by MedalofHonorwinner69 on Stolenvalorvets.com

Jam and Jim were positively giddy—so giddy, in fact, that they both called in sick to work, forcing the newest hire to work a triple shift. Today was the day their uniforms would be delivered. Then it would just be a simple jaunt to Somalia followed by a quick search for General Fonzi, and from there they would get the treasure. It was all going to be a very leisurely, cheerful, and orderly affair, which, like every other trip to an exotic locale, needed no advance planning.

Before the postman could even ring the bell, Jam was already swinging open the door, grabbing the signature form, hastily scribbling his name (which resembled more the erratic movements of a stroke victim than any legible letters), and grabbing the package. The postman himself didn't even have the chance to ask Jam how the weather was treating him before the door was promptly slammed in his face.

Tearing open the package, they found the objects they so desperately craved—the clothes that would lead them to riches. Holding the uniforms up, they admired the Chinese craftsmanship. Craftsmanship was a rather dubious word to use to describe the clothing in question. The seams on the uniforms were hardly sewn tight, the color patchy and faded in parts. It all seemed to be hastily put together (probably in the most horrendous sweatshop conditions imaginable). To Jam and Jim, though, the uniforms were a godsend, and they hardly noticed any issues with the sewing, coloring, textures, or that weird chemical smell.

The front of each blouse had "U.S. Army" emblazoned over one pocket and their last names above the other pocket. An American flag was on the right arm, and on the left was the SEAL logo mounted below a winged and skulled insignia whose legend read "Task Force 141."

On Jam's uniform, the officer tab was emblazoned with a silver oak leaf. It was actually the rank of U.S. Navy Commander and several ranks higher than what Jam had selected. Jim's rank tab was placed on a red background and had a single inverted V above that of crossed rifles. This insignia is not even used by the Navy, but is that of a Marine lance corporal and several ranks lower than what Jim requested.

They blinked as they took in their new uniforms, examining every inch of them and continuously ignoring the very blatant defects. Soon, smiles spread across their faces.

"Task Force 141!" Jam exclaimed.

"Call of duty!" Jim saluted.

"Fuck, yeah!" they both yelled as they exchanged high-fives.

Faarax sat hunched over the table, examining the pieces he still had left. He had lost his queen early in a risky gambit to end the game quickly. It was a move that had cost him dearly. His remaining pieces were picked away, and he was left with only a rook, a bishop, and a handful of pawns, and hardly enough of them to get into any favorable positions. It would only be a matter of time until he lost. He moved a pawn up a square, hoping he would be able to slip it by his opponent and get the queen. Otherwise he would just be delaying the inevitable.

Shadya smiled, picked up her queen, and slid it across the board to take Faarax's now undefended rook. "Mate in five moves."

Faarax knew he was lucky that his sister was born a woman. She was far too smart for him. Not to mention, she was also far too cunning, ruthless, and bold. She had been the one to suggest the plan that had led to them obtaining the treasure. When Faarax insisted that the plan couldn't be executed, she'd come up with a novel way of accomplishing it—novel, and quite frightening as well. Even for someone like Faarax, it had seemed risky, but she'd said they could do it, and they did. If she had been a man, she would be the one running the gang and not Faarax.

By now the pirate leader was flustered. His hand moved his only remaining strong piece, the bishop, across the board. He didn't have many options left.

She moved her rook into position. "Mate in four moves."

The pirate leader saw the trap his sister was setting up for him. There was no way to stop her from winning, and he could only delay it for a few moves longer and hope she would make a mistake. A mistake that they both knew she wouldn't make.

Their game was interrupted by a knock at the door. "Boss," Ali said through the closed door. "I got to talk to you. I have bad news."

Ali's news, even if it was bad, would at least give Faarax a respite from the game. "Come in," said the pirate leader.

Ali entered, his AK tucked under one arm. You never knew in a pirate village when you would need to utilize the Russian gun, or in this case a Yugoslavian bootleg knock-off of the Russian gun. "Bad news, boss," Ali said again. "You know Adan's gang from down south?"

Adan was an aggressive leader. He was known for launching weekly, sometimes even daily, raids and hitting the best targets with the best loot. He was also the most prolific kidnapper in the region. Just last week they'd made off with some very valuable cargo from a container ship that had sailed too close to the port. Adan had also played a small part in helping Faarax secure the treasure that was now safely in the bunker.

"Of course," Faarax said.

"Well, they're gone now," Ali replied.

"Gone? What do you mean gone?"

"They got bombed to hell by the United States Navy and raided by the SEALs. They're all dead or captured. Word is Adan took two to the face when he tried to attack the SEALs with a machete."

That was indeed troubling news. Some of the men from Adan's crew knew about the treasure and might break under the pressure of interrogation. Faarax could only hope that the men they captured didn't know anything, or else they could be coming for him next.

"This is the third time the navy has attacked this month. What is the sudden interest?" Shadya asked.

"Their new admiral has taken a strong interest in destroying our gangs," answered Faarax. "He has declared that he is going to wipe out all of us by the end of the year."

"Who is this new admiral?" she asked.

"Admiral Fitzroy." He was, in fact, a third cousin thrice removed from Welch's Fitzroy, the owner of the Watering Welch.

It turned out that trips to Somalia were far harder to book than the pair thought. Apparently not that many people wanted to fly to the East African nation, and even fewer air carriers were willing to fly into said nation. And, of those carriers that did, the price for even a one-way ticket was prohibitively expensive, with the total cost coming in at six thousand dollars for both tickets. After checking their bank accounts and clearing out all other sources of funds, the pair was still $5,636 short. This included busting open Jim's much-loved Mickey Mouse piggy bank.

It again seemed that their plan was completely derailed, and Jim was utterly despondent. This despondency was mostly due to the destruction of his beloved Mickey Mouse bank, more so after the fact when Jam pointed out that there was a rubber seal on the bottom that could have been opened to get the money out.

"Man, I guess this was all for nothing," Jim said. "We spent five hundred bucks on SEAL stuff for nothing."

Jam shook his head. He wasn't going to quit on this big deal. He already had too much invested. The only way to turn bad money good was to throw more money at it. "No, we got this. We can still get to Somalia."

"How is that?"

"I'll just ask Grandma Jelly for the money."

Jim's mood instantly turned around. Of course—Grandma Jelly. She always gave her Benjamin whatever he wanted and supported him on his big deals. Though there was some doubt in his mind whether or not she would let the two go to Somalia. "I don't know, Jam. Do you think she'll pay for us? She probably knows it's dangerous there."

Jam rubbed his hands together. "I won't tell her where we're going."

"What are you going to tell her?"

"Don't worry. All you need to do is keep quiet if anyone asks what we're doing or where we're going."

Keeping quiet was something Jim was very good at, and he readily agreed.

Since Jam's recent visit, little had changed at Ample Hills except for the bulletin board. The stolen or missing double-ended dildo had either been returned or forgotten. The grandchildren's crafts day had proved to be a success, with many photos of proud grandmothers posing with their grandchildren and their accumulated works, many of which were phallic in nature, a coincidence of course to anyone concerned. A new notice was posted regarding the sale of rubber ducks, which carefully noted their vibrating abilities. Another notice seemed out of place, not in the sense that it wasn't appropriate for the community, but in the sense that the age group wasn't often targeted by these types of posters. It was a missive from the CDC on how to avoid contracting STDs by practicing safe sex. It highlighted various teenagers learning about condoms and other forms of protection.

In the corner was King Al, still in the same dirty shirt and pants, with his legion of groupies about him.

Grandma Jelly wasn't in her usual spot. Jam knew she would be back soon and sat down on the couch next to the chair she always occupied.

Jam wasn't alone for long, though his new companion wasn't his grandmother. Instead, it was feisty Gertrude, that octogenarian horndog. She sidled up against Jam on the couch.

"Are you the rabbit salesman?" she asked.

Jam was quite confused by the line of questioning. "What?"

"The rabbit salesman," she repeated.

Jam gave her a funny look. *Why would I be selling rabbits in an old folks' home?* he thought. "I don't have any pets for sale."

"Not those types of rabbits. The other kind," she said.

Jam was growing more and more confused by the moment. "What other kind?"

"The vibrating kind."

Jam hadn't the faintest clue what she was talking about. "I don't understand what you're talking about. I'm not here to sell anything, I'm just waiting for my Grandma Jelly."

Gertrude snorted in a manner very similar to a horse. "Fine," she snapped. "I guess my money is not good enough for you." With that she stormed off.

Grandma Jelly appeared wearing her usual floral-print dress, carrying her usual knitting tools and a half-completed multicolored scarf. "There's my sweet Benjamin," she said cheerfully. "What have you been up to? You haven't come by in weeks."

"Sorry, Grandma Jelly. I've been working on a big deal," Jam said.

"That's wonderful. You've always had big dreams and ideas. It's a shame that they never seem to work out. One day, though." She had a wistful look of optimism in her eye. "Is it the Venezuelan timeshares?"

Jam huffed at the mention of that particular failed big deal. "No, that turned out to be a scam. I got an even better idea."

"Well, what is it, Benjamin? Don't leave your dear grandmother waiting."

Jam leaned in close, almost conspiratorially. He didn't want anyone to hear this one. It was still a brilliant idea and what he would be working on next if the whole Somalia thing didn't work out, but, of course, he knew Somalia was the deal that was going to make him. He said one word: "Water."

"Water?" Jelly asked with some measure of confusion.

"Flavored water." Jam put his hands and fingers together and drew them out long and slow as he said the words.

Jelly put down her knitting utensils and looked at Jam curiously. "Benjamin, they already make flavored water."

Jam looked around to make sure no one was eavesdropping on his multimillion-dollar idea. "This is different. It will be the Starbucks of water."

"The Starbucks of water?"

"Yeah, the Starbucks of water. It is going to be like a Starbucks, but for people that don't want to drink coffee. So they'll go there to do business meetings and their work and drink flavored water. Flavored water made with real fruit—like it is going to have the fruit floating in it. It is going to make millions. It is probably going to make us billions."

Jelly clapped her hands together in delight. "Oh! My Benjamin, that sounds like an amazing plan!"

Now was the time for him to ask for money, and Jam knew he had to phrase it just right. "Only thing is we need to go to California with this. The people out there love stuff like this. But me and Jim don't have enough money to set this up. I was hoping you could help us out."

"Of course, anything for you. How much do you need?"

Jam had read somewhere once that you always ask for an outrageously large number first, that way when you ask for what you really want it seems that much more reasonable. With this in mind, he blurted out the first large number to come to his head. "Five hundred thousand, Grandma Jelly."

Jelly didn't so much as blink as she pulled her checkbook out of her dress pocket and started writing. "That seems to be a very reasonable amount to open a store with."

It was the largest amount of money the two had ever seen on a check outside of giant novelty checks on TV. They'd certainly never held a check with so many zeros on it before. It was almost an unfathomable amount for anyone in Welch, much less for Jam and Jim. Even though they dreamed of numbers like this it was far beyond their comprehension. They waited nervously in the parking lot of First Bank of Welch, which was the only bank in Welch.

Jim asked the logical question: "Does Grandma Jelly even have this much money?"

Jam didn't know. It was one of the few questions that Jam didn't have an answer for—not even a wrong answer. Growing up they'd had the same type of house as everyone else, driven the same car, and worn the same clothes. He'd gotten some extra Christmas and birthday gifts, but he figured that was only because he didn't have any siblings and not because Grandma Jelly was secretly sitting on half a million dollars. "I don't think so."

"If she doesn't have the money in the bank, how are they going to give it to us?"

Jam thought for a moment. Some half-remembered and partially wrong facts about banks drifted through his head. "We'll ask them to cash the check instead of putting the money in my account."

"That will work?"

Jam was, as always, supremely confident in believing that he was right. "Yeah, bro. We don't have to wait for the check to clear then. They just give us the cash and we'll be gone before they notice Grandma Jelly doesn't have enough in her account."

"That's genius, Jam."

Adam McKnight leaned over the teller's counter of the First Bank of Welch. He had been a teller there since the day he had graduated from high school and reckoned it was a far better existence than working at the plant or in the mill. Hopefully, the easier career would allow him to subvert the Welch curse and live slightly past fifty if all went well. It wasn't a glamorous life by any means, but it definitely provided all the means needed to live in the sleepy town of Welch, and Adam McKnight was quite fine with that, thank you very much.

It also didn't hurt that the day thus far had been a quiet one at the First Bank of Welch. For a small Midwestern town of no importance, it did have its fair share of calamities of various sizes. Old ladies' bank accounts being drained by young gigolos was an ever-common occurrence, as well as disputes of payments over lawn service—the fights over improperly promising "McCormack quality" grass could get quite vicious, with multiple accounts having been shut down. Not to mention that nothing could compare to the massive row over payment for the McSmith fence when a more pearl than white paint was used by the painter. That particular incident had taken the intervention of McKnight, two other tellers, the bank manager, and a representative from the homeowners' association to decide whether or not pearl was an acceptable shade of white. In the end it was decided that it was, and the parties went away satisfied that it was acceptable to the community standards. He certainly didn't want to deal with that one again.

The idyllic Welch day of normality was shattered by the arrival of Jam and Jim. Jam had some notoriety around town, truth be told, but for Adam McKnight, that should have been some infamy. Since their high school days, Jam had been consistently taking credit for the accomplishments of McKnight, and no one would ever believe evidence to the contrary. Such was life in Welch: if it made the *Welch Watcher,* it was gospel. Adam McKnight had been the quick-witted teller who'd spotted the scammers attempting to scam Jam out of his life savings, but Jam had come in and stolen all the credit that was rightly his.

"How's the weather treating you?" Adam McKnight said through half-gritted teeth.

"Uh, yeah, I'd like to cash this check," Jam answered, paying no heed to proper civil decorum nor two decades of knowing Adam McKnight as he slammed the check down on the counter.

Adam McKnight's eyes dilated as he looked at the check. That was a lot of zeros. Far more zeros than Adam McKnight had ever seen. Far more zeros on a check than the bank had ever seen. The median weekly salary of Welch had two zeros, and a leading number in the high single digits was a source of talk. A check in the low four digits seemed almost scandalous and merited increased scrutiny.

"Cashed?" Adam McKnight choked.

"Yeah, cash it," Jam answered and looked to Jim. "Hundreds should be good right?"

Jim nodded his head absently. "Yeah, let's do it in hundreds."

"You . . . you want to cash a five hundred thousand dollar check?" Adam McKnight said.

"Well, yeah. That's what you do with checks," Jam answered with a sense of self-assuredness.

Words sprang into Adam McKnight's mind. Words like: "elder abuse," "fraud," "counterfeiting," "extortion," "wire fraud." All the words and dirty techniques they taught tellers about and how to spot— words those tellers almost always ignored as they went through the monotony of their clerical duties. Adam McKnight was not one for monotony, and even those other tellers who were would not be able to ignore such a blaring example of fraud. Not to mention that there wasn't even five hundred thousand dollars in cash in the bank, much less the entire town of Welch.

Adam McKnight had Jam now. The alleged hero who'd stopped the credit scammers, the man who'd shut down the pot-growing ring, the man who'd killed the school's prized turtle and shifted blame to Adam McKnight. In the end, Jam was just a common criminal.

"Just a moment, Jam," Adam McKnight said with a smile.

Check in hand, he walked into the office of the bank manager, one Mr. McBride.

"Mr. McBride, Benjamin Fitzgerald came in with a check from his grandmother that he wanted to cash," Adam McKnight said, almost gleaming with pride.

McBride was not amused by the distraction. He looked up from the computer screen, where he was perusing a list of mail-order brides from a variety of Eastern European countries, and grumbled, "Just cash it."

"You really need to look at the amount, Mr. McBride." Adam McKnight placed the half-million-dollar check in front of his boss.

McBride went white. His collar seemed tight around his neck. The glimmer of a potential heart attack washed over him. Beads of sweat condensed upon his forehead in the air-conditioned office. "Oh . . ."

"I believe this may be a case of elder abuse," Adam McKnight said a bit too happily.

McBride nodded. With a shaking hand, he picked up the office phone and dialed out. "Mrs. Fitzgerald, this is Mr. McBride from the First Bank of Welch. I'm calling you about an exceptionally large check you wrote to your grandson."

McBride grabbed a piece of paper, crumpled it, and dabbed at the sweat that was now pouring down his brow. "Yes . . . yes . . . I understand. I was just concerned about the amount and that he wanted it to be cashed . . . No! Please don't close your account with us. We are very thankful for your loyalty."

This certainly wasn't proceeding the way Adam McKnight had

intended. It now all seemed to him that it was just a mistaken amount on the check. The dream of Jam being dragged off in handcuffs quickly evaporated in his mind. How wrong he would soon be.

"We don't actually have that much on hand," McBride continued. "No. No. What I'm saying is that we will need time to get that type of money. I'll need to arrange an armored car to transport it. I'll make sure it is delivered as soon as possible." With a shaky hand, McBride placed the phone back on the cradle. "Adam, tell Mr. Fitzgerald that he'll have his money within the next three days. Wait, I'll go tell him myself. I don't want him thinking that the bank doesn't care about him."

How could something go this wrong? thought Adam McKnight. There was certainly no way that an account from Welch could cover such a withdrawal. "Mr. McBride, you can't be serious. How much money does she even have that you're considering this?"

McBride pulled up a new screen on his computer, punched some letters on the keyboard, and spun the screen around. Adam McKnight's jaw dropped. He had thought the amount of zeros on the check was large and wasn't prepared for what he saw now. He had never seen so many zeros in his life. "Where did she get it all from?"

"Some old billionaire, some guy who was in love with her when they were teenagers. He screwed up when he was writing his will and put her as his sole heir. The family tried to fight it, but in the end the court agreed she should get everything."

Truth be told, Grandma Jelly's money was the only thing still keeping the First Bank of Welch afloat. The bank's management was just as prone to falling for scams as the average Welcher. Several bad investments in the 1990s and early 2000s would have shuttered their doors for good and left the Welchers without a bank and—more importantly—without any savings or pensions if not for Grandma Jelly's millions. A large portion of that mismanagement came from McBride himself. Four failed marriages to four different mail-order brides from four different countries had left him with serious alimony obligations—obligations he could only keep afloat by dipping into the bank's coffers. It was only Grandma Jelly's money and her complete lack of desire to spend it that kept the town and bank going in their meager existence.

Jam shifted impatiently, waiting for Adam McKnight to return. Adam McKnight was nothing but a troublemaker and a stool pigeon, at least according to Jam. Adam McKnight always had it in for Jam—and with no reason whatsoever, again, at least according to Jam. Jam just knew that Adam McKnight was back there right now trying to squash their big deal.

Could General Fonzi have called Adam McKnight as well? The thought crossed Jam's mind and seemed to be a very strong possibility. General Fonzi wouldn't be able to spend all this time waiting for Jam to contact him again. He would have had to move on and look for other people to help him get the gold out of Somalia. Jam knew he would need to move fast and get to Somalia and find General Fonzi before anyone else could get all the money to him and get the gold out of the country.

Jam leaned over the counter, looking for Adam McKnight, but couldn't see into the back room. To Jam it seemed like Adam McKnight had been gone for hours, but in reality it had only been a few minutes. Jim whistled absentmindedly and rocked on his feet, seemingly unfazed by this burdensome delay.

"Something is up, Jim. I don't like this," Jam said.

"Huh? Why's that?" Jim said before going back to his mindless whistling.

"This is taking a long time. Too long. I think McKnight is up to something."

Jim's brow furrowed up in furious thought. "Maybe they're just counting the money. It's a lot to count. It takes us a long time to count out the register sometimes."

That's a very true statement, thought Jam. But in actuality their inability to count out the register in a reasonable amount of time had more to do with their general lack of understanding of numbers and inability to focus on a task for more than a few minutes at a time, forcing them to keep starting over from the beginning.

"I don't know. The bank should have all that money stacked up in a safe ready to go. I think McKnight knows about the gold and General Fonzi. He's trying to cut us out of our own deal!" Jam said.

Jim's whistling and rocking came to an abrupt halt. "Shit, man, you're probably right. He's probably stealing our money and on his way to Somalia right now."

"Fuck, man, I knew I should have had Grandma Jelly write down 'for flavored water' on the check memo. I'm an idiot."

"What should we do, Jam?"

Jam banged on the bell on the counter, hoping that Adam McKnight would magically appear with the cash in hand. Frantically, he banged on it until the poor bell gave out and produced no more sound. "Okay. You run around to the parking lot and see if he's going out the back door. It's going to take a lot of time to load up all that money. I'll wait here if he tries to come out the front."

"Got it, Jam." With that, Jim was in a run toward the front door and looping around the back to lie in wait for the dastardly Adam McKnight.

Again, what seemed like hours for Jam passed. He was getting nervous—more nervous than he already had been. He hadn't heard from Jim. Maybe Jim was fighting with Adam McKnight right now and couldn't call out? It was a thought that was hanging in Jam's head, but he couldn't leave his post in case Adam McKnight was waiting for Jam to leave so he could sneak out the front door.

Finally, after hours—but really just a few minutes—the door to the back office opened. Mr. McBride came hustling out, out of breath, anxious, with Adam McKnight following behind.

"Mr. Fitzgerald," McBride said, "I am so sorry for the delay. When we are dealing with a sum as large as this, we have to fill out a lot of forms, you see."

"Uh, of course," Jam said. McBride took Jam's hand in a sweaty, awkward shake.

"Rest assured, though, you will be getting your money."

Victory, thought Jam. Adam McKnight wasn't going to be able to screw him over this time. "Can you just put it in a duffel bag for me?"

McBride still hadn't relinquished Jam's hand from that sweaty shake. "Well, we don't have the money right now, but we will have it for you within three days. We will make sure it gets delivered right to your door."

Another delay? That's not good, thought Jam. *That's not good at all*. They needed that money right away before some other lucky bastard was able to get all that Somali gold. "I can't wait three days. I need to leave for my trip to Soma—" Jam caught himself and cleared his throat. "I mean, I need to leave for my trip to San Diego tomorrow for my flavored-water business."

"Tomorrow?" McBride's face dropped. "Yes, yes, of course tomorrow. I will put a rush on it. And let me be the first one to say that your business idea sounds like a remarkable investment, and I hope we will have the great fortune of handling all your banking needs in the future."

Jam finally pulled his hand away from McBride's sweaty grip. "Uh . . . thanks."

"One more thing, Mr. Fitzgerald, please do give our regards to your grandmother and let her know everything we did for you. Her money—uh, she—means a lot to us. Far more than she knows."

The concept of waking up before nine was quite foreign to Jam. It was completely anathema to him, and on the few occasions he had been forced to do it he'd heavily voiced his dissent and made it known to everyone about the excess hardship that was being levied upon him. But today wasn't a normal day for Jam. Today was the day that Jam was going to get half a million dollars in cash that would propel him toward fulfilling his champagne wishes and caviar dreams. As such, Jam, quite willingly and eagerly, rose from bed at the ungodly hour of eight in the morning. Not even the alcohol-induced stupor he and Jim had drunk themselves into the night before proved to be a barrier to his cheerful and energetic demeanor. In record time, he managed to take care of his morning routine (shit, shower, and the occasional shave), and before the clock struck nine, he was already leaning out the window waiting for the arrival of the armored car.

It was at exactly 8:59 a.m. that Jam placed the first call to the bank. The phone rang several times before the answering machine picked up—the bank wasn't open yet.

"Yeah, this is Jam," he said, oblivious to the fact that he might need to provide a last name. "It is morning, and the armored car hasn't arrived yet. Call me back when you get this."

Jam hung up the phone and peered out the window. He drummed his fingers together and watched as Welchers drove and walked by on their way to work or their morning errands. Something wasn't right. Jam had a feeling in his gut—a feeling that wasn't producing any sort of positivity. McBride's handshake had been just too clammy for Jam yesterday. It had been the handshake of a man who was guilty of something. Jam knew that McBride was planning something and was probably going to abscond with the money and McKnight to Somalia to get the treasure themselves.

Within a minute, panic was rising through him as he quickly called the bank again at exactly nine a.m. Once again, the call was shuffled to voicemail, and Jam left another panicked message. "This is Jam again. I am calling about the armored-car delivery and want to know where it is. Call me back!"

Jam began pacing the living room, constantly looking out the windows, trying to spot the arrival of an armored car that increasingly didn't seem to be arriving. He grabbed his phone again and dialed a different number.

"Hello," Jim answered in a long, drawn-out, groggy voice, obviously awoken from a deep slumber.

"Jim, the armored car isn't here yet." Jam rushed through the words. "No one at the bank is answering. They're stealing our big deal—we need to get over there."

"Wait." Jim let out a long yawn. "What?"

"The money! McKnight and McBride are going to steal the money so they can get the treasure!"

That snapped both the hangover and the sleep out of Jim. "Are you serious? We can't let them get away with it!"

"We got to get over there. Are you ready to go?"

Jim let out a long grunt. "I need, like, ten minutes."

Ten minutes was too long. For all Jam knew, McBride and McKnight could be halfway to Somalia by then. "I'll meet you at the bank. I'm heading over now."

Jam didn't wait for a response before hanging up the phone. There was too much at stake.

Jam puffed away at a Lucky Strike as he glared into the window of the bank, waiting for Jim. If shit went down, he would need Jim there as backup. From the outside, everything inside the bank seemed to be normal. But Jam knew that looks could be deceiving. He'd played far too many video games and watched far too many movies and knew just how fast things could turn to shit or how much could be hidden behind the scenes.

Just as Jam was finishing off his third Lucky Strike, Jim came running up, still half disheveled from a hangover and a disrupted sleep pattern. "Do you see anything?" Jim asked.

"Nothing." Jam crushed his cigarette beneath his heel. "McKnight is working today. So they must be up to something. Let's do this," he said resolutely, followed by an affirmatory nod from Jim.

The pair strode into the bank and bypassed the line of people orderly lined up, waiting for their turn with the teller. The crowd's Welch sensibilities were offended by the violation of the social order, but their innate politeness prevented them from voicing outrage. After all, for someone to skip the line so brazenly, it must be a critical issue that required an immediate response. After all, why else would someone violate the social contract in such a way unless it was an emergency?

Adam McKnight didn't notice Jam and Jim's approach, as he was too busy explaining to a lady of Ample Hills, between her come-ons to him, that her interest for the month on her account was indeed only five cents and not the six cents she had calculated on her own.

"What's going on, McKnight?" Jam demanded. "Your boss told me that the armored car would arrive this morning."

"I'm with a customer right now," McKnight said in annoyance. His dislike of Jam and Jim increased by degrees with each passing meeting and each additional minute held in their company.

"I need to see McBride right now or else," Jam said and then momentarily got caught up. He didn't really have a threat in mind, but then he had a slight recollection. McBride had seemed especially deferential to Grandma Jelly and made sure to note how important she was. "Or else," Jam continued, "I'll need to tell Grandma Jelly about what's going on."

Even with all the dislike that Adam McKnight held for Jam and Jim, his professional demeanor came to the forefront. Jelly's account was of great value to the bank, and they needed to do everything they could to preserve it. "I'll get Mr. McBride right away," McKnight said.

It only took a moment for McBride to appear from the back. He was as sweaty and clammy as ever; crow's feet deeply lined his eyes, betraying a sleepless night.

"Mr. Fitzgerald," McBride said, his voice hoarse as he grasped Jam's hand in a sweaty, clammy, double-fisted handshake. "I was about to return your call just now."

Jam pulled his hand away and shook the salty moisture from it.

"You said the money would arrive this morning, but," he said as he checked his phone, "it is almost ten and the car didn't arrive yet. What is going on?"

"I just spoke with the armored car company. They said they're on schedule and should be arriving by noon. When we are dealing with such large sums of money, sometimes it takes a while for all parties to get everything in order."

Jam felt slightly at ease—just slightly. With both McKnight and McBride at the bank, he didn't think they were going to steal his big deal and head off to Somalia. Though he wasn't entirely certain they weren't planning *something*—after all, noon wasn't morning, it was noon. Jam still had his trump card, though: McBride's seemingly odd deference to Grandma Jelly. "Well, I guess that's okay," he said. "But if it's late, I'm going to have to tell my grandma about it."

McBride's eyes twitched. The twitch soon descended down his body and was quickly caught in his heart, which a hand soon grasped in obvious distress. "That won't be necessary," the bank manager croaked. "I can assure you that the money will arrive by then."

Jam knew he shouldn't have left the bank. Since he'd arrived home, he had sat by the window waiting for any sign of the money. The clock was striking noon but there was no armored car. Across from him, sprawled across the couch, was Jim, snoring away and catching up on the sleep he had been deprived of earlier.

Jam had no idea how his friend could get any sleep at a time like this. Jam was so nervous about the deal in the works that he couldn't force down cold pizza and taquitos. Even beer felt unsettling to his stomach, and he was never bothered by beer—ever.

Jam snatched up his phone again and dialed the bank.

"First Bank of Welch, Adam McKnight speaking, how's the weather treating you?" the voice answered cheerfully on the other end.

"I need to speak to Mr. McBride about my money," Jam said.

A certain grating sounded over the phone—the noise of teeth being gnashed? "Is this Jam?" McKnight asked.

"Obviously," Jam huffed.

"Just a moment."

Elevator music played for a few seconds before the flustered voice of Mr. McBride came on the line. "Mr. Fitzgerald," McBride said. "We are working as fast as we can to get the money over to you, don't you worry about it."

"You said the money was going to be here by noon," Jam said and checked his phone for the time. "It is now twelve oh five, and the truck isn't here yet."

Jam could almost hear the sweat pouring off McBride through the phone. "Of course, but there were some delays. Delays that were completely outside of our control. I am sure you can understand."

Jam didn't understand. All he knew was that every minute the money wasn't there was another minute someone else could be getting the treasure. "Do I need to tell Grandma Jelly?" he threatened, still entirely unsure why McBride was so concerned about his grandmother and her money.

McBride gasped. "No," he squeaked out. "Of course not, I will make sure to see to it personally that the money gets delivered immediately."

The armored car didn't arrive until nearly two in the afternoon. Because of the lack of signage leading to Welch, the car had made numerous wrong turns and ventured into several surrounding towns while going in confusing loops and constantly missing Welch. In the end, the directional issues had led a terrified McBride to drive out to the armored car himself and escort the vehicle the rest of the way to Welch and up to Jam's door.

An extremely apologetic McBride met Jam at his door, attempting to explain away the multiple delays, which a very disinterested Jam ignored as he quickly signed the necessary papers, took hold of the package, and promptly slammed the door in McBride's face.

A wave of terror washed over McBride. This was the end for him. The end for the First Bank of Welch. Jam was going to tell his grandmother and she was going to pull her money out of the bank, and that would be it—it would be the complete end of the town.

What made it all the worse for McBride was that today was his birthday. It was his fiftieth birthday, to be precise. The end of thirty years of service at the bank would come today.

A creeping, tingling sensation moved up McBride's left arm, and the taste of copper filled his mouth. At least he wouldn't live to see the bank shuttered and have to deal with all those angry Welchers demanding to know where their money had disappeared to.

6

"Willy McBride was a Welcher through and through. He liked his Dewar's on the rocks, his Busch Light cold, and now we can go and sit by his graveside."

—Taken from McBride's eulogy

A minor conflict at Ample Hills was well on its way to escalating into a full-scale war. It all started because Eugenia was jealous of Virginia's apple pie, which had won numerous baking competitions. It was an apple pie that was remarkably invigorating and left all those who ate it in a state of euphoria. Eugenia asked Virginia for the recipe, but Virginia obviously refused on account of it being a family secret and containing a secret ingredient (a soupçon of cocaine) that she couldn't reveal. This, of course, necessitated the stealing of the recipe by Eugenia, who, being a much better baker, improved upon it and beat Virginia in the Ample Hills baking contest.

Virginia, of course, could not take this theft lying down, figuratively at least, and in revenge slept with Eugenia's grandson, giving him an uncommonly aggressive strain of the clap. Of course, both these offenses gained their defenders and detractors, and camps began to form within Ample Hills. At first, this just resulted in snide remarks and sitting at separate tables at mealtime, but it soon developed into a war of pranks and thefts. Most of these pranks involved the ladies' sex toys and sometimes the liberal application of hot sauce to them and a stealthy return of said toy. Not even the intervention of King Al could bring peace to the warring camps.

Now the rec room more resembled the demilitarized zone between the Koreas than that of an old folks' home, with Eugenia's camp firmly in control of the arts and crafts cabinet and Virginia's camp controlling the library and the entire stock of smutty books. This unarmed standoff was the situation Jam found himself stuck in as he walked through the rec room to say goodbye to his Grandma Jelly.

Of course, Grandma Jelly was completely neutral and still sat in her usual seat (right in the middle of the DMZ), knitting her usual knickknacks.

Even someone as clueless as Jam could sense the tension that was thick in the air. "What's going on, Grandma Jelly?"

"My sweet Benjamin, it is absolutely horrible. They're feuding and there is no end in sight. The Cougars broke up and only just a week before the championship. We had to give it up because no one could play together," Grandma Jelly said.

That indeed was the worst possible news Jam could hear. The Cougars had won every championship since Grandma Jelly had joined the team. It was the highlight of Grandma Jelly's year and also always earned them the honor of being featured on the front page of the *Welch Watcher*. "That's horrible, Grandma Jelly. I'm sure you guys are going to win it next year."

"I hope so, Benjamin," Jelly sighed. "There is just no talking sense into them. We've been trying everything to get them to stop. Not even a trip up to the casino could do it. They sat on opposite sides of the bus and didn't talk to each other. Hopefully, the grandchildren's dinner next week will get everyone back together. Speaking of which, will you be coming this year, Benjamin?"

Jam shook his head. "I can't, Grandma Jelly. I'm sorry. I'm leaving for California tonight."

"California?"

"Yeah, California. For the flavored-water business. Me and Jim are going over there to meet with investors."

Grandma Jelly squealed with delight, dropped her knitting instruments, and pulled Jam into an extra-tight hug. It was the type of hug that squeezed all the air out of your lungs. "See, I knew your big deal would come through. Soon I'll be able to tell all the ladies around here that my grandson is a flavored-water billionaire."

Jam gasped for air as his grandmother relinquished the hug. "I couldn't have done it without you, Grandma Jelly. The people at the bank were dicks, though. They made me wait an entire day to get the money."

Jelly waved off Jam's complaint about the bank. "Don't pay them any mind, Benjamin. They're just jealous that your big deal is going to work out."

Jam really hoped no one was going to steal his flavored-water idea while he was away in Somalia. It really was a billion-dollar idea, and he would be able to use the Somali gold to finance it. "I got to get going, Grandma Jelly. Is Vic around? I didn't see her and I should say bye to her before I leave."

"She's off today. You can probably catch her at home, though."

It was an incessant type of knocking—the type of knocking that doesn't take a break, doesn't stop until the door is opened. It was the type of knocking performed by someone who was almost fearful that if they stopped knocking they would forget just exactly the reason they were there. It was the type of knocking Jam excelled at.

Vic didn't hurry to the door. She knew she had time—only Jam knocked like that, and he would wait for her—he always did. She stopped at the mirror by the front door and checked her hair, reapplied her lip gloss, and undid the top two buttons on her shirt. "I'm coming!" she called out.

There was a stilted laugh from behind the door, and Jam yelled, "That's what she said!"

She opened the door with a smile and leaned against the frame. "Hey, Jam."

If Jam noticed her unbuttoned shirt, he didn't give any hint of it. "Hey, Vic. I just came by to say goodbye."

"Goodbye?"

"Yeah, me and Jim are going far away for a big deal. It's really all hush-hush. I can't tell you much about it. But this is going to be the one that makes me millions and gets me out of here."

Vic rolled her eyes. She never had time for or interest in any of Jam's big deals, and he rarely bothered to tell her about them. Everything was always covered in a veil of secrecy. "I don't get why you're always trying to get out of here. Welch isn't as bad as you make it out to be. You just never gave it a chance."

This time it was Jam's turn to roll his eyes. "You don't get it, Vic. Everyone is against me here. Only you, Grandma Jelly, and Jim get me. Everyone else is just jealous of me for being so smart."

"What makes you think this deal is going to be the one?"

"Grandma Jelly gave me money for my mission—uh, business— this time. It can't lose."

One of Vic's eyebrows rose ever so slightly. "So why don't you use the money and start something up over here?"

Jam blew air out through his mouth, making a noise more resembling a horse than a human. "No one gets my ideas here. Everything is the same. That's why I got to go with the money and get out of here."

"What makes you think it's going to be different out there? Where are you going to live?"

"I don't know. It just is. I'll move to a big city somewhere—at least the people are going to be real there and won't judge me."

All Vic could do was shake her head. "You know I lived in the city for college, right? They are the furthest thing from real. Everyone is pretending to be someone else there and just trying to play the role."

It was one of the things that brought Vic back to Welch. The people were all simple and honest. Even Jam, in his own way, despite all his bluster and big ideas, was just a simple, nice guy at heart, even if he didn't see it himself. He would be eaten alive outside of Welch.

It wasn't the first time Vic had seen him so set on his own way, and she knew that when he got like this there was no way to talk him out of it. She would just have to let it pass and wait for his mind to wander on to a different topic. "Where are you going, anyway?"

"Far, real far. All the way to California."

Vic tilted her head. "California? That isn't that far, Jam. I've been to California. It's only a few hours by plane."

Jam shook his head. "Nah, it's going to take us awhile to get there. It's a real trip and a half to get there."

"Where exactly are you going in California? Are you driving or taking a plane? When are you leaving?"

Jam leaned in close to Vic. "Tonight, but that's all I can tell you. You know with these big deals you got to be like the military and keep everything secret so no one knows what you're planning."

All Vic could do was nod. She knew she wasn't going to get anything out of him.

"I got to go," Jam continued. "Jim is waiting and I don't want to be late. I'll be back soon, and when you see me next I'll have millions."

Des Moines was more of a town than Welch was. At the airport there was constant movement, people coming and going, and money exchanging hands. Jam and Jim were momentarily in awe at the size of the place. It was far larger than anything they had ever seen in their entire lives. They were also both relieved and impressed by the complete lack of a weather-based greeting. But they had a mission ahead of them and couldn't get distracted by such triviality.

"Where are we going, Jam?" Jim asked.

Both had decided to look the part from the beginning to the end and thus were dressed in the uniforms they had ordered. The knock-off uniforms were hardly properly tailored and were already beginning to come apart at the seams. Jam's was reasonably kept together and seemed to fit him vaguely. Jim's, however, appeared to hover around him.

Jam pulled a crumpled note from his boot-legged military uniform and attempted to decipher his own chicken-scratch writing. "That's the airline over there."

Neither noticed that the duffel bag filled with cash lay abandoned on a nearby bench as they approached the ticketing line.

The line wasn't unbearable, but even so, they found themselves rocking back and forth and whistling with nervousness as they waited. Everything was resting on the success of this trip.

As they waited in line, a thought pushed itself to the forefront of Jam's mind. It was an issue that had the potential to doom their trip before it even got started.

Passports.

Several years back, the lack of passports had foiled a sure-fire big deal. After hearing about a possible maple syrup shortage, Jam had the idea to cut out the middleman and bring the brown gold directly into the country themselves. Jam and Jim loaded themselves into Jelly's old car and took the long trip up to the northern border only to be turned back for not having passports. The need for them had never crossed their minds. Jam had vowed that they would never miss a big international deal again and made sure that both he and Jim had passports. It was a foresight that Jam was immensely proud of at their current juncture.

Jam knew he had packed his and had checked multiple times that it was in the front pocket of his navy blouse. He tapped the pocket just to make sure and found it reassuringly there. Jim was another matter entirely.

"Jim, do you have your passport?" Jam asked.

Jim ceased whistling and thought for a long, hard moment. "Yeah," he said.

"Are you sure?"

The look on Jim's face told Jam that Jim was entirely unsure of the document's whereabouts. Jim began frantically searching his pockets, working his way from the top down. The sheer volume of pockets in the uniform was slowing down the search to an unbearable degree. Finally, just as he reached the last of his pockets in the baggy pants, he found the little blue book and presented it to Jam.

Jam was able to breathe a sigh of relief as they were called up to the counter. They weren't going to miss this flight and give Adam McKnight time to figure out what they were doing and beat them to the treasure.

"How can I help you?" the clerk said. If the clerk noticed their uniforms, or the state of them, he didn't give any outward sign of it.

"Yeah, we need two tickets for the flight to Mogadishu, Somalia," Jam answered.

The clerk tapped away at his computer. "What departure date?"

"Tonight."

"That's going to be quite expensive."

"That's fine," said Jam. "Say, do you have any first-class seats available?"

The clerk shook his head. "I'm afraid not. It is completely booked. You guys are lucky to get the last two seats. It's going to come out to ten thousand. Credit or debit?"

"Cash."

"Cash?" the clerk clarified.

"Yeah, cash," Jam repeated. "Jim, give me the bag."

Jim looked at Jam quizzically. "I don't have the bag."

This certainly wasn't good. Everything they planned rested with that bag. "What do you mean you don't have the bag? I told you to hold on to the bag."

Jim shook his head profusely. "You didn't tell me that."

"Well, where's the bag?"

The two looked over to the area they had just occupied. A small crowd had formed around the seemingly abandoned duffel bag. The concept of "if you see something, say something" was completely adhered to at the Des Moines Airport. Several travelers pointed and motioned for security to come and check out the bag.

"Quick, Jim. Get it," Jam said, a certain panic filling his voice.

Jim sprinted over to the unaccompanied bag and scooped it up, mumbling apologies to everyone as he sped on by. With the situation seemingly defused by the slovenly dressed military man, everyone gawking went on their way.

Bag in hand, Jim reappeared at the ticket counter and pulled out a crisp bank stack wrapped in tape with ten thousand written across it. He smiled a big, dumb smile to Jam and the clerk.

The security line was the complete opposite of the ticketing line. It snaked its way slowly from the start all the way to the metal detectors. Every step seemed to take an eternity, as someone at the front seemingly always forgot to take off their belt, empty their pockets, or some other sundry issue that was related to traveling in this day and age. It seemed to be that every person flying that day was taking their first flight and was completely unfamiliar with the protocols and procedures of airport security. And, indeed, for Jam and Jim, this was both their first flights and they were already completely disenchanted with the whole process of air travel.

Unbeknownst to Jam and Jim, their tickets were specially marked. The slight scene at the ticketing booth and the not-so-small fact that they'd paid cash for an international flight leaving in only a few hours both were contributing factors for the special attention they would receive.

They handed their tickets over to a TSA agent, who scrutinized them and their passports. He looked at their information, then back to the tickets, then back to them. Finally, he said, "Just wait over here to the side for a minute."

Another TSA agent quickly approached them. "Gentlemen," he said, "can you please come with me?"

Jam and Jim exchanged looks as they were led to a private screening area, made to empty their pockets, go through a seldom-used metal detector, and hand the duffel bag of cash over.

They were then placed in a private room and made to wait. The looks exchanged between the two became more worrisome.

Jim started to speak, but Jam stopped him with a long "Shhh." Jam pointed around the room and said in a whisper, "It's probably bugged."

Jim nodded along to the sentiment. In the movies, the cops were always watching and listening from a secret room.

After several more minutes, another TSA agent entered. He was an older gentleman, a supervisor, still chronically underpaid, but at the very least he had some sort of authority.

"You guys are in the military?" the supervisor asked.

Like most things Jam "knew," what came to mind was misremembered and partially factual, but mostly wrong. He had read somewhere that it was a federal offense to lie to a federal agent about being a soldier. "Nope," he quickly said, "we just like the look."

The supervisor nodded and looked over some paperwork in his hand. "And you're traveling to Somalia with nearly five hundred grand in cash?"

"Yeah, that's correct."

"Can I ask why?"

Jam knew he certainly couldn't tell the TSA boss about the gold. Then they would make note of it and he would have to pay taxes on it when they got back. Jam also wasn't certain about the legality of taking pirate gold. "We are going to open a business."

The supervisor's eyebrow rose to a dramatic degree. "In Somalia?"

"In Somalia."

"Do you have any documentation stating that this money was legally obtained?"

"Huh?" Jam voiced.

The supervisor sighed. "Where did you get the money from?"

Jam pulled the crumpled sheet he'd received from the bank when he'd signed for the money from his pocket. "My Grandma Jelly gave me the money."

Luckily, the primary business of the TSA is to look for explosives and take away sewing kits from little old ladies before they board planes. They weren't in the business of questioning where money was being spent or what it was going to be used for, as long as said money seemed to be legally obtained. Anything that happened to two idiot Americans who got themselves arrested, robbed, or killed (not necessarily all of those or in that particular order) would be the responsibility of the State Department. Or the responsibility of customs when they attempted to return to the United States with copious amounts of cocaine, heroin, or khat strapped to their bodies. With nary a question more, Jam and Jim were released from TSA.

There were only two classes of people who received praise and adoration at American airports. The first was celebrities of all stripes and the second was American soldiers. Americans at airports liked nothing more than laying praise upon those men and women in uniform. Terminals would promptly burst into applause; travelers would call out, "Thank you for your service!" Children would ask them for pictures. It was, after all, the least one could do for those protecting their freedom.

The travelers at Des Moines International Airport didn't fail to pull out all the stops for the two uniformed soldiers, no doubt just trying to make it home after flying nearly twenty hours back from Afghanistan or Iraq.

It was all the adoration and praise that Jam wanted and deserved, and the fact that he wasn't getting it made him all the angrier. The two real uniformed soldiers a dozen yards in front of them were receiving all the attention and not a single person even gave Jam or Jim a second glance. The lack of attention stemmed from the sorry state of their uniforms.

Jim didn't seem to mind it, though. He tugged at the Chinese-made uniform, trying to get it to fit just right. It had all the appeal and shape of a camouflaged garbage bag.

Jam gritted his teeth so hard that it made his ears hurt. Finally, after a long pause, he said, "Come on, Jim. Let's just get to the gate."

They settled into the passenger lounge and waited for boarding to commence for the flight that would take them to Mogadishu and bring them their champagne wishes and caviar dreams, as well as the celebrity adoration that Jam so desperately craved. If Jam wasn't going to be thanked for his service, he was going to try to get some perks for the flight at least. "I'll be right back. I heard that soldiers in uniform get upgraded to first class for free. I'm going to score us an upgrade."

"Jam, the guy said first class was sold out," Jim said.

"Yeah, but we're soldiers. They bump people out of first class for us, or someone will give up their seats for war heroes. It happens all the time," Jam said with utter self-confidence that only he could produce.

With all the military swagger he could muster, which quite honestly wasn't much, Jam marched up to the gate counter. The girl behind the counter was gorgeous. She wasn't fake and made up like Super-Rich's girlfriend. She had a more Midwestern look about her. She actually bore a strong resemblance to Vic. Jam knew he had this one in the bag. If there was one thing he was good at, it was talking to Iowan girls— once again, that was a talent that only existed in Jam's own mind.

The pretty gate agent looked the faux military man up and down and let out a long, exasperated sigh. She had had dealings with these types before. "How can I help you?" she asked sweetly but tinged with annoyance.

Jam craned his neck, cracking it, and leaned on the counter. "I was wondering if there were any upgrades available for me and my fellow soldier over there."

Jam pointed a finger back to Jim, who was now stretched out on the floor, snoozing.

The gate agent smiled briefly. "Boarding pass, please."

Jam handed their boarding passes over and smiled an even bigger smile. He was confident that they were going to get upgraded now.

The gate agent tapped away at her keyboard and then said, "I'm sorry. There don't seem to be any upgrades available."

Absolutely nothing was going Jam's way. "Are you sure? I heard that active duty soldiers get free upgrades to first class."

She smacked her lips together. "You heard wrong."

"This is absurd. Me and my friend are SEALs going on a secret mission and this is how we're getting treated?"

Her eyes rolled over him, focusing on the army tab on his blouse and then the rank tab. "You're a SEAL *and* in the army?"

"Sure," he said with a big smile.

"Sure" is the default answer for any question where the veracity of the answer can be called into question. "Sure" was neither a complete affirmative, nor did it completely deny the possibility. "Sure" was whatever the answerer wanted it to be—an almost get-out-of-jail-free card for the answerer if they got called out on their bullshit.

The gate agent smiled again and gave a condescending wink. "Well, I'm sorry Lieutenant Colonel, it looks like you're out of luck," she said, using the corresponding army rank for the insignia of a silver oak leaf.

Jam pointed at that very silver oak leaf. "I'm a lieutenant, not a lieutenant colonel."

Jam and Jim waited for the boarding call to economy. They were at the far back of the plane and would be the last to be called. *It's all complete bullshit*, thought Jam. He was completely positive that none of those people lining up for the first-class seats had a duffel bag with five hundred thousand dollars in it, but Jam and Jim did, and that meant they should be in that first-class section.

Finally, after first class, business class, then premium economy, economy was called. But only the first rows. Jam and Jim would need to continue to wait. It was only when nearly ninety percent of the plane was already loaded that the zone for the two Welchers was called.

With the duffel bag of cash slung over Jam's shoulder, they made their way down the plane's aisle. They walked past the first-class passengers being given complimentary champagne, past the business-class passengers being handed hot towels, past the premium-economy fliers picking their meal from an actual menu. Most of the economy-class passengers were already comfortable, or at least gave the appearance of being comfortable, in their seats. It was at the very back of the plane, by the bathrooms, that the two Welchers found their seats.

"Well, this sucks," Jam said to no one in particular.

They pushed their way past the passenger sitting in the aisle seat, who refused to budge, and stumbled into their seats.

"Jam, I have a question," Jim said.

"What?" Jam answered.

"Did you remember to tell the boss that we were going away?"

Jam just shrugged at what didn't even register as an inconvenience. "Nah, he'll figure it out and find coverage."

"It's okay, boss. Not a problem at all. I have no problem working a triple. I'm just happy to help," Dante said as he hung up the phone.

It was only his second day on the job at 7-Eleven, and the two guys set to relieve him, Jam and Jim, were both no-call, no-show. The boss assured him that they would show up eventually. This happened every now and then with those two but there wasn't any reason for concern.

Dante didn't mind. He was happy to have a job, and if working the occasional triple shift had to happen, it is what happened. The job, after all, was a stepping stone. If he put in his time and energy working that triple, surely he would get noticed and be offered the position of assistant manager one day. Then, if he worked hard and showed initiative, he would surely be selected for the heady heights of a real managerial position. After that, everything was a sure thing. He would be able to save up his money and open up his own 7-Eleven and then life would be easy. He had the next fifteen years all tracked out, and things were looking good.

A black Japanese-made car pulled into the parking lot. It wasn't a gray, American sedan, so clearly it wasn't a Welcher. The poor driver was probably lost and needed directions. Luckily, Dante was prepared for this possibility and had several road maps at the ready for anyone who needed them. It wasn't store policy to have the road maps—it was his own personal brand of customer service.

A man clad in all black got out of the car and entered the store. The electronic door dinged as it opened. Nope, this man was definitely not a local. Dante got his pocket-sized road map ready to assist the lost driver.

"How's the weather treating you?" Dante said as the man approached the counter.

The man didn't even give Dante the courtesy of a "ho-ho" as he pulled the black gun out from his black shirt. "Give me all the money in the register."

Over the years, airplane seats have consistently gotten smaller and smaller, and over the course of those same years the space between the rows of said smaller seats has also consistently gotten smaller and smaller, all done in the interest of profits and the abandonment of customer service. It was a fact that Jam was intimately getting acquainted with despite this being his first flight.

Jam's knees touched the seat in front of him. One elbow was jammed painfully against the window, and the other rested on Jim, whose head was leaning on Jam's shoulder, a string of drool dripping down. Jim was sleeping soundly, but not soundlessly, as his snores reverberated through the cabin. At least, he was sleeping soundly until Jam launched an elbow into his ribs.

"Oof!" Jim popped up with a start.

"This is some bullshit," Jam said.

Jim wiped the sleep away from his eyes and drool from his chin. "What?" he asked with a yawn.

"All this," Jam grunted. "We should be up there in first class getting served champagne and caviar, not crammed in back here."

Jim didn't pay any attention to Jam, and he closed his eyes.

"Never mind. Go back to sleep."

Heat from the yellow-tinted lights beat down on the bald head of Hassan Ahmed. The assistant deputy from the Ministry of Tourism tugged at the collar of his shirt and jabbed at his forehead with a white linen handkerchief. A lot rode on his shoulders and the assembled welcoming party that accompanied him.

Somalia had a tourism problem. Its problem with tourism was a lack thereof. It was hard to attract tourists when most of the world's knowledge about your country came from a terrifying and tragic 2001 war movie based on a true story. It also didn't help that the rest of the world's knowledge came from a 2013 film about a ship being hijacked and the crew kept captive by pirates—once again based on a true story. This was then coupled with the fact that whenever Somalia was present in the news, it was always about the aforementioned pirates, and usually because said pirates were holding foreigners for ransom.

Hassan's superiors had decided that this image problem would need to be addressed, and they quickly set about it in the only way they knew how. They got Hollywood involved. Movies would be the salvation for the Somali tourism industry. It had, of course, worked for New Zealand, though they hadn't had a pirate problem for centuries. Talks were underway with producers of the aforementioned 2001 film,

Black Hawk Down. In short, a sequel would be produced that would highlight all the positive changes that had occurred since that slight misunderstanding between Somali warlords and U.S. Special Forces.

How could one write a sequel to a historical event with the sequel bearing no resemblance to the previous movie? It was a question that Hassan had asked and been quickly told didn't matter. Everything would come down to movie magic. Movie magic would be their savior, and no one was to question it.

All Hassan needed to do was rather simple. He needed to razzle and dazzle the advance crew coming to scout filming locations. It was imperative, his superiors had said, that the advance crew be exposed to all the best Somalia had to offer so they would follow through with the movie and not base it somewhere else. He was also under strict instructions to make sure the Americans didn't see anything shady or unsightly that might give them cause to not want to stay in Somalia. These Hollywood types were said to be fickle and could make or break someone, even if that someone was a nation state composed of some eleven million people. No expense was to be spared, and Hassan was expected to treat the Americans to a good time and never refuse any of their requests.

It was also made clear to Hassan, in no uncertain terms, that if these Hollywood bigwigs decided not to film in Somalia, then all the blame would rest firmly on his shoulders. He would be stripped of his post and his name would be dragged so deep and far through the mud that he wouldn't even be able to get hired as a water boy for a pirate gang.

Hassan checked his watch. The plane with the film crew would be landing any minute at Aden Adde International Airport. He dabbed again at the sweat on his forehead, his bald head shining in the lights, and pulled at the all-too-tight collar of his shirt.

Hassan motioned for the welcoming party to get ready as the plane pulled up to the gate. Everything rested on this first impression.

7

"For a country mostly known for its civil war, the
whole ceremony is quite similar to a small war."

—FROM THE CHAPTER ON SOMALIA IN *THE HITCHHIKER'S GUIDE TO
WORLD HISTORY*

Airports by nature are very confusing places, what with all the
people rushing about. Hassan almost missed the two Navy
SEALs coming from the gate in the international terminal of
Aden Adde International Airport.

The two men, Jam holding the duffel bag and Jim looking around
with awe, weren't quite what Hassan was expecting. He stood for a
moment, flanked by a welcoming party of men and women in traditional garb, consisting of brightly colored robes and headscarves.

Finally, Hassan spoke. "Are you with the advance crew from the
production company?"

There was a quick exchange of looks between Jam and Jim. "I
don't think—" Jim started.

Jam interrupted Jim with that ever-confident yet evasive answer: "Sure!"

"Welcome! Welcome!" Hassan yelled. He turned to the assembled
party behind him and said, "It's them."

A collective cheer rose up as the welcoming party swarmed the
two Americans, battering them with hugs and kisses, and shoving

bouquets of flowers, boxes of sweets, and other trinkets into their hands. Hassan grabbed hold of both of them and pulled them into a three-way hug.

"What's going on, Jam?" Jim asked.

"Just go with it," Jam replied as he basked in the adoration of the crowd.

Jam was not the type of person to ever entertain doubt. When he did experience doubt, it was short and fleeting, usually right after a big deal fell through. Then it was on to the next big deal. But any possible doubt that had cropped up regarding their trip to Somalia had instantly evaporated. Jam was finally getting the attention he deserved. A moment of real admiration. It wasn't the nonsensical admiration obtained by being featured in the *Welch Watcher*. It was a glorious moment and he intended to bask in it for as long as possible.

Jam held tight to the duffel bag as a waiting attendant attempted to take the load away from him. "Sorry, important documents," Jam said. The attendant smiled and nodded, giving Jam a thumbs-up.

"We are so happy to have you," Hassan said as the welcoming party shuffled them out of the airport and into the hot summer sun of Somalia. "I am Hassan Ahmed from the Ministry of Tourism. Anything you need, just ask. I am here to serve you."

"Uhh . . . thanks," Jam said. Despite all his optimism about Somalia, he didn't expect it to be this grand. He certainly wasn't used to this kind of attention and didn't know entirely how to respond.

"You're going to find Somalia very accommodating. You'll have whatever you need in order to get the film produced."

Jam had no idea what film Hassan was talking about but managed a "That's great."

"You've come at a great time. It is our solar festival: Neeroosh," Hassan said as he led them into a waiting limo. "You will get to experience everything Somalia has to offer."

Quickly bundled up in the limo, Jim and Jam were driven off in unexpected style. Their status as film producers and welcome by the

Ministry of Tourism had let them completely bypass customs and any talk of why they were carrying around half a million dollars in cash or why they were dressed in military attire.

"This is great," Jam said. "I told you this was a great idea. We just got to play along and say we're part of the film crew." *After all*, he thought, *how hard could it be to pretend to be from a film company?* Just talk about some movies, some actors, and bring up cameras and sets. They had seen more than enough movies to do that. It would be quite simple for them to play the role.

Jim got that look on his face again—the look that showed he was thinking hard about something. "Jam, I wonder where the actual film crew is?" Unbeknownst to Jam, Jim, and Hassan, the two real film advisors, two actual Navy SEALS, arrived several hours later, were arrested for being imposters, and were immediately sent back the U.S.

The streets of Mogadishu were filled with celebrants. Massive bonfires burned throughout the city, as men and women leaped over them, dousing each other with water after completing their jumps to wash away any of the burning embers that may have caught on them.

The entirety of the city was a cacophony of colors: reds, yellows, purples, and blues. They were all the colors that were missing from Welch, with its white picket fences, gray sedans, and brown pants. It was like nothing the two Welchers had ever seen. In Welch, parties and festivals were quiet affairs with a grill going and a potluck set up—certainly no colorful and wild festivity in the streets. Welch had nothing that could compare to the near riotous assembly they were now driving through. They rode with their faces pressed against the windows of the limo, eyes wide as they took in everything around them, their brains barely able to comprehend the vast array of sights and sounds. This was nothing like what they had expected when they'd originally planned to come to Somalia. This was something completely different—something they would never have been able to imagine, even in their wildest dreams.

Celebrants swarmed around the limo, cheering and waving and throwing water at the two dazed and astounded Americans. The water bounced harmlessly off the closed windows, but Jim still managed to flinch from it.

"Jam, this is crazy," Jim said as he gawked out the window.

"Jim, you don't get it. This is all for us. They're doing it for us." Jam beamed. Well, technically they were doing it for the film producers, but as far as Jam was concerned, they were the film producers now. After all, maybe with the treasure in hand they could go into film production. It was a very glamorous life, and they would be able to rub elbows with celebrities and other rich people. It would sure beat hanging out with all the boring people in Welch.

"What if they figure out we aren't the film producers?"

Jam shook his head. There was nothing to prove that they weren't. "Just go with it. We are the SEALs that the film company hired for the movie."

"What if they ask what movie we're making? What are we going to say?"

There are certain times in the universe when an idea is released into the ether and somehow migrates to another mind that had nothing to do with the original conception. This was one of those moments, and that idea, albeit a bad one, now seeped its way into Jam's mind. "Just tell them it's a sequel to *Black Hawk Down*."

The limo came to a halt in a large fairground, where a sizable group of Somalis had gathered in celebration of the arrival of summer. The fairground was lined with dozens of carts and tents with vendors selling their wares, festive costumes, perfumes, and the finest clothes, toys, and foods that Jam and Jim had never seen before. In other parts of the fairground, dozens of rides were set up for the children. But the main attraction of the festival was in the center of the grounds, where dozens of bonfires filled the field and shirtless men raced toward the fires and leaped over them, as women covered in flowing robes and scarves waited at the other side with clay pots filled with water, prepared to shower them with liquid and praises. Each man who leaped the flame had his own style. The more cautious of the bunch just ran and jumped over the flames without much fanfare. Those slightly bolder extended their arms and legs midair. The even bolder spun and twisted their bodies as they crossed the flame, or even performed flips to let the fire tickle their heads. The boldest of the bunch would stand with their backs to the flame and, without any running, perform a backflip over it that would make an Olympic gymnast jealous, to the adoration of the crowd.

Hassan appeared at the limo door and opened it. "Please come," he said. "You must participate in the festival."

"I'm good," Jim tried to protest, but the hands of festivalgoers reached in and extracted him from the limo.

The smell of smoke and cooked lamb and goat filled the air as the two Welchers were pulled into the crowd by Hassan and the other celebrants.

"Take your shirts off," Hassan said. "You must be shirtless to jump the flame."

Jam had no intention of jumping over any fires, but he wasn't going to not participate in the rest of the festival. It was all too grand— all too different. He would never be able to go back to Welch after this. *How would anyone be able to go back to Welch?* he thought. *Especially after being in a place that parties like this.*

Jim was far more hesitant. "I really don't want to."

"You must," Hassan insisted. "It would be rude not to."

"Come on, Jim," Jam added. "Don't blow it."

"I really can't because—" Jim didn't get a chance to finish as multiple pairs of hands pulled the cheaply made knock-off military blouse off him.

A group of girls giggled at Jim and then grabbed him, dragging him into the crowd.

"Jam!" Jim called out.

"He will be fine," Hassan said as he pushed Jam toward the nearest bonfire. "Now it is time for you to jump the flame."

The fire danced in Jam's eyes. For the first time since arriving in Somalia, he was actually nervous. Maybe this was all a very bad idea after all. He could deal with pirates, but jumping over a roaring bonfire was another thing entirely; it was almost suicidal.

Jam backed away from the flames. "Nah, I'm good, really," he insisted.

"It is an insult not to. You must jump or we will throw you," Hassan countered.

"Wait, what?" It was too late. Strong arms grabbed Jam and before he knew it, he was on the ground, one set of hands holding his arms outstretched and another set holding his feet. They started to swing him like a hammock.

"No! Please!" Jam begged as he twisted and turned, trying to break free of their vise-like grip.

They didn't listen to Jam's cry and continued their back-and-forth swinging as the crowd around them chanted. With one final "Hurrah!" they let Jam go flying.

Jam soared over the bonfire, flames licking at his back. On the other side, he landed unceremoniously in a heap. Women waited with water-filled pots that they hastily dumped on him. A great cheer went up in the crowd as they chanted, "Again! Again!"

"Yes, yes, I understand. I will let you know if I see anything. Let me know the same on your end," Faarax said as he put down the encrypted satellite phone.

Shadya sat by the chessboard, her first play already completed, a simple moving of the king's pawn two spots. It was a basic opening from someone who was far from a basic player. "What was that about?"

Faarax was careful with his opening move. His sister was a sly one, and such a simple volley almost invited him to be bold. Instead, he was cautious and moved the king's knight out. "Mungab's camp to the south was just bombed to smithereens by Fitzroy."

Shadya moved her queen into the open area of the board. "This Fitzroy is a bold one. I've never seen the United States target so many camps at once."

Her brother shook his head. "Mungab is a fool. He invited this on himself. He should have released his prisoner after the last bombing. He wasn't even asking that much for the prisoner, it would have been no big loss. He also didn't help himself by making his village look like a pirate camp. He flew a giant Jolly Roger flag over the camp."

A quick series of moves played out on the chessboard, moves that were already putting Shadya in an advantageous position. "Do you think they know about the bunker?" Shadya asked.

"No one has said anything about it." Faarax examined the board carefully. "I told the men not to go anywhere near the bunker in case the Americans are watching with their drones. I also told everyone that they are not to leave the village until all this has blown over."

"A wise move."

Faarax wasn't sure if she was talking about his bishop or the bunker.

"There has been some talk in the camp," Shadya said.

The pirate leader picked up and then put down his queen. "What type of talk?"

"Some of the women are getting restless. They want their men to get their share of the treasure so that they can go and buy some nice things."

Faarax forgot about the game and leaned back in his seat. "You will tell them that they will need to wait. I can't have them running down the road to the next town to flaunt their wealth in the shops. Then the Americans will know we were the ones responsible."

"That's what I already told them."

Grandma Jelly wasn't in her usual spot in the rec room of Ample Hills. The tension that had led to the creation of the DMZ between the feuding camps of Eugenia and Virginia had exploded into a full-blown war. Vicious battles played out in the common areas. There were fights in which slippers served as makeshift bludgeons and canes became hooks to trip up members of the opposing camp. No one was exactly sure what led to the final escalation, but the sudden death of King Al (a heart attack during sex) was certainly a contributing factor.

The hostilities forced Jelly to give up her spot and retreat to the relative safety of her private room, a location where she only had to contend with the occasional screams and fights that took place in the hallway.

It was after one particular row between Eugenia and Virginia, which required the intervention of orderlies and the liberal application of sedatives, that Vic came to visit Jelly.

Vic rolled the medicine cart into Jelly's room and greeted her cheerfully, "Hey, Jelly. How are you today?"

"I'm good, Victoria," Jelly said as she worked away at knitting a hat. "How are you?"

"I'm good as well." Vic placed Jelly's plastic cup of medicine down. "Have you heard anything from Jam since he left?"

Jelly just shook her head. "Not since he left for his trip. I'm sure he's very busy working on his big deal. Has he called you?" Jelly asked the last part almost hopefully. Vic was a nice girl, and Jam would be very lucky to have her—very lucky indeed.

Vic shook her head. "Not a word. He was acting very strange when he came to visit me before he left. Do you know where he was going?"

"You know Jam doesn't like anyone knowing about his big deals," Jelly said. The grandmother placed her knitting tools down on the bedside table and smiled. "But I know you'll never tell anyone. So I'll let you in on the secret. Close the door."

Vic closed the door as Jelly put on the TV and raised the volume to an ear-shattering level. Anyone who wandered by would only be able to hear the sound of a couple fighting over a DNA test on *The Jerry Springer Show*.

"He has a great idea this time," Jelly continued. She was quite happy to finally be able to tell someone about her grandson's pending success.

Vic sat at the foot of the bed and rolled her eyes out of habit. As far she was concerned, none of Jam's ideas were any good. "What big deal is it this time?"

Jelly looked toward the door to make sure it was still closed and no one was eavesdropping. "Flavored water," she said, barely above the din of the arguing couple on TV.

Vic blinked. "Flavored water?"

"That's right, flavored water. He said it is going to be the Starbucks of water. My sweet Benjamin has finally struck gold. That's why he had to go to California to meet with investors. They're going to set up over there."

Vic shifted on the bed to face Jelly. "Did he tell you where exactly they were going in California?"

Jelly pondered for a moment and scratched at her mustache. "I think he said he was going to Los Angeles."

"Los Angeles?" Vic shook her head. "That's funny."

"Why's that, honey?"

"I was at Mr. McBride's funeral the other day and—"

"That poor man," Jelly interrupted. "Just dropping dead like that— and on the lawn of my old house. I would hate to see the letter that horrible homeowners' association is going to send to my grandson over it. They're always complaining about the house for no reason."

"I know. It was just terrible." And rather expected; he had just hit fifty after all, though no one talked about the Welch curse out loud. "I was talking to Adam McKnight there, he works at the bank, and he said that Jam mentioned going to San Diego."

"That Adam McKnight," Jelly said with deep disdain, "is a snake. He's always trying to get my Benjamin in trouble. He probably lied to him so that Adam wouldn't be able to steal his idea."

"I suppose," said Vic.

Something gnawed at Vic's mind. This didn't seem like one of Jam's usual harebrained ideas. There was usually more craziness attached to his plans. This flavored-water thing seemed downright normal compared to some of the ones that had failed. He was probably covering for something. She just wasn't sure what exactly Jam was covering for.

"Jelly, do you still have the spare key for Jam's house?" Vic asked.

"Of course, dear, why do you ask?"

"I just want to make sure the house is in order. You know Jam, he was probably all excited and left everything on when he ran out."

Jelly laughed. "My grandson is so absentminded when he has his mind set on something. The keys are in the bottom drawer. Help yourself."

Vic rummaged through Jelly's dresser for the key. She was quite fortunate that the bottom drawer only contained various knickknacks and mementos instead of the copious collection of dildos and vibrators that inhabited the top drawer.

A thought crossed Vic's mind as she found the keys, something else that Adam McKnight had said. "Adam mentioned something about Jam withdrawing a lot of money from the bank."

"Oh, yes," Jelly hummed. "I gave him the money. He needed something to show to the investors in California."

Vic's hands curled up into fists, the keys digging into her palms. It was one thing for Jam to throw his money away on these get-rich-quick schemes, but it was entirely another thing to rope his grandmother into them. Vic hoped it was only a small amount. "How much did you give him?" she asked.

"Oh," Jelly mused. "Only five hundred."

Vic let out a sigh, relaxing her hands. The way McKnight had described it made it seem like it was a fortune. "Five hundred dollars, that's not so bad."

"Not five hundred," Jelly said without a care in the world. "Five hundred thousand."

"Dollars?" Vic's mouth went slack.

Ali hurried over to Faarax, a mask of worry plastered across his face. The last few weeks had brought nothing but bad news, and nothing seemed to suggest that was going to change anytime soon. If this trend continued, they might have to give up pirating and get even less legitimate jobs. The very thought of being forced to operate a pyramid scheme sent a cold chill down Faarax's spine. There were few things less honorable than tricking people into harassing their friends and family into buying workout supplements or dull knives and then trying to get them to sign up as salespeople themselves.

"I just spoke with Beyle's base to the north," Ali said.

"What did they have to say?" the pirate leader asked. Faarax somehow knew that whatever news they were bringing wasn't positive.

Ali shifted his AK from one crooked arm to the other. "Nothing good."

Nothing good could mean a lot of things, from the relatively benign to a massive calamity. "What do you mean?"

"Beyle said they saw some SEALs snooping around their base. They haven't gotten close yet, but they seem to have set up a camp a few miles away and are watching them."

That was far closer to the calamity side of the scale than the benign side. The pirate leader pulled his aviator glasses off and proceeded to clean them with a soft cloth. "I hope they're not planning on doing anything foolish."

Ali let out a long grunt and sucked in air between his teeth. "That's the problem. Beyle is planning on attacking the SEALs's camp."

An attack on the SEAL camp would assure that it was going to be a full-blown calamity. Faarax dropped his sunglasses to the table. "Is he mad? Does he want to draw all the attention to himself and all the other gangs in the area?" Faarax knew that Beyle was a hothead, but didn't realize until this very minute how far his foolishness went. "Get him on the phone now."

Ali produced a satellite phone and tapped in the encryption key and Beyle's number before handing it over to Faarax.

"Beyle, this is Faarax," he said. "What is this I hear you're planning to do?"

The voice was distorted by the encryption, but the underlying fear was clear as day. "I'm going to show these fucking Americans that they shouldn't be messing with us."

"You are mad. You are going to draw their attention to all of us. Just ignore them. Admiral Fitzroy is trying to get a reaction out of you."

"That is easy for you to say," Beyle growled into the phone, the encryption making it sound almost cartoonish. "You don't have them breathing down your neck, watching everything you do. I can't even relax and enjoy my wives without some American watching me through a telescope."

"Beyle, I am warning you. You're making a mistake. This is going to make it worse for all of us."

"Fuck you," Beyle sneered, his voice digitized by the encryption. "Fuck your village. Fuck the Americans. And fuck Admiral Fitzroy. You're not in charge of me, Faarax. I will do as I please." With that, Beyle severed the connection.

Faarax twisted the satellite phone in his hand, almost breaking the precious device. The phone was the best technology China had to offer. It possessed a world-class encryption chip that was believed to be unbreakable and untraceable. It had cost a small fortune and was well worth it with the U.S. Navy snooping around.

It was a good thing Beyle didn't know about their raid and the trea-sure that was hidden in the bunker. Even so, if he was dumb enough to attack the Americans, it would draw more attention to the area, and being a mere twenty miles south of Beyle's camp would mean his town of Tuulada Mussolini would soon be in the Americans' crosshairs.

"What should we do?" Ali asked.

There wasn't much they could do if that pigheaded Beyle decided to go through with his plans. "Double the patrols and tell the men to keep their eyes open for anything out of the ordinary."

"Got it, boss."

"Wait," Faarax said. "Another thing—tell them not to shoot at any-one without my express orders."

Ali nodded and trotted away.

A certain buzzing sound came from overhead, probably just a congregation of insects flying a bit too close to Faarax. Or it could have been American drones scanning the area for the sign of any-thing unusual.

"Another thing!" Faarax yelled to Ali. "Tell everyone to stay away from the bunker! The Americans are watching."

There was a certain level of luxury one could expect while being on vacation. Then there was a certain level of luxury that one could imag-ine potentially existing. Then there was the level of luxury that Jam and Jim found themselves surrounded by in the premier hotel that Mogadishu had to offer. It went beyond what they had seen on *Lifestyles of the Rich and Famous*, the type of place where servants were ever at the ready and a quick snap of the fingers would lead to a procession of trays of food being brought in for the honored guests present.

Put up in the presidential suite, they had access to around-the-clock room service, massages in the morning, and anything else they could ask for. The suite was larger than both Jam's and Jim's houses combined. This is exactly the lifestyle that Jam wanted—no, the life-style that Jam knew he deserved.

Trying to test the waters of room service, Jam asked for a fish tank with tropical fish to be placed in the living room of the multi-bedroom suite, and within two hours it was set up. Jim was deeply and utterly confused by the presence of the fish tank, asked for it to be removed, and within thirty minutes it was gone.

It seemed as if the only thing they couldn't get their hands on was their beloved Busch Light, or any beer in fact, and it took several calls before they finally learned that all alcohol was banned in Somalia.

Jam poured orange juice into a crystal flute. "I could get used to this," he said.

Jim poked at a serving of sabaayad, a Somali flatbread, that was brought to their room for breakfast. He wasn't entirely sure how to eat the bread dish coated in honey. It had no resemblance to the taqui-tos or cold pizzas he normally ate for breakfast. "I have a question, Jam," Jim said.

"What's that?"

"Now that we're here, how are we going to find General Fonzi and the treasure?"

The answer seemed all too obvious to Jam. "We're going to ask Hassan where we can find pirates for the film."

"Do you think that will work?"

"Of course," Jam said, completely self-assured. "He said he was here to give us whatever we needed."

Jim nodded along in the way he always did. "We might need things before we visit the pirates. Don't SEALs usually have guns?"

Jam said, "Right. We'll just ask Hassan where we can get that stuff."

As if on cue, there was a knock at the door and Hassan let himself in quietly. "I hope you are finding everything to your satisfaction," the Somali said.

"Yeah, it's great," Jim replied. Though he was not so thrilled with the food, he had been told to always be polite as a guest. "We're going to need to go to a market and get some supplies later. You know, for the movie?"

"Why, yes, yes, of course," Hassan agreed. "But first we must go to Dabshid."

"We really need to get this stuff for the film," Jam said.

"I understand," Hassan pressed on. "But you have not experienced a summer in Somalia until you have participated in Dabshid."

Jam wasn't sure he could survive another festival. He had been tossed over that fire half a dozen times. It certainly wasn't an experience he wanted to repeat.

8

"When we first saw the English troops advancing, we asked, 'What has Mussolini ever done for us?' and agreeing that it wasn't much at all, we quickly decided we would rather be guests of the British than the heroes of Mussolini."

—An interrogated Italian defender
of Villagio di Mussolini

There are certain immutable laws of the universe. Things like entropy, gravity, and that the minute you get in the shower the phone will ring. This was also one of those immutable laws: when Jam was excited and in a rush, there would be lights left on in the house. This wasn't a solitary light waiting out its meager existence in a tiny bright spot of pitch darkness—this was an entire constellation illuminating the whole house. Even the refrigerator took part in this light show, as Jam had left the door open. Luckily for Vic, the fridge was only stocked with beer and nothing fresh or perishable. The only food to be found in the entirety of the house was in the freezer.

It was only after Vic went about shutting off all the lights and closing the fridge door that she began her search for any information regarding Jam's big deal or where they were. It wasn't going to be an easy search, as Jam wasn't known to keep records or notes on any of his big deals.

She knew something was up. Jam had been far more evasive than usual about his idea. He was a talker, and normally he would let something slip when he was drunk around her. This time was different. He was purposely more tightlipped, which gave Vic a creeping feeling that was made only greater by the revelation that Jam had asked Jelly for five hundred thousand dollars, and what made it all the more shocking was that not only did Jelly give him the money, but that she had so much to spare. None of Jam's previous plans had involved great sums of money. Sure, there was some money involved, but never anything life-changing.

The focal point of all of Jam's planning was always the living room, and that was where Vic began her search. Many a big deal became a semi-reality through long hours of playing *Call of Duty*, drinking a huge amount of beer, and consuming an even greater amount of taquitos.

There was no order to the living room. It was a chaotic mess. The only two surfaces that weren't littered with clothes, beer bottles, discarded food wrappers and boxes, or miscellaneous papers were the TV and the top of the Xbox.

Vic carefully moved through the clutter. She shifted aside piles of clothes and pizza boxes, looking for some clue as to what Jam and Jim were actually up to. There was an ever-present fear in the back of her mind that some small, furry, scaly, or slimy creature would bite her as she went through everything. She made sure to move methodically and slowly while making as much noise as possible to give those creatures time to scatter.

It was under half a dozen pizza boxes and a dozen discarded taquito wrappers that Vic found something that seemed out of place. It was a box covered in Chinese writing.

Within that box was a receipt that Vic couldn't hope to decipher, as it was entirely in Chinese. The only English anywhere on it read: STOLEN VALOR WARE. A quick Google search revealed a website that was incompatible with her iPhone. This, of course, didn't give her any information, aside from Jam ordering things from shady websites, a fact she already knew.

She searched the room for Jam's laptop, and peeking out from underneath a pile of video game magazines on the coffee table was a wire that connected to a surge protector. She knocked the magazines aside, revealing Jam's old beat-up laptop.

She was in luck once she turned it on. Jam didn't have his computer password-protected. Even if he had a password, it would have only been a small obstacle, as it would have been something simple and easy to guess.

Once she got the website open, she knew for certain that whatever Jam was up to, it wasn't about opening up the Starbucks of flavored water. It was a whole lot stranger than anything Jam usually subscribed to. Whatever this website was selling wasn't on the up and up, that much was certain.

"Oh, Jam," she said to no one as she buried her head in her hands. "What did you get yourself into this time?"

Next to the computer were other piles of magazines that had previously escaped her notice. The title *Soldier of Fortune* was emblazoned across their covers.

Vic knew these magazines had to be related to Jam's new scheme and the shady Chinese website. Even with Jam's obsession over playing *Call of Duty*, he never expressed any interest in actually ordering military equipment. The link between the magazines and the shady website was too strong to ignore. She started flicking through them.

The issues went nearly a year back, but Vic knew that Jam's attention span was far too short to be working on a deal for that long. Indeed, his attention was often lost in a matter of minutes. He had to have come up with this recently.

The magazines themselves didn't offer Vic any clues as to what Jam was up to. He hadn't circled, highlighted, or marked anything. There were no dog-eared pages, and there wasn't anything torn out that he might have taken with him. The whole thing was a complete mystery, and the only thread she had to go on was that Jam's latest big deal somehow involved buying tacky Chinese knockoffs of military uniforms. Considering the craziness and weirdness of Jam's usual plans, it somehow seemed to fit.

As she filtered through the magazines, a note fell out of one of them. It was written in Jam's chaotic handwriting. The note read:

AD IDEA

Wanted: Navy SEALs

For an adventure to retrieve treasure

Payment to be discussed

It all made sense now to Vic, or as much sense as was possible when dealing with Jam and his big deals, which was a step above complete confusion. There was no flavored-water business—they were going to California looking to hire Navy SEALs and have them help search for treasure. If only she knew where exactly they were going after that, she would have all the pieces of the puzzle.

At the very least, she thought, there was no possible way they were actually going to be able to hire SEALs to go on a treasure hunt with them. Still, the thought of the two of them on the loose in California with half a million in cash was deeply unsettling. They could get into a lot of trouble with an amount that large, given their general spontaneity.

She would have to tell Jelly what she'd found, and maybe Jelly would be able to reel Jam and Jim back in before they got themselves into real trouble in California.

Jam and Jim were half the world away, again stripped down to the waist, holding sticks while standing at the banks of a river. They were surrounded by a whole company of likewise stripped-to-the-waist Somali men, also holding sticks. Across from them, on the other riverbank, was another company of Somali men stripped to the waist holding sticks. Behind the two forces of men armed with sticks was a whole host of singers, poets, and musicians.

Hassan had explained to them that this was Dabshid, a centuries-old ritualistic combat ceremony to ring in the Somali New Year. The whole affair was meant to symbolize one's community and honor.

It began with the singers, poets, and musicians entering into competition against one another. The poets began their assault first, eviscerating the other side with their words and jest. They extolled the virtues of their side and lambasted those who opposed them. As both sides dug into each other in their verbal sparring match, the musicians took up their instruments and provided the orchestra to the rhythmic verses of the poets. Finally, the chorus of singers joined in, encouraging the men armed with sticks on to victory.

Suddenly, the opposing side surged forward to the river, chanting and bashing their sticks against their hands, goading the Welchers' side into advancing. The Welchers' side called back their own taunts and insults, and the opposition retreated to the riverbank.

"I'm scared!" Jim cried out.

"Just stay with me and it will be fine," Jam said, even though he didn't believe it himself. Somehow Welch was looking better and better every minute. They were never forced to beat each other up with sticks at any of the social events back home. The only time they fought each other with sticks was if both parties were bored and quite drunk.

A great force pushed the pair into the river, as it was their side's turn to advance and then retreat as they were blasted by the chorus of the opposition. Jam and Jim stumbled in their combat boots, water and silt quickly filling them and making every step a squishy, uncomfortable mess.

Finally, as one, both sides began chanting and yelling. The musicians dueled, the poets threw insults and ripostes at each other, and the singers goaded their men on to victory. It had all the pomp and circumstance of a Somali rendition of *West Side Story*, with the added bonus that the dance battles quickly became real battles.

Both sides advanced into the river, beating their sticks against their hands and exchanging insults. This time there was no retreat. They stopped within spitting distance of each other and hurled put-downs and chants. It was a game they were all used to. Sticks rattled at each other as insults were spat. Over the din of banging sticks, splashing water, and chanting, the chorus of poets, musicians, and singers still sounded. Their voices were growing hoarse from the constant word game, but neither side would be the first to give up.

Then, with a final roar, the two lines charged. Jam and Jim were caught up in the swell and could do nothing but join in with the wave. Sticks swung around them, and the artists in the rear kept up their singing, poems, and playing. Their feet weighed down by the river, Jam and Jim precariously kept their balance in the surge around them, completely unsure how to proceed and where to go. The melee quickly lost any semblance of sides or order. All the two Welchers could do was go with the flow of battle and hope not to take a stick to the eye.

A stick came for Jam's head, and he couldn't do anything but duck, scream, and swing wildly back. He thought he hit something, maybe a person, or maybe the stick just bounced off the water. Jam couldn't tell and couldn't care to be bothered to know. All he wanted to do was get out of the fracas that swarmed around him.

At first, Jam and Jim were side by side, but the tidal wave of chaos soon swept them apart.

"Jim!" Jam yelled over the din of screaming, banging of sticks, and splashing water, all the primal sounds of battle. "Work your way to me!"

"I'm trying!" Jim called back as he ducked wildly swinging sticks.

Jim waddled through the river, his water- and silt-logged boots dragging him down. He ducked between two combatants and caught a mouthful of muddy water before recovering and continuing his slog toward Jam. That was, until he took a stick to the chest and then another to the back. He went down, and a stream of bodies washed over him as they moved to engage each other, ignoring the man beneath their surging feet.

"Jam!" Jim cried in a panic. "Help! I'm drowning! I'm drowning!"

"I'm coming!" Jam yelled back. "I'm coming!"

Jam ran through the river, cutting between dueling combatants, trying to desperately get to Jim who, despite all claims that he was drowning, still had his head and most of his shoulders above the surface of the shallow river. Jam shoved aside men from both companies as he pushed his way toward the bobbing head of Jim, who was gasping for air.

Jam was just about able to grab Jim. Then he saw the stick coming right for his face.

"Ouch," Jam said preemptively before the stick hit him and everything went black.

Hours later, Jam and Jim were back in the hotel, covered in bruises, and with an extremely apologetic Hassan begging them for forgiveness.

"It's fine," Jam said, stretching out one arm and wincing. He had landed on it bad after taking that hit to the face. Luckily it wasn't dislocated. That would have screwed up all their plans of pretending to be SEALs.

"I should have warned you," Hassan said. "It gets very energetic."

"It's fine," Jam repeated. They really needed to get going. If they didn't leave soon, there was the very strong possibility that someone else would get to General Fonzi and get the treasure. "We need to get some supplies."

"Yes, yes of course. What do you need? Somalia is ideal for films. We have all the filming equipment you need, so you don't have to bring anything in. Cheap, too." Hassan adopted the smile of a salesman.

"Guns," Jam answered.

"Guns?" Hassan questioned.

"Yeah, guns," Jam reaffirmed.

"Cigarettes," Jim called from the couch, where he was applying a soothing balm to his cuts and bruises.

Hassan tugged uncomfortably at his collar. "I was under the impression that the studio was going to be bringing all the props for the weapons."

Jam just shook his head. "No, we do all that."

"We also need a car," Jim chimed in. "Something military like."

Jam hadn't thought of that. A military vehicle was exactly what they needed to complete their act. After all, they couldn't go rolling around in a Prius and expect people to think they were SEALs. "Yeah, that too," Jam added.

It was an area of the city that Hassan had hoped to never find himself in. An area where the police decided not to go—an area that was left off of maps so tourists wouldn't purposely go there to see what all the fuss was about. They would have to wander in randomly by themselves and then be lost, with no way of knowing how to get out. It was in this part of the city that everything illegal, unhealthy, and sinful could be purchased for a modest, or sometimes not so modest, sum.

The sight of the two Americans caused a small uproar. Americans meant American money, and that meant the pair from Welch were quickly the most popular men in the bazaar.

Every illicit substance known to man was shoved in Jam and Jim's direction: cocaine, khat, opium, those devilishly delicious, dangerous, and highly illegal Kinder Surprise eggs. However, unfortunately for Jam and Jim, the one thing that they apparently still couldn't obtain was their beloved Busch Light beer. Even in the most lawless outpost of Mogadishu, the black market still agreed that the governmental laws against alcohol should be followed. It was a sentiment that Jam and Jim couldn't appreciate, but their livers certainly did.

Hassan profusely apologized to every vendor as he pushed the two toward a stand selling cigarettes. The stand had every brand that Jam and Jim had ever seen, and a few more they'd never heard of, all of which were missing their tax stamps. Of course, it had their preferred Lucky Strike. But there was another box that immediately caught their eyes.

Treasurer Luxury Black.

The two thought collectively, *Why not?* They had the money for it, and they would only go on to make more once they got the treasure. Plus, those cigarettes would show General Fonzi that they were serious about business. After all, only the most successful people smoked them, like Super-Rich show-off who bought them back in Welch.

"Treasurer Luxury Black," Jam said and pointed toward the carton. He loved saying those words and to be on this side of the transaction.

The vendor picked up the carton and said, "Pricey."

"No problem," Jam said as he pulled a thick wad of cash from the duffel bag. "I'll take them all."

A huge cheer went up from the vendors as the Americans paid for an entire case of the cigarettes. More and more vendors tried to peddle to them as they were pushed through the crowd by Hassan. Drugs and other illicit substances in the forms of endangered animal aphrodisiacs were offered to cure any sexual ailments. Gold watches, chains, and rings were hawked with abandon. Even blue jeans in every make and cut were on sale and offered at cut-rate prices.

The next item of business was the procurement of firearms. In this they were not disappointed. The vast array of weaponry to be had would have given even the most diehard Montana militiaman a moment of pause to consider the possibility of gun control. There were pistols, rifles, shotguns, grenades, machine guns—even a Gatling gun. There was also a mortar launcher designed to launch small nuclear weapons (nuclear weapons not included). If it had been used in the past 150 years, it was for sale in the bazaar.

Jam and Jim had their pick of whatever they wanted, and like a video-game fantasy come true, they went for everything they had ever seen in *Call of Duty*. M4 carbines with grenade launchers? We'll take two. An RPG-7? Sure, why not. AK-47? Why not, you can't go wrong with those, we'll take three, just in case one breaks. They capped it all off with the purchase of two Colt 1911s, each adorned with gold-inlaid ivory handles, all at only a slightly extra expense. Of course, the pair had no real knowledge of how to use any of what they bought.

It was then that they had to look for their means of transportation. They found it at the end of the bazaar. An old American military Jeep left over from the peacekeeping mission. It was loaded with the latest music and movies that Somalia had to offer, also known as the worst of the 1980s America had to offer.

The owner of the Jeep at first refused to sell his prized possession. After all, how would he transport his collection of music and movies? He offered them a first-edition laser disc of *Howard the Duck* instead. This refusal led to an incessant back and forth between Jam and the purveyor of music and movies, delivered through the intermediary translation of Hassan.

It was during this heated negotiation that Jim's notoriously short attention span kicked in and he wandered off in search of something that would keep him entertained. It was at a nearby stand that he found that entertainment. The merchant was selling drones. Not the large drones that the military uses to rain death down on people, obviously. These were drones of the smaller, personal variety, the type that unruly teenagers fly over airports, forcing them to shut down for hours and stranding thousands of travelers. He had seen one just like it at RadioShack in Welch right before it went out of business. He had sworn to himself that he was going to buy the drone, but before he could, the doors of the store were already shuttered. It was a toy that Jim had to possess.

Through a series of pantomimes, Jim and the merchant were able to negotiate a price and then Jim was the proud owner of a drone.

Jim, with the drone's box tucked under his arm, rejoined Jam just as he was insisting upon the purchase of the rundown, old Jeep by handing over a sum that could have purchased them a state-of-the-art, top-of-the-line BMW. With that giant overpayment, they were now the proud owners of American military surplus.

While Hassan made sure the proper title documents for the Jeep were filled out, Jam and Jim huddled in a corner deciding best how next to proceed, but first the box that Jim was carrying caught Jam's eye.

"What's that?" he asked.

"It's a drone. I got it from that guy over there." Jim motioned to the nearby stall and a very happy Somali counting out the crisp hundred dollar bills Jim had paid him.

"Huh," Jam shrugged. "I guess we can use it to help us look for the treasure."

It was a statement that raised an interesting point. Just exactly how were they going to find General Fonzi and the treasure? Somalia was a rather large place, and they hadn't a clue where to begin their search.

"How are we going to find General Fonzi?" Jim asked again.

"Let's ask Hassan," Jam told him again.

Jim nodded along.

The Jeep was soon unloaded of laser discs and cassette tapes and was quickly loaded with guns and cigarettes. Hassan stood about waiting for the next impulse purchase of the two Americans.

"Hassan," Jam started. "Do you know General Fonzi?"

"General Fonzi?" Hassan stared. "Fonzi from *Happy Days*?"

Jam and Jim looked at each other. "That's what we thought," Jam said. "Do you know where we could find pirates?"

Hassan tugged nervously at his collar. "Pirates? Why would you want to find pirates?"

"We need to find pirates for the trea—" Jim blurted out but was quickly stopped by Jam placing his hand over Jim's mouth.

"We want authentic pirates for the movie, of course. You can't have a sequel to *Black Hawk Down* without pirates," Jam finished.

"That's not safe. I wouldn't recommend it," Hassan responded.

"Didn't you say you were here for everything we needed?"

A sweat caused by terror appeared quickly across Hassan's head, a terror brought on by a fear of unemployment. "Well . . . yes."

"So where can we find pirates?" Jam pressed.

Hassan pulled at his shirt's collar again. "Well, there is Tuulada Mussolini." The Somali said it with a tinge of embarrassment.

"Mussolini?" both the Welchers said at once.

Hassan looked down at the ground instead of meeting the pair in the eye. "The government has been meaning to officially change the name."

"Why?" both asked again.

"Well, you know." Hassan dabbed at his forehead with a handkerchief. "Because of the implication."

The two Welchers blinked in confusion at the implication of the implication.

"What implication?" Jam asked.

"The political implication."

Again the two Welchers exchanged a series of confused blinks.

Finally, after a long pause, Hassan continued. "That doesn't matter. It is only a few miles north of here."

That was something the Welchers understood, and they were quite satisfied with the answer. They smiled and high-fived each other.

With a cloud of dust in their wake, Hassan watched as the two Americans sped down the road toward Tuulada Mussolini. The grim terror of being fired and unemployment loomed over him. There was nothing he could have done otherwise. He was told by his bosses to give them whatever they wanted, and they wanted to visit pirates. If he had said no and they'd complained, he would have gotten in trouble for it as well. He was damned no matter what, and all he could do was watch them drive off to their doom as he pondered his own.

He knew he was doomed—doomed not only to be fired, but also to never be able to get a job again. Even if that job was being water boy to some pirate gang.

The mood in Tuulada Mussolini was grim—far grimmer than even a pirate camp should be. There were talks that drones were flying over-head keeping watch on them. One of the men had claimed to see something in the air, though it could have been a large bird, but the accompanying buzzing sound made it more likely to be some sort of drone spying on them. Like most talk of ill tidings, it quickly spread through the rest of the village, and the unverified drone spotting be-came gospel.

That sullen mood of the pirates even extended to Faarax, who sat slumped in his chair in the old church. Not even the arrival of the season five DVDs of *The Sopranos* could relieve him of the anxiety that gnawed at him because of the American intervention. He found himself constantly rewinding the DVD as his attention kept lapsing. Faarax was so zoned out, he didn't even notice the arrival of Ali and his sister.

"Bad news, brother," Shadya said.

"Terrible news," Ali corrected. He moved his AK from hand to hand nervously.

Over the past month, Faarax had become accustomed to getting bad news. It seemed to be the order of the day. All he wanted to do was crack open the bunker and enjoy the treasure and live luxurious-ly, but it seemed to be an ever-distant possibility as each day passed. "What now?" Faarax said.

"It is Beyle," his sister said.

"What did that idiot do now?" Faarax asked. Though Faarax had a dread feeling in his gut that he knew exactly what Beyle had done.

"That idiot," Ali said, "went and attacked the American encamp-ment. He hit them with everything he had and it wasn't good enough. The Americans fought them off and then destroyed Beyle's camp."

It was exactly what Faarax had feared would happen and exactly what he had told Beyle, but that hardheaded fool had refused to listen and now he had gone and gotten himself blown up. *Maybe*, thought Faarax, *maybe it's a blessing in disguise.* Just maybe, now with a bunch of camps destroyed, the Americans would be satisfied and dial back their operations. But given the circumstances, Faarax could not give in to optimism.

"It gets worse," Shadya said. "We confirmed that there have been drones flying about."

"So?" Faarax said. "We've been hearing talk about drones for weeks now and nothing has happened."

"One was overhead only thirty minutes ago, and it came in low over the bunker and made several passes around it."

Indeed, that was much worse. Faarax had no idea of the capabilities of those American drones. For all he knew they had infrared and X-ray cameras that would be able to look into the bunker and discover the treasure they had captured. If the Americans knew about the treasure, then they would all certainly be done for. The treasure was far too valuable to ignore. Faarax knew his men would not be able to stop a full-blown assault, much less offer a defense against a drone strike.

"What should we do, boss?" Ali asked.

There wasn't much they could do. "Just tell the guards to stay alert. Have everyone else stay inside." Faarax thought for a moment and then decided on what was the most important way to not draw the Americans. "And remind everyone not to shoot at anything or anyone without my approval. No matter what."

The Jeep roared down the dirt road alongside the coastline, kicking up dust and leaving a long cloud trail behind it, more reminiscent of a cartoon than anything natural. It was just like how Jam pictured it and wanted it. They were on a larger-than-life adventure to find thirty million dollars in gold. It was the stuff that movies were based on. That, in fact, was going to be Jam's next big deal—he was going to make sure their story became a movie. Forget about the Starbucks of water, movies were where the real money and all the fame were at.

Jam drove like a maniac through the small coastal villages, honking the horn of the ancient Jeep as people gathered in the street to behold the strange sight of the faux SEALs passing through. Jim, sitting shotgun with an M4 draped across his lap, tossed packs of cigarettes to the crowds.

Jam gave Jim a curious look.

Jim shrugged and tossed another pack of Treasurer Luxury Black at a small Somali child, no older than ten. "I saw them do this in a movie once when they entered the town."

That was all the explanation Jam needed as he grabbed several packs of his own, Jeep swerving all over, and tossed them to the villagers. Villagers yelled their gratitude and called out to their neighbors, who quickly flooded the streets as well, hands stretched out waiting for the gift of cigarettes. Jam and Jim were all too eager to comply and tossed packs to the crowd, which responded with a chorus of cheers, thumbs-ups, and okay signs. It felt to Jam as if he were a conquering hero rolling through the town—a feeling he could easily get used to.

It was upon their exit of that small village that they encountered a slight problem, meaning small in stature but quite large enough to completely impede their progress.

The entirety of the road was blocked by a herd of goats. They stood about, picking at grass, basking in the summer sun, and generally being a nuisance to the two Welchers. The goats paid the approaching Jeep no mind and quietly continued about their day, confident in their place in the world and their dominion over the road.

Jam stopped the Jeep about twenty yards away from the goats and lay on the horn, hoping it would cause the livestock to disperse.

The goats simply stared at them.

Jam again honked wildly, and Jim waved aggressively, standing on his seat in the roofless Jeep.

The goats just stared back. One yawned and decided to lie down in the sun directly in front of them. Others decided to bleat back at the Jeep, a sound that in no uncertain terms told the Welchers they would have to wait.

"Maybe we can scare them away with this?" Jim said as he held up the M4.

With the horn and their waving not working, it seemed to be the only sensible plan to get the herd of goats moving. "Just make sure to shoot over their heads, soldier," Jam said.

Jim gave Jam a sloppy salute and jumped out of the Jeep. He marched to a position a few feet in front and checked the rifle in his hands. He struggled a bit, but he managed to make sure it was properly loaded and flicked the safety off.

Standing with legs shoulder-width apart, Jim held the M4 at his hip, ready to fire. He looked back at Jam and flashed a smile. This was going to be good, they both knew. The goats were going to freak out and scatter all over the place and they would get a good laugh from it.

The only mishap was that instead of the sound of gunfire there was in its place a dull pop that offered a brief moment of confusion before a deafening explosion ripped through the herd of goats, obliterating them from this world.

"Holy shit! What the fuck!" Jam yelled. "What the fucking fuck?"

Jim was dumbfounded. The barrel of the grenade launcher on the M4 was smoking. "Fuck! I pulled the wrong trigger!" Jim yelled.

"What the fuck? How did you pull the wrong trigger?"

"I don't know, man. I just fucked up. I had my fingers on both. I thought that's how you hold it and pulled the wrong thing. What the fuck do we do now?"

Jam looked out onto the road. Aside from the small crater and the heavy coating of goat giblets, the road was clear and drivable. "I don't know. I guess we just go, right?"

Before they could make their decision, they were interrupted by the quite irate screams of the local shepherd and now former owner of what used to be whole and living goats. He descended on them in a stream of curses, waving his shepherd's crook around.

Jim dove back into the Jeep, the staff narrowly missing his behind. "Shit, Jam, I think we're in trouble."

The shepherd banged on the Jeep with his crook and gestured wildly at the slaughtered goats that previously were worth a small fortune and were in many ways like family to him and now were just a mess waiting to be cleaned up on the road.

The Welchers hadn't the faintest clue what was being said, but they could clearly comprehend that it wasn't good.

"What should we do, Jam?" Jim asked.

There was only one way out of a predicament like this that Jam knew of. That way was the application of cold, hard cash. "Just give him some money!"

Jim reached into the duffel bag and pulled out two stacks of cash equaling twenty thousand dollars and thrust it at the shepherd. The shepherd stared hard at it for a long moment and then accepted the currency in exchange for the loss of his goats and ended his assault against the Jeep's hood.

With that semblance of peace established, the pair made their way down the goat-slicked road as the shepherd counted out his money.

The scene at Ample Hills still very much remained that of two belligerent nations. Jelly was the last neutral party and attempted to orchestrate a peace deal between Eugenia and Virginia.

Initial talks were off to a good start, and there seemed to be room to reconcile. With both sides controlling their own portions of the retirement home, it was becoming quite cumbersome and difficult to get around or do very much of anything. Everyone realized that the current state of affairs wasn't tenable in the long run.

Jelly was in her room trying to figure out how to end the feud when Vic came in.

"Oh, Vic," Jelly said. "It is just horrible out there. I need to figure out a way to end this warfare nonsense. Maybe a trip of some kind will set their minds straight and end it all."

"That's not going to work," Vic said with a sigh. "You saw what happened last week when we had the monthly casino trip. A full-scale riot nearly broke out."

It wasn't every day that riot police needed to respond to octogenarian ladies in motorized scooters jousting each other with their canes in the lobby of a crowded casino. It also wasn't every day that those same octogenarian ladies mistook those very same riot police for a gaggle of police-themed strippers and began pelting them with dollar bills.

"It's only because they're used to the casino," Jelly said. "They need to go someplace new and exotic. Maybe an island somewhere—somewhere where there are young men to distract them from all this nonsense."

Vic just shook her head, knowing it was impossible. "The home is never going to pay for something like that."

"I'll pay for it," Jelly insisted.

"Jelly, you already do too much around here."

"I insist—"

"Have you heard from Jam?" Vic asked, changing the subject.

"I haven't."

"I'm worried about him. I don't think he went to California to start up a water business."

"Why would you say that?"

Vic sat on the foot of Jelly's bed and tried to figure out just how to explain everything she'd found. "I found some things at Jam's house. It looks like he purchased some military uniforms and tried to place an ad in *Soldier of Fortune.*"

"Why would he do that?"

"Jam wrote an ad saying they wanted to hire SEALs to help them look for a treasure. I think they went to California to try to hire them."

Jelly's face lit up. "A treasure? What type of treasure?"

"I have no idea. I couldn't find anything about what they were exactly looking for or why they needed SEALs to help them."

Jelly let out a long sigh. "Oh, Benjamin," she said. "At least they're in California. What's the worst that could happen to them in California?"

9

"In the latest scandal to rock the military, it has been reported that military operatives have been using drones to spy on women changing."

—Taken from the Welch Watcher, page seventeen

Along the side of the old dirt road stood a sign. It was a relic of a time when Somalia was considered part of the Italian Empire. It said:

Villagio di Mussolini

2 Kilometers

Jam brought the Jeep to a halt as he and Jim gawked at the sign. It was the first they had seen in miles. They wiped the accumulated dust from their faces and tried to make sense of the old metal sign.

"Villagio di Mussolini," Jim said, sounding out every letter in a slow, pronounced manner as his dyslexic mind sorted through them. "Do you think this is the village we're looking for?"

Jam spat out a chunk of dust and rubbed the back of his hand across his lips. "Nah," he said. "Hassan said it was Tuulada Mussolini. The sign says Villagio di Mussolini. It's probably the next village over. Like Welch by the Bay. I bet they can give us directions to Tuulada Mussolini though."

With a resolute nod from Jim, Jam hit the gas again, propelling the Jeep down the road toward the village that definitely was not Tuulada Mussolini and instead a completely different town known as Villagio di Mussolini, at least in Jam's mind.

It was slightly before sunset when the old Jeep came barreling through the square of Tuulada Mussolini and screeched to a halt mere inches away from two nonplussed Somali pirates lazily holding AK-47s. It was the first time in decades that a vehicle of that make had entered the town, and indeed it could have very well been the same exact Jeep from the previous visit.

There was a collective moment of silence as the two Somalis and the two men in shoddy uniforms stared at each other, each group deciding how to proceed. Neither party had expected the other. The pirates hadn't expected a pair of soldiers in an ancient Jeep rumbling into the middle of their village, and the two Welchers certainly hadn't expected to stumble upon a pair of armed sentries outside a nondescript village.

The Somalis acted first, raising their AKs and pointing them at the occupants of the Jeep as they screamed in Somali. From the surrounding Mediterranean-style houses, a flood of pirates all holding AKs came storming out, forming a circle around the Jeep.

Jam and Jim leaped to their feet on the seats of the Jeep, M4s grasped nervously in their hands. They spun around, trying to face the force that was surrounding them all at once, but that was quickly proving impossible, as more pirates joined the cordon, trapping the Americans.

"Holy fuck! Holy fuck!" Jim yelled. "What do we do?"

Jam wasn't listening to Jim at all. "Drop your weapons!" he yelled back, trying to sound defiant and brave and not like he was consumed by a pants-shitting level of terror.

The two groups continued to yell at each other and shake their guns in anger, to no avail. Neither side was backing down, nor were they going to be the first to pull the trigger. One side, because they were ordered not to and knew that to defy that order meant death— and the other because they were only playing soldier and had no idea what to do. This wasn't how things happened in *Call of Duty*, and Jam and Jim were both at a complete loss. They were supposed to just explode onto the scene and take everyone by surprise, not the other way around while also getting themselves surrounded. Not for the first time in Jam's mind, there was a sense of regret in coming to Somalia. They should have stayed back home and worked on a different big deal.

A regal figure approached them, AK in arm, aviator sunglasses concealing his eyes. Another man cradling an AK was close behind him. The pirates all seemed to defer to the man with the aviator glasses and made way for him to approach the Jeep.

"What are we going to do, Jam?" Jim whispered.

"Just leave this all to me. I got it." Jam said it in that self-assured way that really meant: "I have no idea what I'm doing, so I'll wing it."

The man lifted up his aviator sunglasses and appraised the two Welchers. "Who are you?" Faarax said in his heavily accented English.

"We're SEALs looking for the treasure," Jam replied.

If there were only two words that every pirate knew in English, those words would be "SEALs" and "treasure." The pirates looked at each other nervously and then to Faarax.

"What treasure are you talking about?" Faarax answered, his voice strained.

"General Fonzi said there was a treasure here," Jam said.

"*Happy Days* Fonzi?"

Jam grunted in indignation. "No, not *Happy Days* Fonzi," he said for what felt like the hundredth time. "General Fonzi of Somalia."

Faarax looked to Ali and said in Somali, "Do you know this General Fonzi?"

Ali shook his head. "I never heard of him."

"Find out who he is," Faarax said before turning back to the Americans. He motioned for his men to lower their guns.

Faarax continued in English. "I am Faarax the . . ." He paused, searching for the right word. Words like "pirate captain," "pirate leader," and "pirate boss" were out. Finally deciding on the right word, he continued, "I am the mayor of this village."

Jam and Jim smiled at each other. This was going all right for them, they thought in unison. What had seemed to be a disaster had quickly reversed itself into an opportunity.

"Good, we need directions," Jam said.

Faarax squinted at the faux SEALs and pulled his sunglasses back down, even as the sun dipped lower under the horizon. "Come with me."

Women dressed in brightly colored clothing looked out from the houses, trying to catch a glimpse of the two Americans as they were led into the old church by Faarax and Ali.

"Wait by the door," Jam said to Jim. "You'll be the guard. That's how they always do it."

Jim nodded and stood by the door, holding his M4 and trying to appear soldierly instead of slovenly.

Faarax took his usual seat on the altar and motioned for Jam to sit.

"What are you looking for?" Faarax asked.

"Tuulada Mussolini," Jam said.

Faarax's face dropped. "Here?"

"No," Jam said. "Tuulada Mussolini." He drew out each syllable.

"Yes, this is Tuulada Mussolini."

Jam shook his head. "The sign said this is Villagio di Mussolini. I'm looking for Tuulada Mussolini."

No one noticed that during this Abbott and Costello exchange, Jim abandoned his post and slipped out the back door of the church. As usual, his mission was quickly abandoned by whatever caught his momentary fancy—a fancy that needed to be delighted immediately and without regard for anything else.

Faarax shook his head, figuring his English was failing him. "Get the Doctor!" he yelled to one of his lackeys. The man went running from the church.

Before the Doctor could arrive, Shadya entered the church and sat next to her brother. She was one of the most beautiful women Jam had ever seen: dark skin, pure white teeth, perfectly high cheekbones, and bright, piercing brown eyes tucked underneath long eyelashes.

Faarax could not help but notice Jam's gaze toward his sister and gritted his teeth. "This is my sister, Shadya."

Shadya held out her hand gracefully for Jam to shake. "A pleasure," she said.

Jam smiled and took her hand. Then he pointed to the oak leaf on his chest and said, "I'm Lieutenant Jam Fitzgerald of the SEALs."

She batted those long eyelashes at him and he felt a flutter go through him.

Their moment, however, was quickly interrupted by the arrival of the Doctor. The Doctor wasn't his real name, of course, but no one in Faarax's gang had ever bothered to learn his name, and he was simply referred to as the Doctor. Nor was he a doctor of medicine, but that distinction was lost on the pirates, and in between writing press releases and ransom notes, he was often called upon to treat coughs and patch up bullet holes.

The Doctor and Faarax engaged in a quick-fired conversation in Somali before the middle-aged balding man in a fine suit turned to Jam. "What village are you looking for?" he asked with a posh British accent.

Jam rolled his eyes. "Tuulada Mussolini."

The Doctor tugged at his collar slightly. It was very similar to what Hassan had done when the village was brought up. "Yes, that's this village."

"The sign says Villagio di Mussolini," Jam insisted.

"Yes," the Doctor said and tugged at his collar again. "That is the old name. We are now Tuulada Mussolini, but we've been meaning to change that name and sign for some time."

"Why does everyone want to change the name?" Jam asked, still just as clueless.

"Because of the implication."

"What implication?"

"The political implication."

Jam rolled his head back and blinked hard. *Why does everyone keep saying that to me?* he thought. "I don't care what it means. All I care about is that this is Tuulada Mussolini."

The issue was finally resolved and they were ready to proceed to a much more important topic—a topic that concerned the treasure and what would come of it. A topic that was of great importance to both Jam and Faarax.

Jim didn't want to leave Jam behind, but he had to. He felt it in his chest: the tightness, the shortness of breath. These were the symptoms of a rising wave of anxiety that hadn't left him since a dozen guns were pointed at him. He needed to have a cigarette to calm down. Someplace he wouldn't be seen and could get away from all these pirates.

Across from the church was an old stable, though all the horses were long gone and now it was just a darkened building that only served as storage. It seemed to Jim the perfect place to light up. It was an out-of-the-way spot where no one could see him in the rapidly encroaching darkness of night.

Within the stable, Jim sat down on a barrel that had he read the label he most certainly wouldn't have sat down on. Since the pirates had no horses, the stable was now used to house their cache of explosives, fuel, and ammunition. The barrel that Jim was sitting on contained a not-so-small amount of gasoline—gasoline that was slowly leaking out of the old and rusted fifty-five-gallon drum.

Jim took out a Treasurer Luxury Black and lit it up. He coughed from the acrid taste of the cigarette. He was quite disillusioned with the flavor and texture of Treasurer Luxury Black. For all the fanfare and price, he had expected them to be much better. They tasted dry, old, and stale. Certainly not the cool, refreshing taste he'd anticipated. The thought that perhaps an open-air Somali market wasn't the best place to keep cigarettes fresh never crossed his mind.

Still, even a dried-out, stale cigarette was better than no cigarette at all, and Jim happily puffed away. The tightness in his chest was washed away by the warming, cancerous smoke, and soon his anxiety was a thing of the past as he devoted himself fully to focusing on his cigarette. Smoking was the closest thing to meditation that Jim practiced.

He held his head back, eyes closed as the smoke pulled the tension away from his body. The confusing jumble of his mind slowed down to clear, calculated thoughts and then finally into nothingness, just a serene sea solely occupied with the act of smoking. If Jim could experience this all day, he would have no objections.

A shout from outside broke Jim from his reverie, and he remembered the mission he was tasked with. He had to guard the door for Jam. Failing to extinguish his cigarette, he dropped it to the floor and dashed out of the stable.

At the same time, a trickle of leaking gasoline was making its way toward the still-burning Treasurer Luxury Black.

Jim slid back into his place by the door, completely unnoticed, just as the discussion regarding the treasure was in full swing.

Jam was in rare form, gesturing wildly. "I told you already," Jam insisted. "General Fonzi told us about the treasure."

The Doctor conferred with Faarax and nodded along as Faarax explained something to him in Somali. Then he said to Jam, "Yes, we know that. But how did you find us and the treasure?"

Jam had a slight moment of epiphany. An epiphany brought on by something Fitzroy had said and from years of playing *Call of Duty*. It was one of those rare times when he was able to weave a truly masterful tale—the type of tale that would land him on the cover of the *Welch Watcher*, or in this case a tale that might just prevent him from getting shot in the head.

"We found it with drones," Jam said.

That was the magic word and probably the third word every pirate knew in English. A sheen of sweat quickly formed across Faarax's face. "Drones?"

"Yeah," Jam said with far more confidence as the quickly formed lie grew larger and larger. "Drones have been watching over this place for weeks now. They're overhead right now waiting for us."

Neither Faarax nor the Doctor responded, giving Jam time to spin more of his fanciful tale. In *Call of Duty*, the drones were always there, ready to help the good guys if they needed it. "They're waiting for us to report in right now about the treasure."

Somewhere not so far away, a stream of gasoline crept closer and closer to a slowly burning, overpriced cigarette.

"What if we don't cooperate?" Faarax asked.

Jam called upon years of card playing and gave the best poker face he could muster. "Then they're going to have to start dropping bombs."

A Hollywood actor wouldn't have been able to time the delivery and execution better. Just as the final words were leaving Jam's mouth, the cigarette heated the trickle of gasoline enough to produce a flame, a flame that raced upstream toward the barrel. The fuel within the barrel went up, creating the pressure needed to cause an explosion of some force. That explosion tossed flames across the rest of the stable. Those flames caught the accumulated explosives, and the ammunition contained within was set aflame. In the span of a few seconds, each went up with its own explosion, each larger than the last. The stable, which had stood for nearly ninety years, was obliterated.

The concussive blast of exploding stable hit the church, and with that blast, the stained-glass windows that had survived rock-throwing youths, cleaning mishaps, and a war finally gave way, pelting the Somalis and the two Welchers with shards of rainbow-colored glass.

It would take several hours for the pirates to put out the inferno that consumed the stable, and then several more to clear up the debris. In the meantime, they put Jam and Jim up in the nicest room in the church—Faarax's room—and dutifully, with all the efficiency of the Four Seasons, brought in a roll-out bed for Jim.

"I got a good feeling about this one," Jam said as he tested out the softness of Faarax's bed. "I think they know about the treasure. Now all we need to do is convince them to give us part of it. We're going to be millionaires."

Jim cocked his head slightly to the side. "But how are we going to convince them to give up the treasure?"

It wasn't something Jam had entirely considered. He knew there was treasure, and even if there wasn't a General Fonzi around to give them half, they should still be able to get some of it for all their effort. His mind rolled over all the possibilities as he bounced on Faarax's bed. It was incredibly soft and comfortable—not as comfortable as the bed in Mogadishu, but far more comfortable than his bed at home. Jam could certainly get used to this.

It was only after significant bouncing that an idea bounced into Jam's head. "We'll tell them they need to give us part of it or else we're going to have them blown up!"

Jim wasn't paying any attention. Instead, he was going through Faarax's carefully sorted DVD collection and spreading the discs out across the floor as he searched for something he wanted to watch. "Do you think that will work?" he said absentmindedly. It was less of a question and more of a statement of acknowledgment.

Jam scratched at his chin for a moment, contemplating the question that wasn't really a question. "Of course it will work," he finally said with the confidence that only an idiot could muster. "They already think we're the ones that caused the explosion."

"So we're going to blow up the place?" Jim said as he stared at a bootleg Indian DVD version of *Fifty First Dates* with a look of confusion.

"No, we're not going to blow the place up. We're just threatening to. We don't have any explosives." It was something that, now in hindsight, Jam realized they had forgotten on their shopping spree. Sure, they had the M4 grenades, but those weren't real explosives that could do a lot of damage. All they seemed to be good for was blowing up cans—and goats—and costing them money.

An electronic chirp sounded.

The pair stared at each other in confusion for a moment and then Jam's mouth formed an "Oh" of recognition. He pulled his cell phone from his cargo pants. It was the first time they had gotten reception since they'd left Mogadishu. There was a new text message from Grandma Jelly.

How's California?

Jam furrowed his brow. He had no idea why his grandmother was asking him about California. They were as far away from California as possible.

California?

For the flavored water business?

Jam had almost completely forgotten about the Starbucks of water. He wasn't quite yet ready to tell his grandmother about the big deal they were working on. He wasn't going to jinx it. There was still too much up in the air for it to be a done and set thing; he couldn't reveal his genius to everyone yet. For now he would have to wait a little bit longer.

We're about to close on our big
deal. We're having an important
meeting soon.

That's wonderful! Call me!
I want to hear all about it!

Jam's phone flashed with a message that the battery was critically low. It was just the excuse he needed. Not that he didn't want to talk to Grandma Jelly, but he was rather worried that he would let too much slip about their current situation in Somalia.

> Can't! Phone dying!
> I'll call you soon once the
> deal is done!

Jelly knew that her grandson was lying to her. He might be in California, but everything Vic found pointed toward something far different than the Starbucks of water. Her little Benjamin was a bright boy, despite everything his teachers and numerous tests said, but she was smarter and knew when he was up to something, and right now she knew he was up to something.

If only she had given him her credit card instead of a check, then she would have been able to check up on him and see where he was. For now though, she would just have to trust him to do the right thing. He always had a knack for getting out of tricky situations—it was a family trait after all. He was also only in California, so how much trouble could he actually get himself into? Surely, whatever happened there, it was nothing that a Fitzgerald couldn't handle.

Plus, she still had to deal with the war that was engulfing Ample Hills. This was, at the time, a far more urgent concern to her own well-being and day-to-day routine. With no end in sight, it was going to take all of her own genius to come up with a course of action to restore peace and tranquility to Ample Hills.

Faarax paced the room, or at least attempted to pace the room. Having given his room up to the SEALs, he had been relegated to Ali's much tighter space. It wasn't a condition that suited the pirate leader at all. But he had to be careful. They were SEALs after all, or at least they claimed to be SEALs. A certain deference to them had to be maintained if Faarax and the rest of the pirates were going to get out of this alive. He had Ali now contacting the other pirates to see if they had seen or heard anything regarding this particular group of SEALs.

Faarax had made at least a dozen rounds pacing the cramped room before Ali returned.

"Has anyone heard anything?" Faarax asked.

Ali shook his head. "Nothing," he said. "I spoke with every camp within a hundred miles and no one has seen any SEALs since they took out Beyle's camp."

That wasn't good at all for Faarax. That meant they were focusing on just him. "Anything else? Anything at all?"

"Just the usual drone sightings. Nothing else, no bombings or anything of the sort."

This was all just getting worse and worse for Faarax. He dropped down on Ali's bed. It was a hard mattress, a personal preference of Ali, who needed more back support, a preference that Faarax didn't share. "Any press releases from Admiral Fitzroy or announcements from the navy?"

Once again, Ali shook his head. "Nothing at all. Not a press release or any other announcement. Nothing has been leaked either. Whatever he is planning, he is keeping it close to his chest."

Faarax slammed his fist against the hard mattress. He had nothing to work with. "What do you think of those two SEALs?"

"They don't look like what I thought Navy SEALs would look like."

The pirate leader was thinking the same thing. They very much seemed like two idiots pretending to be in the military joyriding around the country. Then again, Faarax couldn't deny that their ammunition and fuel dump had just been blown up—that couldn't be just a coincidence. Not to mention that SEALs were also known to be tricky. It could all be a set-up to lull them into a false sense of security.

"I thought the same," Faarax replied.

"Do you think they are really from the U.S. Navy?" Ali asked.

Faarax mused on that for a moment. Truth be told, he didn't have much to go on by how SEALs looked or acted aside from movies, and anyone he knew who had encountered them wasn't around to talk about it. "I don't know," Faarax said honestly. "This might all be a ruse and they are trying to see how we respond."

"What do you want to do?" Ali asked.

Faarax rubbed at his chin. There was only one thing they could do. "We will wait and see what these Americans want and see if they are who they say they are."

"And if they are actually SEALs?"

"Then we may be forced to negotiate with them about the treasure." It was a truth that stung at Faarax. The treasure was the result of months of planning, and to give it up would hurt, but it would be better to be alive without it than dead.

"And if they are faking it?" A smile spread across Ali's lips.

"Then we kill them."

10

"It is this author's belief that the scientific community is specifically avoiding a discussion on the aquatic ape hypothesis because it will challenge decades of so-called 'scientific fact.'"

—An excerpt from the paper that resulted in the Doctor being shunned by and expelled from academia

It was slightly after six in the morning when the Doctor came to collect the two Welchers for breakfast. In addition to the Doctor's other duties, he was also called upon to be a sort of butler in the case of guests. His British education, at least in the minds of Faarax and the other pirates, made him eminently qualified to serve at the behest of their guests. But since the vast majority of the "guests" brought to Tuulada Mussolini were shackled and chained, it was rather rare for the Doctor to perform this function.

Only after some moaning and groaning and a great deal of cursing did the two Welchers finally rise and get escorted to breakfast.

"So, you're a doctor?" Jam asked.

"Of anthropology," the Doctor clarified.

"What's that?" Jim asked.

"The study of humans and societies," the Doctor said.

A brief look of confusion crossed Jam's face as he tried to comprehend what the Doctor had said. He looked to Jim for some sort of insight into the statement and found none. "Are you studying the pirates?" Jam asked.

"What?" the Doctor asked. The next line was delivered with a hint of both shame and pride. "No, I no longer work in the field because of the closed-minded individuals in the community who refuse to debate the aquatic ape hypothesis."

It was Jam's turn to ask: "What's that?"

The Doctor's eyebrow rose noticeably. "It is the belief that humans evolved from marine primates as opposed to the commonly held and wrong notion that they evolved from plains primates."

Jam and Jim shared a moment of confusion but Jim, always wanting to be polite, said, "That seems like a reasonable theory."

Jam agreed with Jim's assessment.

For once, the Doctor found some validation in his beliefs and not the mockery of his former peers, or the bemused smirks of the pirates.

Breakfast was held, as always, in the priest's rectory. Luckily for the pirates, the stable explosion the night before hadn't destroyed the stained-glass windows that lined that hall, and they were able to continue to eat in the rather luxurious hall without having to worry about stepping on a stray shard.

Jam and Jim were the last to arrive. The pirates, accompanied by their wives and girlfriends, had waited for them, as proper dining etiquette trumped all notions of hunger. The seat at the head of the table, normally reserved for Faarax, was given to Jam.

Faarax's jaw was clenched tight as Jam took his seat. He gave a withering stare at Jam, one that the faux SEAL could not see from behind Faarax's ever-present sunglasses.

It was only after the Americans had taken their seats that breakfast truly began. Before them was an array of breads and pastries, a feast that Jam dug into with gusto. Jim, on the other hand, let out a sigh and picked at a piece of bread. Once again, the meal was an uncomfortable change from his usual taquitos and cold pizza.

Faarax hardly touched the food in front of him, his cold gaze directed solely on Jam.

Shadya held her own gaze on Jam as well. It was a different sort of gaze, a gaze far more similar to how Vic stared at Jam. She leaned in close, watching his every move and hanging off his every word.

Faarax tore a piece of bread in half. "So why have you come to Tuulada Mussolini, Lieutenant?" he asked rhetorically, beginning again the conversation that had started the night before.

Jam stopped stuffing his face. This was it—this was the moment where everything they were working toward was finally going to pay off. All he had to do now was convince Faarax that they should be given part of the treasure. "For the treasure that General Fonzi told us about."

General Fonzi had quickly become a damnable name within the pirate community of Tuulada Mussolini. Though no one knew who exactly General Fonzi was, he had become a very prominent thorn in their side.

"There is no treasure here, I promise you that," Faarax said.

Jam wasn't buying that at all. After all, he had spoken to General Fonzi about the treasure. "That's not what General Fonzi said. He called us. He said there was a treasure he was trying to get out of the country."

"He called you?"

"Well, yeah," Jam said, holding up his phone. "How else would he have told me about the treasure?"

Faarax leaned in close over the table, wringing his hands. "And he told you where to find us?"

Jam's mouth was full. He gulped down half the food, coughed, and said in a jumble, "Hassan told us where to find you. General Fonzi told us about the treasure."

Something wasn't syncing up about their story. Faarax was becoming more and more confident that these two men were some sort of imposters or con men. He was going to very much enjoy killing them himself. His hand slid beneath the table and wrapped around the AK that was hidden there. The cool metal and wood finish felt soothing in his hand.

Before Faarax could pull the gun out and send the two imposters to meet their maker, Jim leaned across the table to Jam and said something that would completely change Faarax's perception of events: "I don't think we're in the right place. They're far too nice and nothing like what Fitzroy said they would be like."

The name of Fitzroy caused a mild disturbance amongst the assembled pirates and they engaged in a series of quick, fearful conversations.

Faarax dropped the AK with a clatter. "You know Fitzroy?"

The two Welchers, unaware of just how close they were to certain death, answered in the affirmative.

"You know Fitzroy, too?" Jam asked back.

"Yes, we know Admiral Fitzroy."

All Jam and Jim knew was that Fitzroy, their bartender at the Watering Welch, had been in the Navy and for all they knew he could have very well been an admiral. Not knowing anything about the military aside from what video games and movies had taught them, they thought it was perfectly reasonable for someone who said he spent twenty years in the navy to be an admiral. *After all, isn't that how it works?* Jam thought. *If you put in your twenty years you leave at the highest rank.* "Yeah," Jam said. "He told us all about you."

Once again, this revelation caused a commotion amongst the pirates, and Faarax quickly silenced them with the wagging of his hand. "What did he tell you about us?"

It was here that Jam's preternatural luck again came out in his favor. "Just that the only thing pirates understand is getting bombed," he said, quickly adding, "but we wanted to come and talk first about the treasure."

This time the commotion was much greater, and some of those

sitting at the breakfast table made for the door. Faarax didn't stop them. "Yes, we can talk about the treasure," Faarax said.

"So the treasure is here?" Jam asked.

"Yes, we do have a treasure here."

"Is it buried?"

In a way, yes, as the old bunker where the treasure was stored was built partially into the hill. "Yes," Faarax said with a growing concern that the two SEALs knew a lot more than they were letting on. He was almost certain that the foolishness of the SEALs was just an act.

"Right," Jam said. "That's what General Fonzi told us."

Faarax and Ali exchanged glances. The other pirates and their partners were quickly making themselves scarce. Besides the Americans, the only people left in the hall were Faarax, Ali, and Shadya. Even the Doctor, who was supposed to stay nearby in case his services were needed, quickly found an excuse to leave the room. Shadya seemed undisturbed by the revelation and kept the same coy, almost gleeful look as she continued eye contact with Jam.

"What do you want with the treasure?" Faarax asked.

"We want to take a share of it," Jam said. "We are here to negotiate or—"

Jim interrupted with, "Or otherwise we're going to have to blow the place up." He slammed his fist down on the table for emphasis.

Faarax and Ali went pale. "Give us a minute," the pirate leader said as he pulled Ali from the room.

It was only when the two pirates were in the privacy of the hallway that Faarax dared to speak again. "We need to find out what everyone knows about these SEALs and what Fitzroy intends to do, and we need to do it quickly. Get in touch with all the other camps nearby."

"Of course, boss," Ali said as he reached for the satellite phone that was clipped to his belt.

A thought crossed Faarax's mind. The visiting SEALs had said that

Fitzroy knew all about their camp and was talking about him. More importantly, they knew the treasure was buried—none of the other pirate camps knew exactly where they were keeping the treasure. *Could it be possible that the Navy is listening in on our conversations?* he thought.

Faarax eyed the satellite phone in Ali's hand. He'd never entirely trusted the Chinese technology. After all, every other Chinese product they purchased arrived broken or broke soon after arrival. Even the nearly indestructible AK-47 was tormented with mechanical issues if purchased from a Chinese vendor. It was a very real possibility for Faarax that the phone wasn't as secure as the vendors had made it out to be and that the Americans were eavesdropping.

Faarax grabbed Ali's hand as he was in the middle of dialing out. "No," the pirate leader said. "They could be listening in."

"The encryption is unbreakable. They can't possibly be listening in," Ali said.

"You heard what they said in there. Fitzroy was talking about us and they know the treasure is buried. No one but us knows where the treasure is."

Ali looked at the satellite phone with a mix of concern and suspicion. "What do you suggest?"

Without an encrypted phone, they were basically cut off from the world. They couldn't use regular phones or the Internet because the Americans were definitely listening in on those communications. "Send runners out to the camps. Tell them to tell the other gangs not to use their phones as well. We don't need any more attention," Faarax said.

"That will take a long time. What are we going to do about the SEALs in the meantime?"

"We will just have to stall them until we find out just how much they know." It wasn't an idea that Faarax relished. He wanted the Americans out of his hair as quickly as possible, but he wasn't about to let the treasure go simply from fear of who they might be.

Ali turned to leave before Faarax stopped him. "One more thing,"

Faarax continued. "Tell the men not to carry any weapons. I don't want the people operating the drones to think we're a threat to the SEALs."

With the absence of her brother and the other pirates, Shadya wasted no time in occupying the empty seat next to Jam. She leaned in close to the American and gave a look to Jim that read: Get lost. He either didn't notice or didn't care and just sat there picking at his breakfast.

She decided to ignore the enlisted man and focused her entire attention on Jam. "So," Shadya said, "Lieutenant, how are you liking your stay here in Tuulada Mussolini?"

Like always, when his alleged rank was brought up, Jam pointed at the silver oak leaf on his uniform. "It's good, especially that you're here," he said, mustering his most charming and suave tone, which wasn't very charming or suave, especially coupled with the fact that his mouth was again stuffed with pastries.

Shadya perched her chin atop her hand and smiled at Jam. "How long have you been a SEAL, Lieutenant?"

Jam choked a little on a pastry. He hadn't prepared for that. He didn't think anyone would ask follow-up questions—once they saw the uniform and gun they wouldn't ask anything else. "You don't have to call me Lieutenant, you can call me Jam. It's what everyone calls me," he said as he stalled for time.

"Of course, Jam." She said his name slowly, letting the lone syllable roll off her tongue. "So, how long have you been a SEAL?" she asked again.

Jam's eyes widened and he blurted out, "Just about ten years now."

"Oh." She smiled, flashing perfectly sculpted ivory. "You must have been on plenty of adventures and have some amazing stories."

"Oh, yeah," Jam said, returning her smile, but nowhere near as perfect or white. "We've been all over the place, haven't we, Jim?" Jam slapped Jim on the shoulder.

It was a routine that Jim was used to when Jam was talking to girls. Being the dutiful wingman, Jim answered, "Yeah, this guy right here saved my life in . . ." Jim searched his mind for a suitably exotic-sounding place and then settled on, "Budapest."

"Budapest?" she said as she batted her eyes toward Jam. "I would love to hear all about it." She glared at Jim. "In private."

Before Jam could offer an answer, they were interrupted by the return of Faarax. The look that crossed over the pirate leader's face showed that he did not approve of his sister sitting so close to and getting so friendly with the two Americans. "Shadya," he said in Somali, "I need to speak business with the SEALs in private."

Shadya stood up and smiled at her brother and then turned her attention back to Jam. "I do so hope to see you later and would love to hear all about your adventures." Without another word, she left her brother and the Americans to their business, but she was sure to flash a smile and a wink to her brother before leaving the room.

The pirate leader knew this would be a difficult negotiation and called for the Doctor to return. After a few moments of awkward staring and silence, the Doctor came in from an adjoining room.

Faarax sat across from Jam and asked, "How much of a cut?"

It wasn't a question that the Welchers had considered they would be asked. They leaned in together and did their best to be quiet, but it very much amounted to a drunken whisper as Jim said, "How much are we going to ask for?"

"We should probably ask for seventy-five percent. You know, in case General Fonzi comes back, because he wanted to split it fifty-fifty."

It all seemed very reasonable. They couldn't cut General Fonzi out of the deal considering that he was the one who brought it to them.

"Seventy-five," Jam said, even though Faarax and the Doctor had already obviously heard them.

That number was absurdly high—way too high for the pirate leader to agree to. After giving the Americans that much of the treasure, he wouldn't be able to evenly divide the remains amongst his men.

And with pirates notoriously strict about equal distribution of wealth, such a violation would lead to the ousting of Faarax.

Faarax shook his head and said, "Twenty-five."

Math wasn't Jam or Jim's forte, as many report cards and frustrated math teachers throughout the years could attest to. They took out their phones and started typing in numbers, trying to figure out exactly what a quarter of thirty million was. After several failed calculations, they managed to agree that a quarter of thirty was seven and a half. It was only after several more wrong calculations that they managed to figure out what their shares would be after potentially splitting it with General Fonzi. The number didn't excite them at all. It was less than two million for each of them. Hardly enough to get them their champagne wishes and caviar dreams.

The two pirates looked at each other in silent confusion as Jam and Jim pointed at each other's screens and exchanged concerned whispers over what apparently seemed to be a very difficult math equation.

"Not enough," Jam said.

"Thirty percent?" Faarax countered.

The proper calculation of thirty percent took even longer for the Welchers. It was only after multiple failed attempts and mixed answers that they decided they couldn't accept that amount. Not because it was too small, but because they couldn't properly arrive at a number and their phones couldn't agree on what constituted thirty percent of thirty million. Finally, the two Welchers agreed it would just be simpler to ask for half and have that be their final answer.

"Half, no more or less, though we really wanted more," Jam said with a smile.

It was now time for the two Somalis to conduct their own calculations. Being that one of those men was an Oxford scholar, the calculations went much more quickly and completely without errors. It was after some additional calculations concerning the proper disbursement of the treasure to the other pirates that they reached a conclusion.

Faarax and the Doctor determined that they would be able to part with half of the treasure and still be able to maintain, if just barely, proper equity with the members of the gang. It wasn't ideal but it would do.

"Agreed," the Doctor said. "It is a good compromise. A great man once said that 'a good compromise is when both parties leave dissatisfied.' And we both wanted more but can agree that this is the fairest outcome."

There were very few topics that Jam could categorically claim to know. Pop culture references were one of those rare topics. "Larry David said that," Jam said.

"I believe it was actually Franklin Delano Roosevelt," the Doctor responded.

"Nope," Jam said with confidence. "Larry David."

But Jam didn't care about being correct about comedian quotes. His primary concern was getting his half of the treasure as soon as possible. "Let's go get that treasure now," he continued. "Jim, go get the Jeep and bring it around."

"Wait," Faarax interrupted. "The treasure isn't ready yet."

That was something that took Jam by shock. He wondered how a treasure could not be ready. Gold was always ready to just be picked up and moved. "Not ready? How can it not be ready? You said it was here."

The pirates had to stall for time to see if their fears were confirmed that the Americans were indeed SEALs playing dumb or just mere fraudsters. "It . . ." Faarax struggled to find the necessary words. "It needs to be sorted."

"Just general accounting," the Doctor added. "We need to make sure everything is up to speed so that it can be properly divided. It will only take a few days for everything to be cleared and all the proper paperwork to be sorted out." Faarax whispered something into the Doctor's ear. "And, of course, Faarax, being a most gracious host and friend of the United States and of the United States Navy, will extend every hospitality to you during your stay so that you are comfortable."

Jam and Jim were businessmen, of a sort, and this arrangement seemed on the up and up to them. Plus, what were a few more days when they would soon be millionaires. There was also the not-so-small fact that this was the first and only time any of their big deals had even gotten to this point of success. They couldn't jeopardize it now. Not to mention that Jam and Jim were also known to never turn down free food.

"Of course," Jam said as he looked toward Jim with a huge grin. "That seems very reasonable."

"Very reasonable," Jim parroted.

The old church certainly wasn't the presidential suite in Mogadishu, but that didn't stop the pirates from putting in the same commitment of service in making sure that the Americans' needs and whims were accommodated. However, the one thing that the pirates couldn't provide was their beloved Busch Light. Even here in the supposed lawlessness of a pirate camp, the prohibited-alcohol law was still strongly abided by. Nor did the pirates know where to acquire any of the hoppy elixir. The two Welchers were forced to resign themselves to the fact that they wouldn't be able to imbibe any beer until they returned home, a true hardship if there ever was one.

Faarax's room now firmly belonged to Jam, and another room was being prepared for Jim. Such was the commitment to the needs of the Americans that the Doctor was unofficially officially declared their butler.

The Doctor was taking it all very much in stride and seemed to be enjoying himself quite thoroughly, now that he had an audience that didn't mock him or laugh at him about his theories on aquatic evolution. "The premise of evolution of humans on the plains of Africa is deeply flawed in that it doesn't account for a need to walk upright.

Also it completely disregards that the nutritional needs for proper brain development don't exist within the interior," the Doctor lectured as he made up Jam's bed, adding the extra pillow Jam had requested.

Like riding a bike, a good lecturer never loses the ability to keep students engaged, and the Doctor was one of the best lecturers Oxford had ever produced. The two Welchers sat in rapt attention on the floor like diligent schoolchildren.

"That makes a lot of sense. I never thought of it that way," Jam said, even though he had understood almost none of it.

"It really does," Jim agreed with an even lesser understanding of the subject matter.

The Doctor, finally having some validation for his theory, smiled and placed his hand on his heart and bowed slightly. "But if you could excuse me. I need to go make up the other room now. I can continue telling you about my ideas at a later time."

Both Welchers agreed that they would want to hear more about his theories, and the Doctor left happy, knowing that he was slowly, even two people at a time, converting the world to a theory that was falsely and irrationally shamed and disregarded.

The two processed what they had learned for a minute, and then it dawned on Jam that he had made a promise to his grandmother to call her. He pulled his phone from his cargo pants.

"Remember not to say anything about the treasure," Jam reminded himself. "We finally did it. Nothing can stop us now. We can't jinx this one by letting it out into the universe."

"We finally did it," Jim agreed. "After all the big deals that fell through, we got one to stick."

Ample Hills was now in a temporary lockdown. This lockdown was caused by what some would consider a domestic terrorist attack— not one of those elaborate attacks that makes the news and calls for thoughts and prayers, but the more minor and benign type that creates an inconvenience and prevents you from attending your afternoon shuffleboard session. And for the residents of Ample Hills, an interruption of shuffleboard carried the same weight as Notre Dame Cathedral burning down.

It appeared that someone in one of the two camps had decided to lace the lunch's soup with laxatives. Luckily, because of the quick intervention of Jelly, who smelled the Ex-Lax, none of the soup was served, and there were no explosive bouts of bowel distress to be had. Even though the attack had been thwarted, the administration still decided that the home would need to be put in lockdown until a perpetrator could be discerned.

Both Eugenia's camp and Virginia's camp momentarily decided that the real enemy was the administration of Ample Hills and turned their focus to impeding the case. It was in this cessation of hostilities that the old ladies began working together, if somewhat reluctantly. A code of silence that would make any mobster proud quickly took hold in Ample Hills, and all the ladies were tightlipped about seeing or hearing anything. Working in tandem, they dumped all their laxatives and other assorted pills into the hall in giant piles to prevent the staff from seeing who had access to what. Even the security footage that would have exposed the perpetrator had conveniently gone missing.

With nothing else to do as the orderlies conducted their search, Vic found herself in Jelly's room, helping her crochet a blanket. Though considering the pride Jelly took in her craftsmanship, Vic's helping consisted mostly of holding the yarn for Jelly and watching her work.

"Would you believe that the sex tourism group said we were too old?" Jelly said as she crocheted, her fingers working away on the vibrant red yarn.

"I didn't know you called," Vic said as she helped arrange the half-completed blanket.

"Of course, I wanted to surprise the ladies and get all the info first. They said that their insurance wouldn't cover us in case someone got hurt. They said we were a liability." Jelly blew air out between her lips.

"They've never met us. Those men are the ones who would have to worry about getting hurt once we were let loose on them."

Before Jelly could continue on her rant about the sex resort, they were interrupted by the chiming of FaceTime on her phone.

Her face lit up and she proclaimed, "Benjamin's calling!"

Vic crowded on the bed with Jelly as she answered. On the screen, Jam's face appeared, with Jim peeking in from the side.

"Hey!" Vic and Jelly said in unison.

"Hi, Grandma Jelly! Hi, Vic!" Jam said.

Jim waved excited at the camera.

The first thing Jelly and Vic noticed was the odd state of dress that the two were in. Both were wearing matching military outfits adorned with tags and patches. None of it appeared to possess good craftsmanship, and if Jelly had the misfortune of knitting something so shoddy, she would have burned it in shame before anyone could see it.

"What are you guys wearing? Are those uniforms?" Vic asked.

"Yeah," Jam said, as if the answer was obvious.

"Why are you wearing them?" Jelly asked.

"We're pretending to be SEALs." Once again the statement was delivered in a matter-of-fact manner, as Jam was wondering why it would even be questioned.

Jelly and Vic exchanged looks, and then Jelly continued. "Is this about the treasure?"

"How do you know about the treasure?" Jam asked.

"I found your note for the ad in your house inside *Soldier of Fortune*. What type of treasure is this?" Vic said.

It was now time for Jam and Jim to exchange looks. "I guess we should tell them," Jim said. "Since they know about the treasure already."

"We're going to come back with half of fifteen million dollars once we split it with General Fonzi," Jam said.

"*Happy Days* Fonzi?" Jelly and Vic asked in unison.

"No," Jam corrected. "General Fonzi of Somalia!"

"Somalia?" Vic exclaimed.

"Yeah," Jam continued. "He got in touch with us about a treasure they needed help getting out of the country. The pirates have the treasure now, but we're getting half of it from them."

"Pirates!" Jelly yelled. "Are you safe? Is everything okay?"

"Yeah! That's why we have these uniforms. The pirates think we are SEALs, so they're afraid we're going to blow them up and they're going to give us the treasure to make us go away. It's all secret, though, so don't tell anyone." Not that there were many people they could tell who would care about the affairs occurring in Somalia.

A knocking in the background put a quick end to the conversation, and a voice with a British accent was faintly heard saying, "The other room is ready now if you would like to see."

"We got to go," Jam said. "Bye, Grandma Jelly! Bye, Vic!"

"Wait!" Vic yelled louder than she'd intended. "Where in Somalia?"

"Yes!" Jam said. "We're in Somalia!"

Jam and Jim burst out laughing as they hung up the call.

Jelly and Vic stared as the screen went blank and then looked to each other in obvious confusion and with some degree of apprehension.

"At least it seems like they're safe," Jelly said.

Jam lay sprawled on Faarax's bed. The extra pillows that the Doctor had brought him were excellent. While the pirates went through their treasure and inventoried it, Jam had all the time in the world to indulge in the best entertainment American cinema had to offer, and he leisurely sorted through Faarax's DVD collection, stuck between watching *Forrest Gump* or *Dumb and Dumber*.

Just as he was about to make his decision, he was disturbed by a knock at the door. He hoped it was the Doctor with the taquitos he had requested. Despite enjoying the food given to him, he was getting rather homesick for his usual diet. It took some explaining to the Doctor as to what exactly a taquito was, as well as a Google search, but eventually the Doctor had figured it out and assured Jam that he would do his best.

"Yes?" Jam called out.

"It's Shadya," a woman's voice answered.

A momentary wave of sadness washed over Jam. The taquitos weren't ready yet. Then that wave of sadness was replaced with a wave of optimism. There was only one reason for a woman to come to your room alone, and that reason was never to just have a casual chat.

"Come in," he said.

Shadya slipped into the room and closed the door quietly behind her. "I trust you are enjoying your stay," she said.

"Much better," Jam said with all the suaveness he could muster. "Now that you're here."

Shadya giggled and plopped herself uninvited but not unwelcome on the bed. "I believe you said you would tell me about some of your adventures before my brother interrupted us the last time."

There was a certain beauty to having over a dozen years of gaming experience under one's belt, and especially with many of those years occupied by playing the various *Call of Duty* games. It provided Jam with a rich source of stories to draw upon, and over-embellish, for his fraudulent career as a SEAL.

Jam's face turned to stone and he stared off into the distance. "There was this one time in Russia a few years back," he said stoically, "where we were monitoring these Russian ultranationalists with satellites and drones."

"Is that common?" she asked.

"What?" Jam asked, genuinely confused. He wasn't expecting an interruption and already had his thoughts thoroughly focused on the story.

"Do you watch everyone with drones and satellites?"

"Oh," Jam said. "Yeah, we do it all the time."

Shadya looked toward the open window with its open blinds and quickly closed them. She returned to the bed and pulled Jam down next to her.

Jam was paying her no mind and continued on with his fabricated tale. "So the higher-ups decided that the leader of the Russians needed to be killed and that Task Force 141 was the right unit for the job. That's who we belong to, and since me and Jim are the best at what we do, we were sent into Russia to take out this guy."

Shadya slid closer to Jam, her fingers playing with his hair. "That sounds very dangerous."

Jam was almost oblivious to Shadya's intentions, as he was fully engrossed in the story that he was quickly fabricating based on the video game's mission. "Very dangerous," he confirmed. "We had to crawl through the grass outside an old nuclear power plant, dodging guards. We got attacked by a bunch of guard dogs that we had to take out quietly. The grass was so high we couldn't even see anything, so they had to radio in to us what the drones saw—that way we didn't bump into anything that we couldn't handle."

Shadya leaned in closer, her hair hanging in Jam's face.

"Then finally we got the Russian leader in range," Jam continued. "I took out my sniper rifle while Jim was watching my back, and I got the Russian leader in my sights. I held my breath and steadied my aim—"

Shadya smothered Jam's lips with a hard kiss, putting a quick end to the story just moments before its climax.

Faarax and Ali stood outside the church, their AKs hidden away in case the Americans were watching. They had to keep up the illusion that this was simply a peaceful village and not a pirate camp, though both men doubted the Americans would fall for it. At least, they hoped, if they presented themselves as nonviolent, the Americans would largely ignore them if they cooperated. There were far more outlandish pirates for the Americans to take out first.

"This is not good at all," Faarax said. "Did you send the messengers out?"

"Yes," Ali affirmed. "I sent our quickest men out to get news from the other gangs. They should be back in two days—three at the most."

"Good, I want to solve this as quickly as possible. Hopefully, the Americans will be satisfied and we will be able to get back to business as usual. Did you tell everyone else how to act?"

Faarax didn't need Ali to answer that question for him; he could see that his orders were implemented with his own eyes. Gone were the sauntering men with their AKs at the ready. In their place they set up market stalls attended by wives or girlfriends. Other members of his gang perused them, hunting for bargains. It all had the veneer of a happy, coastal fishing village, the citizens just trying to live their day-to-day lives, and in no way resembled a murderous pirate camp.

Faarax lifted his aviator glasses over his forehead and looked toward the sky. "Do you think they have any drones watching us now?"

Ali didn't get to answer.

"They do," Faarax's sister said.

She was exiting the church, her hair in disarray even under her scarf. It was clear where she was coming from and whom she was coming from. "The lieutenant told me that they have drones and satellites watching us as we speak."

The trio craned their necks skyward, all looking for something they couldn't see, mostly because of the fact that those satellites and drones that were supposedly watching them didn't exist.

Though, as often is the case, when you look hard enough for something, you will manage to find it. Backdropped against the hillside that contained the bunker was a drone. The black shape wasn't flying steadily, but it definitely wasn't a bird. It juked and weaved, plummeted and pulled up unnaturally. Seemingly it was always on the verge of crashing, but at the last minute managed to right itself. Despite all its unsteadiness, it was clearly surveying the area.

The trio held their breath as they watched the drone disappear around the far side of the hill.

On the far side of the church, away from the gaze of Faarax, Shadya, and Ali, Jim leaned out the window of his room. His tongue was out and twisted as he struggled with the controls in his hands. Flying the drone was nothing like how the videos on YouTube made it seem. The drone he had purchased was harder to control than he had anticipated, and he had quickly lost sight of it after he'd sent it barreling out the window. The shaky video feeding back to the controller's screen was making him nauseous, but he was doing everything within his power to keep it from crashing. He had, after all, paid good money for that drone, but far less than he would have paid in the United States, meaning he had to keep it in one piece if he was going to bring it back home. The thought that with the millions he would soon have he would be able to buy hundreds of drones never crossed his mind.

With shaky hands and a shaky stomach, he whipped the stubborn drone around the hillside, barely avoiding the ground, and brought it zooming back toward the church, where he hoped he would at least be able to land the thing instead of having it crash into the side of the building and shatter into a thousand pieces.

Most dinners at Tuulada Mussolini were a communal affair. Everyone would gather in the old church and sit at large tables sharing food and stories as Faarax looked over them from his central seat at the main table that dominated the church's altar. There Faarax would sit with Ali and his sister and anyone who had proven themselves worthy of the honor, be they visiting pirate leaders or members of his own gang who had performed exemplarily. It was a dynamic that had existed for years in the village, one that rarely changed and one the pirates had grown quite accustomed to. Having an orderly house was important to the state of pirate affairs, and slight disruptions in the social order there, just like in Welch, could have far-reaching consequences—though in Welch those consequences usually didn't involve the use of AK-47s, but only the judicious application of complaints administered by the homeowners' association.

Recent events had caused dramatic changes to life in Tuulada Mussolini, and the current state of dinner showed just how dramatic. Faarax no longer commanded the room at his central seat at the main table atop the altar. Instead, he was relegated to the side of the table, nearly at the end, as Jam and Jim took the chairs normally reserved for Faarax and Ali. Shadya held her usual seat but was now draped across the arm of Jam, a perpetual smile stuck on her face as she clung to every word the American said. Just the sight of it all made Faarax grind his teeth.

Jam and Shadya weren't the only things that caused Faarax to grind his teeth. There was also the matter of the food. When he had instructed his crew to go along with everything the Americans requested, he hadn't realized it would go this far. The SEALs had virtually commandeered his kitchen and his cook. Instead of the delicious and traditional cambuulo he was expecting for dinner, they were instead served American-style pizza and taquitos. The food that the two SEALs were shoveling into their faces with gusto was turning Faarax's stomach in loops. It was for the pirate leader just a greasy mess, and given the look of most of his pirates, this was something they all agreed upon.

Worse yet was the violation of the social order—a violation that Faarax was forced to endure in order to assure his continued survival. He had never imagined that Jam would so fully take control of everything that occurred in Tuulada Mussolini and how easily his pirates would look to Jam to approve every order that Faarax issued.

The latest affront was when they were deciding on the night's entertainment. By tradition, every night a big-screen TV was rolled out during dinner and everyone watched a movie. There they would sit in silence and then, following the screening, have a civil discussion on the cinematic merits of the film. Faarax always picked the movie, and this night he had chosen the cinematic masterpiece *Caddyshack*. Jam was thoroughly uninterested in the idea and instead suggested the far more banal *Happy Gilmore* as the movie of the night.

Even though the pirates were all tired of Adam Sandler and his antics after the previous month's binge-watching session, they quickly acquiesced to the Americans' demands and now were once again, for the second time in a month, watching the exploits of Gilmore. Worse yet was Jam and Jim's behavior during the viewing. They talked loudly over the movie, yelled out advice to the characters, and were generally irreverent during the film-viewing experience.

Faarax wasn't entirely sure how much more of this he could endure and prayed that his messengers would come back to him soon bearing news that these two were imposters so he could dispose of them. But he himself had lingering doubts. They appeared to know far too much and seemed too self-confident about their position with the pirates to be mere charlatans looking to scam them out of the treasure. It seemed very real that he would soon have to part with half of his beloved riches.

"We should have the treasure sorted out shortly," Faarax said, trying to keep some measure of control. "In a day or so you can be on your way."

Jam flashed an affable smile. "We might stay a few days longer," he said. "You all have been so very nice," he added with a laugh while looking at Shadya.

Before Faarax could reply, Shadya interjected, "Lieutenant, why don't you tell everyone about one of your adventures."

Jam couldn't resist the opportunity. He leapt to his feet and stood atop the chair, a sturdy piece that Faarax greatly loved. The movie was put on pause and Jam launched into a story about how he was once dropped into North Korea to rescue a nuclear scientist.

11

"If the girl is that fascinated by your office job in quality control, I have bad news for you. She's only interested in your money and is probably going to rob you."

—A TOUR GUIDE'S ADVICE ON BEING APPROACHED BY STRANGE WOMEN ABROAD

It's going great here," Jam said, holding up his phone so that Grandma Jelly could see the entirety of Faarax's room, which was quickly becoming a shrine to disorder that more suited Jam's taste. What had once contained separate stacks of neatly organized books and DVDs now had everything mixed together in odd, lopsided, on-the-brink-of-falling-over piles. If Faarax had seen his once pristine room, he would have gone into cardiac arrest. "We have everything we could possibly want."

"That's wonderful, Benjamin," Jelly said. "Are you going to be back soon?"

Jam sighed. "Yeah, probably a day or so and then back to Welch."

There was a quick knocking at the door. "I got to go," Jam said as he disconnected the call. He patted down his uniform, attempting to appear soldierly, knocking the crumbs that clung to it to the floor. "Come in."

Shadya looked around the room. She hid her disgust at the accumulating mess and smiled. "Were you speaking with someone?"

"Fitzroy," Jam lied and held up his phone. "He wanted to know how our mission was proceeding."

Her eyebrows rose in a questioning manner, her wide smile plastered on her face. "I loved your story at dinner before, Lieutenant."

Jam smiled and touched the oak leaf that was on his chest. It was a constant reminder to himself what his supposed rank was.

Shadya stretched herself across the bed. "You were so very brave dealing with those North Koreans." She curled her finger alluringly, motioning for Jam to join her. "Did anything else happen while you were there?"

Jam, all too eager to comply, climbed onto the bed with her.

Of course, Shadya had left Jam after three more of his *Call of Duty* war stories but as the first rays of light started to creep over the hills the next morning, she crept back to his room. He was still dead asleep.

Something on Jam's discarded uniform blouse caught her eye. Her spoken English was far better than her written, but even so, she knew something was wrong with the uniform. Holding it up, she examined it and the embroidery that read:

U.S. ARMY

Her analytical mind worked over the uniform, examining every inch of it. Every imperfection quickly became clear to her between the poor stitching and the patches that were faded and barely sewn on. It hardly seemed fitting for a soldier to wear something like this, much less a soldier who was supposed to be part of the elite special forces.

She poked Jam in the ribs. "Aren't the SEALs in the Navy?" she asked.

Jam stirred, coughed, and rolled over to the other side of the bed.

Shadya poked Jam again, trying to rouse him. "Aren't the SEALs in the Navy?" she asked again.

Jam grunted and pulled the sheets over his head. He wasn't an early riser, and it showed by his absolute refusal to budge from bed or acknowledge Shadya.

Shadya jammed her fingers hard into Jam's ribs.

"Ow!" he cried out as he popped up. "Are we late? Did I miss breakfast?"

"Are the SEALs in the Navy?" she asked for the third time.

Jam rubbed the sleep away from his eyes. "Yeah, Navy."

"Then why does your uniform say that you are in the Army?"

If getting out of trouble were an Olympic sport, Jam would have more gold than Michael Phelps. Even in his startled state, his mind quickly and efficiently concocted a lie, a lie that was formulated in some truth, at least the form of truth learned from video games and action movies. A lie about liaison officers. "I am in the army. They sent me over to work with the SEALs, though."

Shadya dropped the uniform on the bed. "They do that?"

"All the time," Jam lied effortlessly. "Sometimes they need someone from somewhere else, and when you're as good as me, everyone wants a piece of you."

Shadya had nothing to dispute Jam's claim, and it did, at least in a small way, make some sense, but that did not account for the shoddy craftsmanship of the uniform. She would have to let that one slide for now. Too many things with the Americans weren't syncing up. She would need to get to the bottom of that—after all, the treasure was at stake.

Work starts early in a pirate camp. There was always something to be done. Boats needed to be maintained, weapons cleaned and loaded, radios listened to to see if any juicy targets would be sailing by. With work starting so early normally, it was rather easy for the pirates to pretend to just be a typical coastal village reliant on fishing. After all, they already had the boats.

Faarax, Ali, and the Doctor were overseeing the conversion of their attack boats into fishing boats. Machine guns were stowed away while nets were brought out. The Jolly Roger was replaced with the colorful flags favored by the fishing fleets of Somalia. The most difficult part of the ruse would be in the actual collecting of fish, but it was a necessary precaution if they were to be believed to be a tiny coastal village. If it weren't for the blast that had destroyed their store of explosives, they would have at least been able to dynamite the fish out of the water. Now, though, they would have to do it the old-fashioned way and actually catch fish using nets. It wasn't the sort of task the men were accustomed to, and there were some grumblings about the indignities of fishing, but in the end, fear of Faarax and—more importantly—fear of destruction by the SEALs kept them in line and playing the role of fishermen.

Ignoring the goings-on around her, Shadya hurried down the docks toward Faarax and marched right up to him. "Brother, we need to talk," she said.

"Are you done lying with the American?" he spat.

"I did not lie with him. What do you take me for? The Americans, I don't think they're who they claim to be."

That was all that was needed to get the attention of the three men. It was the information they were all looking for.

"What do you mean?" Faarax asked. "What did you find out?"

"It just doesn't make sense," Shadya said. "The SEALs are in the Navy, but their uniforms have U.S. Army on them. I asked Jam about it, and he said that he is in the Army but is working for the Navy."

Faarax and the others exchanged quizzical looks. "Do they do that?"

"He claimed that they did it because he is good at his job."

"Does the military do that?" Faarax asked again, and they all looked to the Doctor, expecting an answer.

The Doctor was hardly an expert on American military procedure and protocol, but an Oxford education had afforded him a well-rounded knowledge, which allowed him to speak on an array of subjects. Though none of those subjects were necessarily militarily inclined, there was overlap between politics and government upon which he could speak.

"There is some precedent for it," the Doctor observed. "Governments and their military wings are known to exchange liaison officers. It is designed to increase communication, camaraderie, and extend cooperation—"

"Enough," Faarax said, cutting off the Doctor. If he had been left to speak, he would have gone on for some time and somehow gotten onto the topic of that laughable aquatic ape theory. "That's all we need to know." He turned back to his sister. "See, it is normal. Don't distract us with nonsense."

Shadya narrowed her eyes and stared down her brother. He was being pigheaded.

"And don't go riling up the American with questions and accusations," Faarax lectured her. "We don't need you causing trouble and jeopardizing everything we have."

"Fine," she said. "I'll stay away from the American from now on."

"No," Faarax corrected her. They needed to keep a sense of normalcy, at least as much as possible, given the circumstances. "He is used to you being around. Just keep him happy and maybe we can come out of this unscathed."

Something dipped over the water. It was the tiny drone they had seen before flying over the hill and the bunker. It smoothly skimmed past the first of the boats that departed from the dock, much to the shock and alarm of the pirates aboard. It flittered around each boat, going from one to the other, quietly observing them as they put out to sea.

"They're watching everything," Ali muttered in dismay.

Jim was getting rather accustomed to flying the drone. What was a clumsy experiment the day before was now a smooth interactive collaboration between man and machine. He was able to effortlessly keep the drone level and even able to perform some stunning maneuvers with it, such as diving and then pulling up seconds before making contact with land.

Sea spray splashed against the drone's camera as he whisked it past the boats. He whipped the drone over the dock and saw the terrified faces of the four Somalis. He didn't have time to avoid them and the drone surged ahead. Their faces twisted into silent screams and they dove off the dock into the water.

Whoops, thought Jim, *maybe I don't have as much control as I thought.* He didn't pay it much mind, though, as he pulled the drone back up over the village and blew over the buildings and the stunned gaze of the pirates below before bringing it back to the church.

Dinner that night was again a large communal affair, though the portions were far smaller, as the fishing boats came in with a rather small catch. It was to be expected, considering the pirates were not fishermen and had no idea what they were doing out on the water if it wasn't raiding ships. Jam and Jim didn't mind, though. As long as the cook was willing to make them taquitos and pizza, they were quite happy with the meal, even if it made Somali stomachs percolate in agony.

Again Faarax was relegated to the side of the main table and he was one of the last to be served, as Jam and Jim dominated the center seats. This time Shadya was far from amused and looked at Jam with veiled disgust, but she adopted a doting and jovial demeanor when talking to the American. Jam hardly noticed this change and was still caught up in the pomp and circumstance of the pirate gang and the adoration they laid upon him and his every request.

For the second time in two days, Jam had vetoed Faarax's selection of the night's entertainment. Faarax had recommended the all-around stunning and moving *Rain Man*. Jam had declared that movie to be boring and instead insisted on *Home Alone*, which, of course, he then wholly ignored and talked through.

And again he interrupted the movie to regale those assembled with his exploits, lifted straight from *Call of Duty*. This time it was how Jam was once captured behind enemy lines in Russia while on a secret mission and was sent to a gulag. It chronicled his daring escape with another prisoner into the frozen wilderness of Siberia. They dodged dogs and patrols hunting them down as they made their way to an abandoned radio station so they could call for help and be extracted just as their Russian pursuers were closing in on them. It was a riveting tale that ended with the Russians pounding down the door that led to the roof just as the extraction helicopter swooped in to rescue them. Jam then waited for the appropriate amount of applause before he sat down with a huge grin etched across his face.

Jim slapped him on the back. "That's a good one. I remember that one from *Black Ops*."

"Black ops?" Shadya asked.

"Yeah," Jim began, "*Black Ops* is a—"

Jam elbowed Jim, making him shut up with a yelp. "It's a term for when you're deep undercover. You don't exist, and if you get caught, the government denies ever knowing you. Only the best guys can get into black ops because they know we won't break if we get caught."

Shadya didn't have time to offer a response before Jam let out a loud, long yawn and stretched his arms wide. "I think it's about time to head up for the night."

"But, Jam," Jim whined, "we haven't finished watching the movie yet. I haven't seen it in years."

"Oh," Jam said. "You can stay. I was offering the lovely Shadya to accompany me upstairs." Jam flashed a toothy smile, with a big chunk of pizza crust stuck between his front teeth. He was thinking, *Tonight's the night. One more* Call of Duty *story and she's mine.* He held out his hand so he could escort her.

Shadya hesitated.

Faarax lifted his aviator glasses above his eyes, which he narrowed at Shadya.

Shadya gave her brother a look. In the end, she acquiesced, took the proffered hand, and was escorted away by Jam with a quite literal cheesy smile.

A certain problem arises when someone is using borrowed stories, especially stories borrowed from a video game series known for its dubious continuity. Eventually those stories contradict or fail to make sense. Far suaver men than Jam had fallen into the trap of overembellishment, and Jam was quickly going down that rabbit hole as he called upon his latest tale to impress Shadya.

"This one time during the Vietnam War," Jam began, as he and Shadya rested on his bed.

While the pirates didn't have access to the latest world news, there were plenty of things they did know, and most of the mid-twentieth century was well within their wheelhouse of knowledge. "Aren't you a bit young to have been in the Vietnam War?" Shadya asked.

Jam froze wide-eyed, like a deer in headlights. His own knowledge of history was far more lacking than hers. "What?"

"Aren't you too young to have been in the Vietnam War?" Shadya pressed. "It did take place during the sixties and seventies."

"Oh," Jam recovered with his usual bluster. "Right, of course I'm too young to have been in Vietnam for the war. I meant I got deployed there once for a secret mission a few years back. We had to go in country to blow up a secret facility there."

Jam then proceeded to launch into a long, rambling tale that was only a source of amusement and interest to him.

Faarax and Ali stood in the market of Tuulada Mussolini, eyeing the tiny drone hovering above them with growing anxiety. Men and women would nervously glance skyward as they left their homes. They would whisper softly when in public, fearing that the tiny machine was able to listen in on their conversations. Since the Americans had arrived, that drone had been an ever-constant presence within the village, watching everything that was transpiring.

"We need to get rid of these Americans now," Faarax said. The duo were horrid for his health. Since their appearance, his stomach had been twisting itself into knots—he couldn't sleep anymore. Much of that lack of sleep had to do with the hard bed he was now relegated to. He needed them gone and he needed them gone immediately—he could no longer go on living like this. "Tell them they can have half of the treasure and leave."

"Are you sure, boss?" Ali asked. "Our messengers should be back soon with any news about them."

"I don't need the messengers to tell me they're bad news." Faarax pointed toward the drone. "That is all I need to know. They are defying my authority, Shadya is disrespecting herself with that, that, that . . . I am tired of this. Half the treasure is a small price to get everything back to normal and get the Americans to stop spying on us."

There was also the cold, dark thought in the back of Faarax's head that the Americans would keep their incessant spying mission going even after the SEALs departed. Then he would be forced to give up pirating, and the ever-growing dread of being consigned to a life of selling used cars brought the bile up from his stomach and into his throat. But, then again, that bile could also be from his newly enforced diet of pizza and taquitos.

"The Americans aren't who they seem to be," Shadya said as she appeared from seemingly nowhere.

"What do you mean?" Faarax asked. He was tired of her accusations and theories. All his sister was doing was making the situation worse with her snooping, and he would have none of it.

"They're imposters," Shadya said. "Jam tried to claim to have been in the Vietnam War."

Faarax again pointed toward the drone. "Does it look like they're imposters? They've been watching us since they got here."

"Can you listen to me?" Shadya demanded. "He tried to say he was in Vietnam during the war. He would have to be seventy by now. When I told him that he said he was only deployed to Vietnam."

"So?" Faarax said confidently. "He said 'war.' It doesn't matter. He's been all over the world and has fought in wars. We can see that they're SEALs. The bombing. The drones. It all points to them."

"Are you blind, brother? Do you not look at them? They look and act like buffoons. Jam speaks nothing but nonsense, and the other one . . ." Shadya was at a loss for words. "They aren't SEALs and they aren't in the military. They are just taking us for fools."

"I am not risking everything on this hunch of yours." Faarax was defiant. "They won't be bothering us for much longer. I am going to let them take their half of the treasure tomorrow and send them on their way. That will be the end of them, and everything will go back to normal."

Shadya stared him in the eyes, or at least stared him in the sunglasses. "You are making a mistake here, brother."

Jim was quickly becoming an expert on the operation of the drone. He had managed to now keep it hovering in place while tilting it on its axis to look toward the ground. He would glide it over the entire village and sweep it in and out, watching and following people as they went about their daily routines. He found it particularly amusing following them from just a few feet away and watching them try to lose the drone by making random turns and running away. For Jim, it was a great game.

Jam was next to him and quite bored with just watching Jim operating the drone in a safe, sane, and professional manner. "Do something exciting, Jim."

"This is exciting," Jim said cheerily. "I got it flying perfectly. I'm able to follow people around with it. It's great."

Jam held out his hands. "Let me fly it."

Jim leaned away from Jam, protecting the precious controller. "No, you don't know how to fly it. You're going to crash it."

Jam reached for the controller as Jim pushed him away with one hand. "I'm not going to crash it. I just want to give it a try," he insisted.

"No!"

Jam grabbed the controller, initiating a round of tug-of-war.

Hundreds of feet away, the drone whizzed chaotically through the sky. Bucking, weaving, diving, ascending, juking in every which direction. Its four tiny motors strained to the breaking point from the conflicting commands sent to its central processing unit. If the object could call out in pain, it certainly would have. Finally, with one hard turn too many, one of the motors gave out with a little pop and a whole lot of smoke and the tiny drone went careening toward the sea.

Jam managed to gain control of the controller just in time to watch the water race up the screen, immersing it in darkness. "Damn it!" he groaned. "It crashed."

"I told you that you were going to crash it," said Jim.

Jam answered the door to his room to find the Doctor patiently waiting, a thick stack of bound papers tucked neatly underneath his arm.

"What's going on, Doc? Is it time for lunch already?" Jam asked, always ready for another meal. The pirate cook had a knack for making taquitos, and Jam had to admit they were even better than the real thing from 7-Eleven.

The Doctor smiled weakly. "I have good news for you," he said. "We have completed the inventory of the treasure, and you will be able to take your share tomorrow at noon."

Jam's eyes turned to sparkling stars as he jumped, his fist pumping the air in victory. "Jim!" he yelled. "Jim! Get in here! We did it!"

Jim came careening down the hallway awkwardly, one hand sticking up through the sleeve of his blouse and the other struggling, trying to find the other opening so he could properly put it on. "What happened, Jam?" Jim asked.

"We're getting the treasure tomorrow!"

"Really? We get to go home! That's great!" Jim looked to the Doctor, who didn't seem all too thrilled about the current course of events. "Why so glum, Doc?"

The Doctor let out a long sigh. "Of course, I am happy that we have reached a reasonable outcome. But I would be lying to say that I am not sad to see you go. You two are the only ones who take my aquatic ape hypothesis seriously."

"You really opened up our eyes about a lot of things," Jam said as Jim nodded along in agreement. Indeed, their trust, what little they had, anyway, in the accepted scientific paradigm had been thrown asunder by the Doctor's lectures. They no longer knew what to believe when it came to scientists.

The Doctor held out the thickly bound pages to Jam. "That is why I want you to have this. It is my paper on the hypothesis. The world must know the truth about the evolution of man from aquatic primates."

If this had been a melodramatic movie, this would be the part where tears would pour down the trio's eyes and they would embrace and promise to meet again someday. Instead, Jam just accepted the paper and said, "Thanks, Doc. Don't worry, we're going to get this to the right people." Truth be told, Jam had no idea who exactly would be the right people, and the deeply researched paper would most likely wind up just another piece of debris under a pizza box in Jam's living room, lost and forgotten.

The Doctor placed his hand upon his heart. "That is all I ask."

With the Doctor gone and the pair alone, Jam grabbed his phone, ready to share the good news with the world, and by the world, that meant Grandma Jelly and Vic.

"This is it, Jim," Jam said, positively bouncing. "We finally got it done. One of our big deals is going to pay off and we are going to be on easy street."

"It's going to be great," Jim confirmed. "I can't wait until I don't have to wear this uniform anymore. It's so scratchy."

That's what Jim's problem was, thought Jam. He wasn't always looking at the big picture and was focused on momentary complaints. "Who cares about that? We are going to be rich!" Jam said.

Jam pulled up FaceTime on his phone and waited for it to dial out. A few rings later and Jelly's face appeared on the screen. "Hi, Grandma Jelly!" Jam said, followed by Jim parroting off of him.

"Hi, boys," she said back.

"I got good news," Jam said. "Is Vic around?"

"I believe so, let me go get her."

The screen went black as Jelly put down her phone.

"I can't believe this is happening, Jam," Jim said, grabbing Jam by the shoulders.

Jam grabbed Jim back. "I told you, all we needed was that one big deal that would pull us through."

"We're going to be fucking rich!" they yelled in unison, hugging each other and jumping up and down.

"Why the hell are you guys hugging each other?" Vic's voice came from the phone.

"Because we are getting a huge treasure tomorrow," Jam said.

"Are you serious?"

"Yeah!" Jam pulled the phone close to his face. "The pirates agreed to give us half their treasure in exchange for the SEALs leaving them alone."

"They're going along with it?" Vic asked.

"Yeah, they think we blew up one of their buildings or something.

It is great here. But we are going to be worth millions by tomorrow and will be coming back."

"When are you getting the treasure?" Grandma Jelly asked.

"Tomorrow at noon. We'll call you when we're about to get it so you guys can see it all. It's going to be amazing! Just wait!"

"Noon at whose time?" Vic asked.

Jam started to answer and then went quiet as he mulled over the question. "You know, noon."

"Yeah, but whose noon? We're in different time zones. Are we talking about your noon or our noon?"

Jam looked to Jim, who looked to the floor. Neither seemed too confident about answering the question. "I guess our noon," Jam said. "That seems right, right?"

"I guess so," Jim said in that way he had of exhibiting no confidence whatsoever.

"What time is that for us?" Grandma Jelly said.

"Uhh . . ." Jam uttered.

"What time is it there?" Vic asked. Then, almost realizing the futility of her own question, she continued with, "You know what, forget it. We'll figure it out. Just call us tomorrow when you're ready to unveil the treasure and we'll be here."

"Will do," Jam said, waving at the camera, with Jim over his shoulder waving also. "Bye, Grandma Jelly. Bye, Vic."

Grandma Jelly and Vic gave their goodbyes, and Jam's screen quickly turned blank.

A thin smile worked its way across Shadya's face as she pulled her ear away from the door. *I have them now,* she thought. This was proof they weren't SEALs and were just two bumbling idiots trying to pull a fast one on her and her brother. She was going to make sure they paid for that.

All she needed to do now was tell Faarax what she had just heard and once again assert her own superiority and intelligence over him. Her brother was the fool who seemingly believed the two Americans fully, and because of his foolishness, he'd let their charade play out for far too long. She was going to relish the chance to force him to admit that he was wrong and she was right.

She smiled all the wider knowing what was going to happen to the two Americans and how much they would suffer until they were made to pay, one way or another.

Shadya's face could not beam any brighter as she made herself comfortable in the small room that her brother had taken for his own since the arrival of the Americans. The room was tiny, cramped, and windowless—a cell previously reserved for a monk who had chosen such quarters as a sign of penance and self-sacrifice. It was hardly the accommodations that someone such as Faarax was used to or normally willing to abide. *That is what he gets for believing the idiot Americans*, she thought.

Faarax and Ali sat hunched over a chess set. All it took was a quick once-over from Shadya to discern that both of them were unaware of several moves that would give them an instant advantage.

Faarax reached for a pawn only to have his hand slapped away by his sister. She took his rook and, sliding it across the board, knocked over Ali's queen.

"Did you come here just to disrupt our game, sister?" Faarax asked, both annoyed by the interference but also slightly delighted to have gained the advantage over Ali.

No," Shadya said. "I came here to gloat."

Faarax ground his teeth together and pulled the sunglasses away from his face. "About what?"

Shadya rolled the discarded queen between her fingers, savoring the momentary delight of keeping the two men waiting. "It is about the Americans who have relegated you to this."

Faarax went to rip the queen from Shadya's grip, but she pulled the figurine back. "They'll be gone tomorrow and everything will be back to normal," Faarax declared.

Shadya smiled and returned the queen to the table. "They've been taking you for fools. They're imposters. They're not Navy SEALs. They are just two con men who pulled the wool over your eyes."

Faarax wasn't in the mood for any of this. He was already banished to what basically amounted to a dungeon and was giving up half his treasure. He didn't need his sister's nonsense anymore. "I already told you not to interfere with them. Just keep that Jam happy and be done with it. You only have to put up with him for one more day."

"Are you completely deaf? I told you once before that I thought they were fake, and now I know they're faking it," Shadya shot back at her brother.

Faarax was tired of his sister's games. "What are you getting at, sister? Spit it out."

"Only that I overheard them on the phone talking about the treasure."

"What did you hear?" Faarax growled, anxiously awaiting the point.

"Nothing much," she said and smiled a conspirator's smile. "All I overheard was Jam talking to his grandmother about how they're coming home with a treasure tomorrow."

Faarax was nonplussed by the statement. "His grandmother? Are you certain? How can you be sure it is not a trap?"

"You can see for yourself tomorrow. I heard him saying that he would call her again when they were opening up the treasure."

Faarax wrung his hands together in vengeful glee. He had them now and would repay tenfold every slight dealt against him by the Americans. Still, he needed to be certain they were indeed imposters. Tomorrow he would get all the confirmation he needed and be able to wreak his vengeance.

Shadya smiled back at her brother, then conducted a quick series of movements on the chessboard and declared, "Checkmate."

12

"Pirates very rarely buried their treasure, historically.
The average pirate was much too investment savvy
to not properly invest their hard-earned fortunes in
interest-bearing accounts."

—TAKEN FROM A HISTORY BLOG OF
LESS-THAN-REPUTABLE REPUTATION

There was a certain smell to the air that morning. It wasn't the typ-ical smell of morning dew, the sea, or the equally sweet smells of breakfast that normally populated mornings. It was a rather metaphorical smell. It was the type of smell that people attached to holidays: "Oh, it smells like Christmas" or "It smells like Halloween." No one could articulately describe what either of those days actually smelled like, and quite often the smell did not differ from the smell of any other winter or autumn morning. But, still, people continued upon their insistence that those days did indeed have a specific and unique smell and any attempt to dissuade them from this belief would be met with the insistence that the dissuader lacked holiday spirit.

For Jam and Jim, today was one of those days. They likewise could not pinpoint exactly what the smell was, but they quickly decided it was the smell of victory. It seemed obvious to them that this was the smell that precipitated the completion of a big deal and would soon be smelled by them on a regular basis, as this big deal would catapult them to success after success. For now they relished the smell as much as they could. They breathed it in deeply with big, long inhalations.

The pair dressed themselves as professionally as they could in their ill-fitting uniforms. The uniforms hadn't held up well over the past few days and were slowly disintegrating at the seams. It was quite fortuitous for the pair that the whole situation had resolved itself so quickly because in a few more days' time there would have been nothing left.

Soon they would be several million dollars richer and on their way home to experience their champagne wishes and caviar dreams, and that is all they had ever asked for.

They completed the ensemble by slinging their M4 rifles over their shoulders and holstering their pistols. They were now ready to collect, in their minds at least, their rightfully earned treasure.

"Jam," Jim said. "I got a question. How much is fifteen million in gold? Are we even going to be able to fit it all in the Jeep?"

It was a thought neither of them had considered before, nor did they have any frame of reference to judge what would be considered a reasonable size for that much gold. Images of a Scrooge McDuck–like vault intruded upon their thoughts. The idea of swimming through the coins was quite pleasant to them, and they had slight hopes that it was indeed in coinage. However, there was the gnawing issue that if the fortune was that vast there would be some difficulty flying home with it. But that could easily be resolved with the chartering of a private jet—something they would easily be able to afford with their millions.

"We might need to make multiple trips," Jam said.

"Do you think so?" Jim said.

"Yeah." Jam nodded in agreement with himself. "You've seen *DuckTales*. It's probably going to be like the vault. If it's all coins, we're going to be able to swim through them."

"I always wanted to do that," Jim said, now even more enthused than he was before.

They both knew that today was going to be a good day.

On the other side of the camp, another smell was in the air. This time it was the smell of vengeance. In the same way that Jam and Jim were breathing in the sweet smell of victory, Faarax was breathing in his own sweet smell of vengeance.

Everyone around the pirate leader was buzzing with activity. For the first time in days, they had taken up their AK-47s and were gleefully cleaning them and preparing them. Before, the pirates had felt naked without their rifles—they had felt as if their very own children had abandoned them. Now, with the return of their rifles, it was as if they were clothed in the finest silks and reunited with their prodigal sons. Just that alone was enough for them to rejoice, but soon the entire charade would be over, and things would finally be back to normal, and they would also have two Americans as bargaining chips. It would be the biggest score since they'd obtained the treasure months before.

"Do the men understand what they're to do?" Faarax asked Ali. He was already sure of the answer, but it was always better to be safe than sorry and confirm that indeed everything was going smoothly.

Ali was rubbing down his AK with a cloth as lovingly as a mother would wash her newborn baby. "Yes, we are to wait on the other side of the hill until you give the signal and then we jump the Americans."

"Remember, I want them alive. If anyone screws up and shoots them, that man is to be killed." Faarax had plenty in store for the Americans.

"Understood."

Halfway around the world and at an ungodly hour, an hour normally reserved for grave robbers, two women eagerly gathered in a darkened room waiting for a phone call. There wasn't any smell to the air—at least there weren't any metaphorical smells such as Christmas, victory, or vengeance. There was, of course, the ever-present smell of antiseptic and K-Y Jelly that permeated the halls of Ample Hills. Though after years of dealing with that odd combination of odors, a certain smell blindness had taken hold, and to Vic and Jelly it was nothing more than a background odor that occasionally hit you but soon passed.

"Do you think they're really getting part of a treasure, or do you think they're getting scammed?" Vic asked as she was setting up her laptop on Jelly's bedside table.

"My sweet Benjamin never gets scammed," Jelly said with all the confidence and pride that only a grandmother could muster when speaking about her only grandchild. "He always comes out ahead in these things."

Vic knew that wasn't really true, but it would have been an uphill battle trying to explain the intricacies of those scams to Jelly. Jam had been caught up in numerous scams, but his almost supernatural luck always saw him working his way back to breaking even at the end.

"I hope so. They're too far away from home this time around in case anything goes bad."

Vic finished setting up her laptop and the two settled in to wait for the call from Somalia.

Jam and Jim were waiting to be escorted to the treasure. They stood outside the church. Their Jeep idled noisily while waiting for Faarax to finally show up. The village was oddly empty for the late morning. Normally it seemed to be a mecca of commerce and activity—now only the women were around. Anyone else would have taken notice of this fact, but Jam and Jim were too excited and just paced impatiently around the Jeep while sucking down cigarettes.

It was only a few minutes before noon when Faarax and the Doctor emerged from the church.

"It's about time," Jam said as he stubbed out his cigarette and got in the Jeep. "Where is the treasure?"

"We were just taking care of some last-minute accounting," Faarax said with a smile. "The treasure is just outside of the village." The Somalis loaded themselves into the back of the Jeep.

Jam was directed to drive out of town toward a small hill in the otherwise flat countryside. On one side of the hill, a concrete bunker protruded several feet out of what was otherwise pristine nature.

"Here," Faarax said, and Jam brought the Jeep to a halt.

The bunker, aside from the wear and tear of age, was unmarred, the product of its defenders surrendering before they ever fired a shot. The heavy iron door had a dozen locks wrapped through it with chains, keeping it quite secure from anyone who tried to break in.

Faarax hopped out of the Jeep and approached the bunker door, only to be stopped by Jam. "No, we have to open the door."

Faarax smiled and held out a keychain that was so overloaded with keys it would have made a medieval dungeon master proud. "Of course," Faarax said.

Jam took the keys and waited for a moment, staring at Faarax. "We need to have some privacy when we do this. You know, to make sure everything is in order."

"Of course," Faarax said again with a sly smile that would put to shame even the most seasoned used car salesman. He motioned for the Doctor to follow him, and the two started walking back toward the village.

Jam and Jim waited for the two Somalis to disappear from sight before breaking into howls of laughter. They grabbed each other in bear hugs and swung around, drunk on the alcohol of victory. They were finally millionaires. Everything was about to change for the better, and they would be able to buy everything they could ever possibly want.

"We did it, Jim! We finally did it!" Jam said as he rattled the keys. "We are rich! Millions, Jim! Millions!"

"I can't believe we finally did it," Jim agreed.

"Take the keys," Jam said as he handed them over to Jim. "I'm going to call Grandma Jelly and Vic."

Jam pulled out his phone and fidgeted with the settings on the camera. "Jim," he said, "stand by the door and act like you're opening up one of the locks, but don't do it yet until they answer."

"Got it," Jim said. He stood by the door, holding up a giant padlock, and kept a key at the ready. A goofy smile spread across his face.

"Perfect," Jam said as he placed the call.

All they had to do now was wait for Jelly and Vic to answer and then they could commence with the grand opening ceremony.

On the other side of the hill, the pirates lay in wait. They crept around the hillside, hoping to catch the Americans in the act, thus proving that they were imposters. Faarax clutched his AK-47 closely and the sweet smell of vengeance continued to fill his nostrils.

Shadya leaned over Faarax's shoulder and whispered, "Soon, brother." Normally, for an event such as this, a woman would not be present, but Shadya had insisted on witnessing this to prove she had been correct the entire time—a request that Faarax had begrudgingly granted, not that he had much choice in the matter, or really anything his sister insisted upon.

From the direction of the village came a lone pirate running as fast as his legs would carry him. It was one of the messengers Faarax had sent days before, finally reporting back. The pirate was out of breath, gasping and wheezing for air as he approached Faarax.

"Boss," the messenger coughed. "I have news about the Americans and Admiral Fitzroy."

"What is it? Speak!" Faarax demanded. Everything they were planning could depend on what was discovered.

"Admiral Fitzroy was forced to resign from his command last week," the messenger said.

"What? Are you sure?" Faarax could feel the anger boiling inside him, the heat building up from his feet and rapidly advancing skyward.

"Positive. Captain Kayd managed to get a newspaper from Mogadishu." He held out a crumpled newspaper for Faarax.

Faarax snatched it from the messenger's hand and read the head-line out loud. "Admiral Fitzroy forced to resign in disgrace." Faarax nearly tore the paper in half but kept reading as the anger reached his chest, sending his heart pumping a mile a minute.

> After allegations that the admiral misused his au-thority and allowed men under his command to use drones to spy on women, he was forced to give up his post. Because of these allegations and the res-ignation, the operations that Admiral Fitzroy had been overseeing in Somalia have been suspended.

This time Faarax did rip the paper in two as the white, hot anger of being tricked by two random Americans boiled up to his head.

The only sound that could be heard was the wind and a faint whis-per of laughter. It was a laughter that mocked the pirates and all they had worked and strived for—it was a direct affront to Faarax himself. None of the pirates dared speak, not even Shadya, who would nor-mally be quite talkative at a chance to embarrass her brother over his follies. All were frozen in place, hoping to avoid Faarax's anger if he decided to lash out irrationally.

A low growl soon surpassed the sound of the laughter as Faarax squeezed his AK tightly in his hands, gnashed his teeth, and said, "We take them alive. I want them to suffer."

"Hi, Grandma Jelly," Jam said. "Hi, Vic, we are here at the bunker now, just about to get the treasure. Can you see it?" Jim waved, jingling the keys at Jam's phone.

"We see you, Benjamin," Jelly responded. She and Vic were sitting close together on Jelly's bed.

"Okay, we are going to open up the bunker now. There's going to be a lot of gold in there, so have your sunglasses ready!"

Jim struggled with the first lock. He tried to force the key but was met only with resistance. "It's not working."

"What do you mean it's not working?" Jam said. "Just try harder."

Jim tried to jam the key into the lock again. "It's not working."

"Are you sure it's the right key?" Vic said.

Jim held up the ring of a dozen keys. "I don't know. Is this the right one?"

All of the locks were the same make and model and each of the keys looked exactly the same. Jim flipped through them slowly. Then, reaching the end of the dozen, he slowly flipped back through them, looking for any distinguishing markings.

Jim shook his head in frustration.

"What idiot doesn't label keys?" Jam said. "Just try them all, one by one."

Jim began the laborious process of slowly going through each key, one at a time—quite slowly actually, as the keys weren't in any order at all. Grandma Jelly and Vic gave each other a look as Jim continued with each key. Each lock was eventually opened one by one with much grumbling from Jam and Jim until they were left with the final lock keeping them away from fortune and fame.

"And now the moment you've all been waiting for," Jam said.

Jim slid the last key into the final lock, but before he could twist it, shadows fell over them. A gun cocked behind them.

Jam spun around, camera still broadcasting everything. "Hey!" Jam yelled. "I said we wanted to be alone!"

Jam was met by Faarax's scowling visage. With a snap of his wrist, Faarax slapped the phone from Jam's hand, sending it whirling through the air before landing in the dirt.

Instinctively, Jam's fist came around and caught Faarax squarely in the jaw. It was a hit that would bring a tear to the eye of every belt-winning boxer. A true knockout blow if there ever was one. No one was more surprised than Jam.

Faarax went down, his signature aviator sunglasses snapping in

two as he hit the ground. A collective "Oooh" of the schoolyard variety passed through the other pirates' lips before they remembered they
were pirates and had a job to do. They swarmed Jam and Jim, dragged
them to the ground, and stripped them of their guns.

The phone kept broadcasting as it lay in the dirt. Jelly and Vic watched
in horror as the pirates descended on Jam and Jim and grabbed them
and dragged them off camera.

"Benjamin!" Jelly screamed ineffectually at the computer screen.
"Are you there? Can you hear me?"

"Jam!" Vic yelled. "Jim! What's happening?"

All they could hear was the sound of struggling before a pirate
picked up the phone and cut the connection.

"Call them back!" Jelly yelled, but Vic was already on the case, tap-
ping away at the connect button on the computer screen, only to be
met with an unanswered call after half a minute of ringing.

"Oh, my god," Vic said as tears welled up in her eyes. "What are we
going to do? They're going to kill them!"

Jelly was nervously unraveling the blanket she had been crocheting.
"We just have to wait."

13

"If we're going to agree to a ransom, we're going to need some proof that you still have them. So we're going to need you to send us a pinky or a little toe to prove it."

—A FAILED HOSTAGE NEGOTIATOR

Multinational soulless conglomerates and authoritarian regimes are similar in that they often suffer from motivational problems. It is rather difficult to motivate a populace to do your bidding when your very business is often grinding the people down into a pit of misery and despair. Unlike with massive conglomerates trying to get the most out of unmotivated employees, authoritarian regimes don't have the luxury of sending their populaces off to fancy retreats in the Caribbean to conduct team-building exercises, complete with trust falls. Instead, these authoritarian regimes often fall back on what they know, and that is the promise of even greater oppression if the people are not properly motivated. If there is one way to get people not to focus on their current misery, it is to threaten them with an even greater future misery.

The fascists of Italy understood this concept quite well, thus the creation of "The Box." The Box was a small prison built of concrete with tiny dimensions, being only a bit over three-by-three-by-three, preventing its "visitors" from sitting properly or lying down completely. The Box was also positioned directly in the sun for most of the day to quickly reach the temperatures of a Swedish sauna with none of the medicinal benefits.

Faarax and his pirates understood this concept of instilling proper motivation through oppression. Though, where once The Box was used to punish political dissidents, it was now largely used to punish those who talked out of line while watching nightly movies or for failing to adopt the proper menacing scowl while raiding ships. Or, in this case, to hold two Americans who had the audacity to play them for fools.

An iron window on the iron door slid open, allowing the sun to beam into the otherwise pitch-black environment, stinging the Americans' eyes. The land beyond The Box was barren and harsh, to remind the occupants of the hopelessness of their situation. The builders wanted the experience to be a full-sensory event, even when the iron window was open.

Faarax stared into The Box at them, his lip quite swollen from Jam's once-in-a-lifetime punch. His broken aviator glasses had been replaced with a fresh pair, as he had a style to maintain, not to mention an image to project. "You lied!" Faarax screamed at the Americans. The swelling in his lip gave him a speech impediment. "You don't know Fitzhoy!"

"Fitzhoy?" Jam said, not realizing what Faarax was trying to say. Jam was oblivious to the fact that the swollen lip could have contributed to Faarax's mispronunciation of a name Jam did in fact know. "We don't know any Fitzhoy."

"You lied about Fitzhoy!" Faarax yelled again. "He fihed!"

"I already said I don't know anybody named Fitzhoy," Jam retorted. "I know a Fitzroy, not a Fitzhoy!"

Faarax banged on the iron door. "You lied about Fitzhoy!"

"We don't know a Fitzhoy. We know Fitzroy! He owns the bar!" Jam insisted.

"You hot in box? You hot?" Faarax taunted.

It was a far-too-obvious question, but Jam wasn't known for understanding the concept of subtlety, especially while in a state of discomfort. "Of course it's hot in The Box!"

Faarax again banged on the door and slammed the window shut.

Ali approached Faarax as he stormed back to the church. "Boss," he said, "we found some things of the Americans that you are going to want to see."

"Show me," Faarax commanded.

They went up to Faarax's room, now a chaotic mess of crumbs and debris left behind by Jam's irreverent treatment of the space. The once perfectly organized display of books and DVD cases was tossed about in haphazard piles. More egregious was that many of the DVDs no longer resided in their cases and instead were strewn on the floor, featuring prominent scratch marks. Faarax would make sure that Jam paid for the disarray his room was now in.

Ali pulled out a box that had a picture of a drone on it, a drone that was identical to the one they had seen flying about the camp. "We found this in the other American's room and the drone washed up on the beach shortly after we captured the two."

No ransom was worth the indignity that the Americans had put Faarax through. They had played him for a fool and didn't even have the basic courtesy to treat another man's prized DVD collection with respect. Ransom was too good for the Americans, Faarax decided. He was going to kill them, nice and slow, in a way that would give even the most sadistic medieval torturer pause. "I am going to kill them both personally."

"They might be more useful alive," Ali said.

"What?"

"We also found this." Ali opened up the duffel bag that still contained several hundred thousand American dollars. "They are very wealthy; they might be worth a large ransom."

Faarax smiled. That amount of money changed everything. Suddenly the idea of killing them outright wasn't the most interesting option. He was still going to let the Americans rot for a bit, just to make sure they properly suffered first, but then he would get a ransom fit for a king out of both of them, even if he had to take their fingers one by one.

Jam and Jim sat hunched over in The Box. Sweat poured off their bodies and pooled at their feet in pitch darkness. They had no idea how long they'd been held for, as time had quickly lost all meaning. Given the rumbling of their stomachs, Jam estimated it had been at least a day.

After what seemed like an eternity, but had in fact been just three hours, the iron window slid open again and Faarax's swollen face stared them down. Faarax tried to flash them an evil smile, but with his swollen lip, he just looked lopsided and foolish.

His gaze fell on Jam, who was holding a hand to his eyes, trying to prevent the light from blinding him.

"You hansom!" Faarax growled at him.

Jam swallowed uncomfortably, a lump quickly forming in his throat. "What?"

"You hansom!" Faarax declared again.

This certainly wasn't going well for Jam. Not only was he in some box in the middle of Somalia, now the pirate leader was calling him handsome. There was only one way Jam could see this ending, and that was being used as a sex slave. "No, bro," Jam said. "You don't want me. I'm ugly. I'm no good in bed. I'm just a princess-lie-there."

"No! You hansom! One million!" Faarax insisted again.

"I'm not worth a million dollars! I won't make a good sex slave!" Jam begged. "Please, no, please!"

"Hansom! Hansom! Both of you! A hansom!" Faarax rattled the iron door in frustration.

"We're not any good. Really. We can't even get laid in America!" Jam tried pleading his case.

Faarax slammed the iron window closed, plunging them into darkness again.

Jam banged on the door. "I'll pay ransom! My Grandma Jelly will pay for both of us! One million for each of us!" He yelled out the first number that came into his head.

The window slid open again—and again blinded them with sunlight. "You will pay hansom?"

"No," Jam corrected. "We will pay a ransom." He was speaking as though to a child. "A ransom for both of us. You just need to let me call my grandmother."

Faarax smiled that lopsided swollen smile and nodded at Jam before passing a cell phone through the gap. It was an old Motorola flip phone, a veritable brick, the type of phone that you could throw against a wall and instead of the phone breaking the wall would break.

Jam eagerly took the phone and dialed out. He knew his grandmother would bail them out—there was no way she was going to let them get sold as sex slaves. Faarax was watching him like a hawk as he dialed the phone. Jam knew he had to play this off just right. They always did it that way in the movies and in video games, so he knew exactly how he could keep everything secret from Faarax.

"Hello," Grandma Jelly answered tentatively, her voiced trembling slightly.

"Andmagray Ellyjay, it'syay emay Amjay. E'veway eenbay idnappedkay," Jam said in Pig Latin, the quasi-language Jelly had taught him as a child.

"I know," Jelly practically shouted. "We saw everything. Are you okay? Why are you using Pig Latin?" The words streamed out of her mouth in a jumble as she tried to get everything out all at once.

"Iyay oday otnay antway emthay otay overhearyay usyay. Ouyay eednay otay eakspay inyay iglatinpay."

"Atwhay appenedhay?" Jelly said, switching to Pig Latin. "Areyay ouyay okayay?"

"Eythay utpay usyay inyay ayay oxbay andyay areyay eateningthray otay ellsay usyay asyay exsay avesslay!"

This entire time they were speaking their nonsensical language, at least nonsensical to Faarax, the pirate leader stared at Jam with a quizzical look. Before Jelly could respond again, Faarax interrupted Jam. "What is this? What ah you speaking?"

"Pig Latin," Jam said as if it were the most normal thing in the world. And, for Jam, it indeed was the most normal thing in the world. He had spent many childhood days yapping away in Pig Latin to either Jelly or Jim.

"Why ah you speaking this Pig Latin?" Faarax asked.

"It's the only language my grandma knows."

"What?" Faarax asked while blinking in confusion.

Sometimes the most outlandish lie is the most believable because the person being lied to doesn't know how to respond, and that's what Jam decided to go with. "We were raised by pigs on a monastery. The priests spoke Latin and the pigs spoke Pig Latin."

Faarax, not knowing exactly how to respond to that, just shook his head, accepted the lie for what it was, and said, "Just get me the money."

"Eythay areyay oinggay otay ellsay usyay asyay exsay avesslay unlessyay eway aypay emthay ayay ansomray," Jam said to Grandma Jelly.

"Owhay uchmay oday eythay antway orfay ansomray?" Jelly said.

"Oneyay illionmay orfay eachyay ofyay usyay. Utbay ehay isyay eallyray admay, eythay ightmay emandday oremay."

"Iyay ancay etgay ouyay ethay oneymay. Erewhay ouldshay iyay endsay ityay? Atwhay isyay ethay addressyay erethay?"

"Oldhay onyay," Jam said before he asked Faarax, "What's the address here?"

"Tuulada Mussolini," Faarax answered.

"The sign said it was Villagio di Mussolini."

"It is the same thing! It is Tuulada Mussolini now!" Faarax tried to explain for what was probably the tenth time since the fake SEALs had arrived.

"Fine, Tuulada Mussolini," Jam said more into the phone than at Faarax. "What's the street name and address?"

"Theh is no name and addhess. Just Tuulada Mussolini." Faarax gritted his teeth as he answered.

"I don't know if the post office can deliver to that," Jam said completely seriously. After all, back home, the post office would screw up all the time if the house number was off just by one, even if the name on the package was correct.

"It is just Tuulada Mussolini! They know wheh to deliveh it!"

"Is there a zip code?" Jam asked.

Faarax had had enough of Jam's inane questioning and ripped the phone away from him, then slammed it shut, cutting off the call.

Jelly needed to figure out a way to rescue her grandson and his friend as quickly as possible. She needed to find Vic.

Vic was in the pharmacy in Ample Hills, mindlessly cleaning shelves. She was just as distracted as Jelly and was cleaning the same spot over and over again.

"Vic," Jelly said, knocking Vic out of her haze. "Benjamin just called me."

"Is he okay?" Vic asked. "What happened?"

"The pirates have them and want a million-dollar ransom for each of them."

Vic spluttered, "We need to pay the ransom before they get killed or worse!"

"What if they don't let them go and keep asking for more money? I couldn't even get the address of where they are before the connection died."

"Do you know where they are in Somalia at all?"

Jelly nodded. "I know the town is something like Villagio di Mussolini or Tuulada Mussolini. Something like that."

For a moment, the worry on Vic's face morphed into one of confusion. "Mussolini? That's an odd name. You would think they'd change it."

"Why?" Jelly asked.

"Because of the implication," Vic said, then continued with, "but that doesn't matter. What are we going to do?"

Jelly was quickly formulating a plan. "We need to go to Somalia and rescue them before the pirates can hurt them."

"How?" Vic asked. "You saw how many of them were on the camera. There had to be at least a dozen of them, and who knows how many more that we didn't see."

Jelly looked across the hall to the cafeteria now in the midst of breakfast service. It was quite full already, and her plan was gaining more traction. "Yeah," Jelly said, "but, look, there are a lot of us, too."

Vic's eyebrows went up quizzically. "What do you mean?"

The plan in Jelly's head was becoming more solid by the second. "If we get everyone from here to go, we'll have the advantage of numbers." She kept looking around the room and the tables, still divided up in feuding camps. "And my idea will put an end to the feud as well. We are going to get Benjamin and Jim back while also making everything here normal again."

Vic just shook her head. "I don't think they're going to agree to go to Somalia to try to rescue Jam and Jim from a bunch of pirates."

Jelly's lips curled up into a little smile. "Don't worry about that. We are all going on the trip."

It had only taken a few hours to get the flyers made up for the XXXventures trip to Jamaica, and once they were posted on the bulletin board, next to the ads for familial events as well as the missing sex toys, they were quickly taken notice of.

Jelly set up a small table with a sign-up sheet in the rec room and within moments a line had formed, filled with dozens of ladies giggling like schoolgirls ready to go on a quest of sexual adventure. The feuding between the camps of Eugenia and Virginia quickly deescalated as they all lined up together, chatting and eagerly waiting their turn to put their names on the list.

"That's it, ladies," Jelly said as she shoved the registration sheet forward. "The quicker we're all signed up, the quicker we can arrange to get flown out to Jamaica. There is no need to worry about the cost. It's free! So just put your name down and start packing your bags."

Free was the magic word for the ladies of Ample Hills. The most curmudgeonly, anti-fun amongst them couldn't resist the allure of anything that was given for free. Even the prospect of a free tote bag would send a tidal wave of women toward the source of the giveaway. The prospect of an all-inclusive trip made certain that every single lady residing in Ample Hills was in line, ready to sign up.

Vic stood by the table with a sense of awe and wonderment. The animosity that had existed between the feuding camps had almost completely evaporated with the appearance of the flyers. There was even talk circulating of getting the baseball team back together. Vic still had some doubts in her mind about how this was all going to play out with the pirates, though.

She leaned in close to Jelly and whispered, "How are we all getting to Somalia without them knowing?"

Jelly just smiled and said, "Don't you worry a thing about that. I'm going to arrange for a private plane."

Vic had learned to never underestimate Jelly, but this seemed like a tall order even for her. Vic knew Jelly had money, but private jet money was a whole other level of money. She realized she was going to have to sit and wait, just like everyone else, and see how it all played out.

Brian McConnell had been bank manager for less than a week and he could already tell that the First Bank of Welch was in dire straits. The previous management—or mismanagement, in the much more accurate vernacular—of McBride had left the financials of the bank much worse than anyone outside the bank could have predicted.

That wasn't to say McConnell was entirely innocent in the endeavor of looting the bank as assistant manager, but at least, he reasoned, his proclivities did not fall under the guise of a series of mail-order brides followed by a string of divorces from said brides, each with a hefty alimony payout attached. Instead, his own vice was the much more benign and socially acceptable one of gambling. And he only took liberties with the bank's funds when he was losing and would always repay said losses when he was winning. Not that he ever won, but McConnell had high hopes for the next World Series of Poker, which would not only get him in the black, but would also let him get out of Welch before his fiftieth birthday, which was quickly approaching. It was the only way to escape the Welch curse, he reasoned. He wasn't going to drop dead of a heart attack at work like McBride had, or McBride's predecessor, old man Fitzpatrick, before that. Fitzpatrick had spat in the face of the curse when he dared paint his fence blue instead of white. McConnell was going to beat the curse one way or another.

Now, though, he was left with the mess of Jelly Fitzgerald's withdrawal of half a million dollars from the bank just as interest was to be divvied up between accounts. This month was going to be tight, but with enough creative accounting, he figured he would be able to get it all sorted out without any discrepancies. There was a certain satisfaction in knowing that he had managed to keep the bank afloat for another month and avoid a lynch mob of Welchers.

That glimmer of hope quickly went out the window with the ringing of his phone. Sweat began to pour down McConnell's brow as he listened to the teller on the other end.

"Put her on the line," McConnell said, his mouth already dry. He grabbed a water bottle as he waited for the call to be connected and chugged its contents to no avail. His mouth was still dry as sandpaper.

"Mrs. Fitzgerald," McConnell said as the call connected. "I heard you're trying to make a large transfer of funds in the range of several million dollars. Can I ask you what the reasoning is?"

In all his years of working at the bank, he had heard his fair share of odd reasons for money transfers. This by far was the oddest, especially coming from someone who until very recently had hardly ever touched any of her money. The chartering of an entire 747 to a destination halfway across the world would raise red flags and cause for concern even in the largest and most stable banks in the world, much less at the First Bank of Welch, which was desperately dependent upon the account of Jelly Fitzgerald.

McConnell looked to his carefully laid out spreadsheets meant to avert the bank from disaster and watched it all disappear in the blink of an eye. "Are you sure that is a prudent purchase?" McConnell attempted to ask.

He was met with the same aggression his predecessor had when asked about the previous large withdrawal. Jelly threatened to take all her money out of the bank if the transfer didn't get approved. McConnell didn't have much choice in the matter, especially if he wanted to preserve what money was left in their nearly failed institution.

"Of course, Mrs. Fitzgerald," McConnell said. "I'll make sure the authorization is approved immediately."

There wasn't much McConnell could do except type out the approval. His heart raced as he hit the "send" button. An unfamiliar taste of copper filled his mouth, and his left arm experienced a certain tingling sensation. He furtively glanced at the calendar that resided on his desk. His fiftieth wasn't for several more months; he was supposed to have more time to right everything. The poker tournament was only a month away.

One of the benefits of flying private was that most of the tedium and trauma of dealing with airport travel was bypassed. The rich, as usual, received a pass when they flew, be it quick access through customs and security, ignorance toward the smuggling of contraband by customs, or just an all-around general luxurious experience by being allowed in exclusive lounges where one doesn't need to pay fifteen dollars for a beer—not that the rich can't afford said beer, they just abhor paying for it and are more than willing to spend multiple thousands flying private in order to avoid the inconvenience of breaking a hundred dollar bill for a drink. There was also the benefit of not having to deal with the general population—aside from "the help," that is—which is just exactly how the super wealthy wanted all their interactions with the general population.

The luxury of private flight was not a convenience the ladies of Ample Hills were used to. And the airport staff weren't used to ladies like those from Ample Hills. Normally, luxury riders were one of two types, each horrible in their own and unique way. The first type was the more refined businessmen who hid their deviancy and debauchery under a thin veil of sophistication. After all, they had reputations to uphold and needed to avoid sexual harassment suits and scandals. They preferred to be condescending and abrupt with the staff while flaunting their wealth in subtle ways, such as casually flashing a Rolex or speaking at a slightly higher tone about their Black Card or asking if they could light up a Treasurer Luxury Black on the plane.

The second type was trust-funded frat boys, the sons of the first type, who made it a contest to see just how publicly debauched they could be while avoiding arrest. They were far more vulgar and rude than their fathers, not having learned the key skills of flying under the radar and presenting a civilized demeanor in public. They would outright grope the female flight attendants or proposition them with money in exchange for sexual acts. Mostly, though, they were loud, rude, and, more importantly, drunk. When confronted about their behavior by any sort of authority figure, they would of course respond with,

"Do you know who my father is?" If that particular gambit failed, they would offer meek apologies and sneak away, not out of any sense of actual embarrassment, only the embarrassment that their familial ties did not absolve them of blame and of not conforming to civil norms.

The sight of grandmothers clad in muumuus, shifts, and house-coats at first put the staff of the airport at ease. They could hardly imagine that these kind old ladies would trouble them in the veiled ways the older men did, or the outlandish ways the young men did.

Unfortunately, looks can be deceiving, and they didn't know what type of old ladies they were dealing with. The ladies of Ample Hills descended upon the male staff with ravenous glee, imparting upon them unwanted touching and lewd comments—comments that were far more lewd and vulgar than even the most outlandish comments the trust-funded sons could muster. At first the female staff laughed and looked on as the men experienced what they handled on a dai-ly basis, but then the ladies of Ample Hills, being equal opportunity harassers, quickly began visiting the same lewdness upon the female staff. Behind the lecherous ladies of Ample Hills followed an exas-perated Vic, offering a series of apologies to everyone she came into contact with.

It was only after several hours of this debauched behavior through-out the airport, and the emptying of the luxury lounge of nearly all its alcohol, that the ladies of Ample Hills began boarding their flight and the staff on the ground could breathe a collective sigh of relief—the old ladies were now the flight attendants' problems.

Few people could tolerate The Box for long, and Faarax figured that after a day in it the Americans would be more agreeable to answering questions instead of stalling with their own inane questions regarding zip codes.

It was an especially hot day—a day where even the locals com-plained about the heat, the feel of which made Faarax smile as he thought about how hot The Box would be for the two Americans. Faarax crouched down in front of The Box and slid open the window on the iron door. Sunlight streamed in, illuminating Jam and Jim exactly where he had left them, though it was not as if they had anywhere to move to in the cramped box. Jam didn't seem much worse for wear after being so confined, but Jim had managed to strip himself down to his underwear.

"Are you ready to pay ransom now?" Faarax demanded. The swelling of his lip had gone down enough to allow for him to once again speak "R"s that sounded like "R"s.

"I told you already," Jam said, wiping the sweat from his face. "Grandma Jelly is going to pay the ransom, but we need to know the zip code so she can mail it."

Faarax rattled the door. "There is no zip code! They know it is just Tuulada Mussolini. Just have her bring me the money."

"Your sign says it is Villagio di Mussolini," Jam said in the same matter-of-fact tone he always used when speaking about the discrepancy.

"It is the same thing! They know where we are!" Faarax repeated, wondering whether Jam was indeed this stupid or if it was all just an act.

"Okay. Well don't blame me if they send the ransom to the wrong town."

Faarax was done with Jam's games and thrust the cell phone toward him. "Call now and tell her to send the ransom. One million for each of you."

Jam took the phone, dialed out, and placed it to his ear. He nodded along for a few seconds and then closed the flip phone. "No good," he said.

"No good?" Faarax questioned.

Jam shrugged as he handed back the phone. "Her phone is off. We're going to have to call back later."

"The phone is off?" Faarax banged on the door. "This is not a game! I need the ransom money or else!"

Jam looked to Jim, who didn't pay any notice as he scratched away. "We'll just have to try back later," Jam said.

Faarax let out a long growl. "The ransom is now two million!"

Jam blinked in confusion. "We were already paying two million."

"Two million each now!" Faarax yelled. "Four million total!"

Jam didn't know how kidnapping worked and whether it was normal for the price to increase over time. "Oh," he said. "I guess that makes sense."

Faarax went to slam the window shut but was interrupted by Jim, who spoke for the first time in a long while. "Wait, can I say something?"

The pirate leader fixed his gaze on the American. "What is it?"

"Can I get a magazine or something to look at?"

Faarax was at a complete loss for words at the audacity of the Americans. *No*, he thought, *it isn't audacity, it is complete ignorance of the magnitude of the situation.* He didn't bother to answer, at least not in words. He simply slammed the window of the door shut. They would have to bake for a while longer to make them more open to paying the ransom.

"I think that went well," Jam said as he sat crunched up in the darkness of The Box. Not that there was ever a hostage-captor situation that could be called ideal, but in the grand scheme of things, it seemed, at least according to Jam, to be far better than it could have been.

"He raised the ransom on us, though," Jim said.

"Yeah, but at least he doesn't want to use us as sex slaves anymore. So that's a plus." It was quite the silver lining given their current predicament.

"Huh," Jim said. "I guess you're right."

A thought crossed Jam's mind. "You probably should put your pants back on, though."

"Why should I put my pants on?" Jim moaned in discomfort. "It's hot in here."

"Think about it," Jam said with a tone of seriousness only used for discussing their big deals. "I convinced them not to use us as sex slaves. If they see you half naked, they're going to think that you're okay with being a sex slave. You got to put your pants on."

"But, Jam," Jim whined.

"You got to put them on," Jam insisted. "We can't have them deciding to sell us as sex slaves again because you felt hot."

"Damn it," Jim groaned. He shuffled around in the dark, struggling to get the pants on in the cramped environment. Several kicks to the wall and Jim finally managed to pull his pants on most of the way. "They're on."

At this point, Jam was no longer paying any attention to Jim. His mind was already working on another task of monumental importance. It wasn't like Jelly to have her phone off.

"I wonder why Grandma Jelly's phone is off," Jam said. The query wasn't actually directed at Jim, it was directed out into the ether, a more open-ended expression of wonderment.

Jim, being the very literal sort that he was, said, "Maybe her battery died on her."

It was as good an answer as Jam could come up with as well. "Yeah, probably."

Somewhere over the Atlantic, a flight crew was being terrorized by a band of horny, drunk old ladies, just as terrifying as any band of pirates, if not more so. The debauchery on the plane was amplified by the prodigious and free consumption of alcohol, which followed the already heavy drinking they had done at the airport, and emboldened the ladies of Ample Hills further. The freely flowing drinks made the already loose ladies far looser, and many had opened up the top buttons on their shifts and muumuus, displaying their cleavages to the staff.

"Oh, steward," Gertrude called out to a tall, blond, and muscular flight attendant. "Oh, steward, could you come over here?" She motioned for him with the curling of her index finger.

The male flight attendant approached with some trepidation, the way one would approach a lion's cage if they weren't entirely sure the door was properly locked and were certain the lion was hungry for fresh flesh.

"What can I get for you, ma'am?" he asked.

Gertrude wasted no time with small talk and instead went right to sliding her hand up the flight attendant's inseam to his crotch, giving it a good squeeze. "You'll do," she said with a gummy smile.

The flight attendant tried to take a step back but was held in place by the surprisingly formidable grip of an eighty-year-old with arthritis. "What can I get for you, ma'am?" he repeated with an even greater measure of trepidation, his body quickly entering fight or flight mode.

Gertrude gave the man's crotch another squeeze. "I was hoping you would help me fill out an application for the Mile High Club."

The flight attendant stuttered and leaped back, breaking free of Gertrude's grip with a yelp. "I'm sorry, ma'am," he blurted, "we're all out of applications." With that, he disappeared down the aisle back toward the galley and away from the hooting and hollering ladies goading Gertrude on.

Jelly wasn't participating in any of the activities, being far too focused on how she was going to get her grandson and his friend back. She sat sober in the seat across the aisle from Gertrude and next to Vic, whose face was bright red and her eyes closed in dismay. Jelly knew she had to keep her wits about her to make sure everything worked out perfectly. She wasn't worried much about the pirates, but more about keeping all the ladies on point until they got to the pirates. Then all she needed to do was turn them loose while she and Vic rescued Jam and Jim.

"What's wrong with this crew?" Gertrude moaned as she undid some more buttons on her shift. "You would think that the crew for a sexual adventure would be a little more flirtatious and amorous. They're all a bunch of prudes on this flight. Jelly, are we going to a sex resort or a monastery?"

"Don't worry," Jelly said. "You saw the flyers. They promised that all of your sexual fantasies and needs would be met and exceeded. You need to save your energy for all the muscular men who are going to be there. Isn't that right, Vic?" Jelly shot a wink at Vic, who quickly adopted a deeper shade of red.

"Oh, really?" Gertrude purred at Vic and ran her tongue over her toothless gums. "Have you been? Tell me everything."

It was Vic's turn to stutter and stammer. "I just read the same reviews that Jelly did."

Gertrude sighed. "She's so shy, Jelly. The resort will do her good." Gertrude paused for a moment and looked around. "This seems to be taking a long time. I thought Jamaica was a shorter flight. It feels like we've been in the air all night and we aren't anywhere close to landing."

"We'll be there before you know it," Jelly said. Toward the front, another of the ladies was attempting to drag the blond flight attendant into the bathroom. "Say, isn't that Eugenia up there? I think she's trying to sneak off with your steward."

"Over my dead body," Gertrude declared. Quicker than a lioness after her prey, she was out of her seat and bounding down the aisle.

Now that Jelly and Vic were alone, they could speak freely. "I'm worried about this, Jelly," Vic said.

"Worried about what?"

"Aren't you worried that when we land they're going to know we're in Somalia and not Jamaica?"

But Jelly had it covered. "Not at all. They're going to be so drunk and excited they're hardly going to notice where they are as we load them into the bus and head to the pirate village."

"What about when we get to the pirate village? They're going to know it is not a sex resort."

"Victoria, once they see all those muscular men, they're not going to care where they are and they'll be all over them. Then when the pirates are distracted by them, we're going to find Benjamin and Jim and free them."

Vic was still concerned. A lot of the plan rested on how other people responded. "They're pirates and everyone here is just old ladies. What if they can't distract them?"

Jelly watched with bemusement as the fight between Gertrude and Eugenia played out over the blond flight attendant. Each was grabbing at him and trying to pull him their way as he desperately tried to pry himself away from their grasp. "I'm sure we'll be fine," Jelly said as her lips twisted up in a conspiratorial smile.

Faarax was flummoxed. His sister had him in a serious bind. For the last several moves, she had been playing him, giving him a false sense of security, and now she'd sprung her trap. His queen, rooks, and remaining bishop were all exposed, and any move he could make would lead to the eventual sacrifice of several of those pieces. He couldn't see any way out.

She gave him a cocky smile and said, "It is your move, brother, or have you forgotten?"

He hadn't forgotten. He was just trying to stall for time. Like usual, when he was in such a bind and stalling, he attempted to distract his sister while formulating a strategy. "The Americans aren't being cooperative about the ransom. Jam is mocking me every time he is given the phone and keeps asking for a zip code. They're still trying to play me for a fool."

"Have you tried some more persuasive measures in order to get them to be more forthright with the ransom money? Also, make a move," she said, growing more impatient with every passing minute.

Faarax's hand hovered above the chessboard in dismay. Finally, his fingers settled on the queen, and he moved her out of danger. "What more can I do? No one has ever handled The Box so well. It seems as if they are too dumb to realize where they are."

Shadya's hand showed no hesitation, and she quickly took one of Faarax's rooks with her bishop in one sweeping motion, a move that once again put Faarax's queen in danger. "The Americans did like putting on a show to get their way. Maybe we should put on a show for them and let them be the fools for once," Shadya said.

Faarax wasn't following exactly where Shadya was going with the idea. According to Faarax there was no bigger show of force than being forced to endure The Box. "What do you suggest?"

"What I am saying is that if they aren't responding to The Box, we must find something that they will respond to. Perhaps we set up a firing squad for them and see if they are still going to be playing games after that."

Faarax didn't know how to respond. What good would they do to him dead? "What do you mean? We need them alive. Have you gone mad, sister?"

Shadya smiled. Her brother sometimes couldn't appreciate her genius, especially when he was so distracted by losing at chess. "We don't actually shoot them, at least not yet. We just make them think we're going to shoot them so they are more motivated to give us the money. If they continue to play games, we can kill one as a message to the other."

It all suddenly made sense to Faarax. It was so simple and had been plainly in front of him all the while. If only he had been the one who had come up with it. With that matter decided, he looked back to the chess set in front of him and scratched his head as he contemplated his next move. The game playing out on the board certainly didn't have a simple solution.

There wasn't much to do in The Box aside from sit in the dark, pretend it wasn't that hot, and contemplate what was happening to them, or at least do as much contemplating as two people with notoriously short attention spans could do. There was little point in talking to one another either, as they had exhausted all topics of conversation, so they just sat in the dark and sweated out the toxins that had accumulated in their bodies from years of drinking and eating fatty, processed foods.

The silence was finally broken by Jim.

"I think we made a bad choice here, Jam."

It wasn't something that Jam could deny. There had been plenty of questionable or sketchy decisions they had made over the years, but they always seemed to just wash over in the end. "I think you're right, Jim," he admitted.

For all the big deals that had fallen through, of which even Jam had lost count, never had they been put in a position as bad as they were now. Normally, at this juncture, things would have turned around for them. Something would be said or done that would mitigate their losses and bring Jam a little notoriety and set him on his way toward plotting and enacting the next big deal.

Every minute they stayed in The Box, that hope was becoming more and more diminished. This no longer seemed like something Jam would be able to talk himself out of like he usually did. Now it seemed that the only thing he could do was sit in The Box and hope Grandma Jelly would somehow be able to get the money for them to be ransomed.

Since being placed in The Box, Jam had had the fleeting thought, though now more constant than fleeting, that perhaps they should have stayed in Welch and pursued other avenues for their big deals. By comparison, Welch didn't seem as horrible as he normally thought it was.

This quiet reverie was broken after an indiscernible amount of time by the window on the door being slammed open. Sunbeams invaded the darkened space, burning their dilated eyes and causing both

Jam and Jim to yelp in pain while trying to shield themselves from the light.

As Jam's sight adjusted, he was able to glimpse the eyes that stared at him from the outside. They weren't the eyes of Faarax but instead were the eyes of his sister.

Jam mustered a smile. This could be the break that they needed to escape. All he had to do was lay on the charm and convince her to release them. "Shadya," he said. "I'm glad you came. This has been a terrible mistake. You need to help us out."

Shadya's face quickly turned into a mask of worry. "What happened? Why did my brother imprison you? It all happened so fast."

"He thinks we are imposters. But he's wrong. If we don't report back soon, the SEALs are going to be all over the village. You need to let us out now before it's too late."

Jam thought he did a pretty good job of making his case to Shadya, and judging by the look on her face, it seemed she believed his story and was actively considering letting them go. Then all they would need to do is grab the Jeep and hightail it out of town.

That was until Shadya's face turned from that mask of worry into one of mocking laughter. "The only mistake we made is we believed you. We should have killed you both the moment you came here," she said.

"No," Jam said, still trying his best to salvage the situation. "You don't understand, Shadya, this is serious. You have to listen to me before it's too late."

Shadya was having none of it. "No, you need to listen. You tried to play us for fools, but you're the only fools here. You are lucky that my brother is in charge and not me. I would have dealt with you already." She smiled even wider and continued. "But that all ends tomorrow. Wait until you see what my brother has planned for you."

With that, she slammed the window shut and plunged the pair again into the thick darkness of The Box.

"Wait!" Jam yelled. "What does that mean? We're getting the ransom all sorted out. Grandma Jelly is going to take care of it."

Silence was the only answer he received.

"I think we should have stayed back home," Jim said, stating the obvious.

At that moment, Jam could not agree more.

14

"Following a quick investigation it should be noted that no money from anyone important was lost in the mismanagement of the First Bank of Welch, and being as such, no fines or levies shall be imposed for said mismanagement."

—TAKEN FROM A FEDERAL MEMO

After an eighteen-hour flight, the private 747 landed in Mogadishu, Somalia. Though heavily intoxicated and sleep deprived, the ladies of Ample Hills were far too energetic and excited to even think about a moment's rest. They stampeded off the plane and into the private terminal, where they then stampeded the customs booth at the far end. The lone customs agent manning the prestigious post looked at the encroaching crowd of old ladies with a cross of absolute wonderment and horror. It was hardly the sight he was expecting with the arrival of a private jet, and the crowd seemed poised to trample him in their excitement. Luckily, just like cattle being goaded through gates, the old ladies slowed down, if just barely, to conform to the laws of international travel.

"Welcome to Somalia," the exasperated customs agent said as he struggled to stamp the heap of passports thrown at him.

"Somalia?" Gertrude asked Jelly. "I thought we were going to Jamaica?"

Jelly was ever quick on her feet when confronted with an issue like this and declared, "It's just a local term for the area. Don't pay it any mind."

Gertrude accepted this logic, thrust her passport at the agent, and eagerly shuffled through the gate.

The ladies were escorted quickly through the private terminal and out onto the street, where buses painted in black and red were waiting for them. The sides of the buses were emblazoned with bold lettering: XXXVENTURES.

The old ladies squealed in joy and shuffled toward the buses, boarding them with glee at the prospect of the whole host of young men they would soon be ravishing with abandon. The ladies jockeyed for position, each trying to get on first to get the prime seats, which would allow them to be the first off and first into the waiting arms of the big, strong men who awaited them.

If the drivers paid any attention to this extremely odd occurrence for Mogadishu, they gave no sign of it and stayed calm and collected, and kept their eyes ahead of them even as the Ample Hills ladies peppered them with questions. Most of the questions were a variation of "Are you on the menu as well?" This was often joined by the ladies slightly tugging at the driver's uniform before giving out a long sigh and moving down the aisle to an open seat.

Jelly and Vic were the last to board the lead bus, and after a quick head count to make sure none of the ladies had wandered off to sample the local "cuisine," they were ready to be on their way.

"Where are we going?" the bus driver asked, keeping the same stoic, stony face while staring straight ahead.

Jelly pulled out the piece of paper on which she'd scribbled the name of the village. "Tuulada Mussolini," she said.

The stony expression of the driver washed away as his face twisted momentarily in recollection. "Mussolini? You'd think they'd change the name of the village."

"Why would they change it?" Jelly asked in all seriousness.

"Because of the implication."

"What implication?"

"You know, the political implication."

Jelly, much like Jam when confronted with the same statements, had no clue what the driver was talking about. "We don't have time to talk politics," she said. "We have a bunch of ladies looking to experience the time of their lives, so we need to get moving."

The small convoy of buses pulled onto the busy streets of Mogadishu. The dark-tinted windows hid the scenery from the old ladies as they drove down the same roads that Jam and Jim had driven before to get to Tuulada Mussolini.

They passed through the same coastal villages where Jam and Jim had thrown the overly expensive cigarettes to small children. Several of these children lined the roads as the buses rumbled past, cigarettes hanging from their mouths as they eagerly hoped these travelers would also throw them some fresh packs. They puffed away at their smokes as they watched the buses depart without even a fleeting glance from the passengers and had to accept the hard truth that they would need to ration the few remaining cigarettes they had left.

The buses rumbled down the road, which was still stained with the goat giblets that had been inadvertently blown up by Jim. The herder was long gone and already moving on to the next phase of his life: a vast empire of goats that he would rent out.

Throughout the ride, the ladies of Ample Hills chattered on and on about the physical delights they were going to partake in, how many men they wanted at once, and how long they planned it all to last. If there was one thing that was certain about Jelly's plan, it was that the trip had worked tremendously in bringing the ladies of Ample Hills back together. There was no longer any talk of the feud that had previously consumed them, and now they only spoke of positive things as they were again united as a team. All Jelly needed was for them to stick together a little longer so she could rescue her grandson and Jim.

Finally, they came upon that old rusted-out sign that had endured for decades, littered with bullet holes, declaring that they would soon be arriving at their destination.

"Tuulada Mussolini is coming up next," the driver said with a sense of relief.

Jelly wasn't entirely sure about that. She had read the sign as well, and it clearly said Villagio di Mussolini. "Are you certain?" Jelly asked. "The sign says Villagio, not Tuulada."

"Tuulada means the same thing as Villagio," the bus driver said, trying to assure Jelly.

"Does it?"

"One is the Italian word for village and the other is Somali," he said confidently.

"I sure hope you're right," Jelly said, still not entirely convinced.

Jelly and Vic exchanged nervous glances. For the first time since they had embarked on this adventure, Jelly began to worry. She knew her plan was going to work out. Her plans had always worked out in the past, just not necessarily in the ways she intended. Now she just had to hope that all the ladies of Ample Hills would be able to play their parts, keeping the pirates distracted so she could rescue Jam and Jim.

Important events always seem to take place at high noon. Whether this is largely because of artistic license or some sort of mystical force that makes sure all important events converge at the same time is completely unknown. Even in cases where the original event didn't take place at high noon, if there was enough historical significance to the event, the narrative would of course be retroactively changed so that it took place at high noon and the cosmic balance of the universe was restored. Being an event of such scale, it is only right that this particular convergence of the fates took place at noon as well.

Faarax and Ali peeled open the door of The Box shortly before noon. Despite the gruesome conditions that Jam and Jim were held in, they weren't much worse for wear. They had lost a few pounds and if they felt at all ill it was probably the result of sweating out the toxins that a lifetime of poor diet, alcohol, and heavy cigarette smoking causes to the body. If their livers, lungs, and kidneys could thank the pirates for the brief respite, they would have.

The two pirates pulled the two Americans out from The Box, Jam fully dressed despite the heat, and Jim still stripped to the waist.

Jam gave the pirates a million-dollar smile, or in this case, a two-million-dollar smile. "I guess the ransom got paid," Jam said.

Faarax stared him down.

The pirate leader was done with Jam's games and pulled him roughly toward the village center. "There is no longer going to be a ransom. We are going to shoot you."

Jim wasn't having any of it. He struggled against Ali, who was trying to drag him to the village square. "What?" Jim said. "No, no, we're going to get the money—you can't shoot us."

Jam likewise added, "We had a deal. You said you would let us go if we got you ransom money. I'm working on the ransom money!"

"You are playing games! We are going to show you what happens when you play games with us," Faarax said.

The pirates pulled the Americans into the village center, where two posts were erected and the remainder of Faarax's pirate gang was eagerly waiting, AKs at the ready. From the windowsills of the buildings surrounding the square, the wives and girlfriends of the pirates looked on in amusement, waiting for the start of the festivities of an execution. Even a faux one would provide all the excitement they needed. It was a very jovial atmosphere. If it wasn't for the grisly nature of the task at hand, it could easily be imagined that someone would be going around selling hot dogs and sodas to those in the crowd waiting for the main event to begin.

Jam and Jim were quickly lashed to the posts as five pirates stepped forward as the honorary firing squad. The crowd cheered and hollered at the executioners, calling for them to kill the Americans.

Faarax stood to the side and smiled with delight at the sight of Jam and Jim struggling against the posts and crying platitudes that they would get the money. He might have to do a few more of these fake executions just for his own amusement, he thought.

"Today," Faarax addressed the crowd in Somali. "Today, we show these interlopers who came here and tried to play us for fools that we will not tolerate their disrespect and their crimes. We will make a showing of them so all will know of our power and what becomes of those who defy us!"

The crowd cheered even louder as Jam and Jim gave each other another round of nervous glances and struggled against their bonds. However, Jam, being Jam, simply had to know what Faarax was saying. "What was that in English?" he asked.

"I said we are going to kill you," Faarax responded.

"Oh." It was the answer Jam had largely expected, but he'd hoped it would be something else—something like it being all a joke and that they were going to get released.

"Take your positions," Faarax commanded the firing squad.

The firing squad arrayed themselves in front of Jam and Jim, their polished AKs glistening in the sunlight as they held them lazily.

"Ready," Faarax continued.

In military-style unison, the AKs snapped up, their butts locked into their owners' shoulders and the barrels pointed at the Americans.

"Aim," Faarax said. His ruse was about to take effect. He would give the order for his men to fire, and they would launch a volley of shots into the sky over the Americans' heads. He wondered whether the Americans would cry or scream or faint or worse when he gave the fake order to fire.

Just as Faarax raised his arm and was about to swing it down, giving the signal, he was rudely and loudly interrupted by a small convoy of buses barreling into town, their horns honking frantically.

The pirates weren't expecting any visitors, much less a bunch of buses wildly driving in for no apparent reason at all.

The pirates didn't know what to make of this odd turn of events, and looked on in confusion as the XXXventures buses came to a halt in the square, smoke rising from their exhausts as the automatic doors slid open. Nor were they prepared for the tsunami of American old ladies that emerged from those buses.

Resembling hyenas more than humans, the ladies of Ample Hills shrieked and laughed as they flooded the village center. Somali pirates were frozen in confusion, but the old ladies weren't. With the force of a hurricane, they surged over the pirates. Not even the guns could dampen their glee, as they heightened the desires of the old ladies, who had for too long been denied carnal satisfaction.

"Oh, my god!" one lady screamed. "Look how gorgeous they are!"

Gertrude wasted no time and grabbed one pirate by his gun, the one for fun not for fighting, and asked, "Are you as handy with this one as you are with the other one?"

Faarax couldn't tolerate this. He was losing command, and he knew that somehow those damned faux SEALs were responsible. There was no way this distraction was a coincidence. He had to take control again, and this time he wasn't going to just perform a fake execution, he was going to kill the damned Americans for real.

"Shoot them!" Faarax ordered the firing squad. "Shoot them for real!"

Fortunately for Jam and Jim, but unfortunately for Faarax, the firing squad was far too consumed by the mass of flesh that had descended upon them, teasing and tantalizing them with sweet words and even sweeter touches.

"Get them back in The Box!" Faarax shouted to Ali.

Ali was rooted in place. But as he was not yet the focal point of the advances of the old ladies, he almost reluctantly followed Faarax's orders, and together they pulled Jam and Jim from the mass that was quickly descending into a joyful group copulation.

"Hey, wait!" Jam said as he was being pulled back to The Box. "That's my Grandma Jelly! She's coming with the ransom!"

"Quick, get them in The Box!" Faarax said as they unceremoniously shoved the two Americans back into their tiny prison.

By the time Faarax and Ali returned to the village center, they were met with a scene that would make Caligula proud. Bodies in the midst of fornication lay all about them. The sound was an orchestra of wounded elephants. Between the flagrant copulation, two figures emerged in the square. One was a lady who bore a striking resemblance to Jam. The other was much younger, beet red, and kept her eyes toward the sky.

"Who's in charge here?" the older woman asked. "I'm here for my grandson."

Faarax got right in Jam's grandmother's face, careful to avoid the masses of flesh that were writhing in pleasure underfoot. "That would be me."

Jelly's face was reflected in Faarax's sunglasses. "Release my grandson and his friend now."

Faarax gave her a cold, calculated smile. "Do you have the ransom money? You can have them when you give me the four million dollars."

It was Jelly's turn to smile. "No," she said. "You're just going to let them go and let us get on our way."

The pirate leader was done with games and this family that seemed to defy him at every turn. Soon he wasn't going to have two prisoners for ransom, he would have dozens. "Seize them!" he ordered his men. "Seize them all!"

Faarax had a look of supreme confidence on his face, while Jelly's was masked with fear and anxiety, her eyes darting around, waiting for the pirates to swarm her. But when nothing happened, the expressions switched, with Jelly's holding supreme confidence and Faarax's fear and apprehension.

None of the pirates broke from their couplings, or in some cases triplings.

Faarax would not be defied. He would have them all in chains, even if they had to do it one granny at a time. "Ali, seize them! Start with these two."

Ali was otherwise preoccupied, with two grannies lavishing him with attention in the corner of the village center.

When all else fails, it is sometimes necessary to resort to rather desperate measures. "Doctor," Faarax said, "help me seize these women."

Unfortunately for Faarax, even the Doctor was preoccupied with two old ladies who were fawning over him like schoolgirls, complete with giggling, as he explained his theories on aquatic evolution.

Jelly put a hand on her hip and leaned to one side with a look that said, *What are you going to do now, hotshot?*

Faarax wasn't one to back down, but without his pirates in tow, he wouldn't be able to detain all of the ladies. He would now need to buy himself some time to figure out a plan.

"Let's discuss this," Faarax said. "Follow me."

Jelly looked to Vic and smiled. "I look forward to it."

Faarax grabbed both Ali and the Doctor by their ears, pulling them away against the protesting ladies, as well as the protests of Ali and the Doctor, and toward the church.

Shadya was already waiting for them in the main church hall, having seen everything from the window. She was pacing the marble floor incessantly as her brother arrived.

"What's going on, brother?" Shadya demanded.

"You already saw what is going on," Faarax fired back.

Jelly and Vic exchanged bemused smiles. "What did you want to discuss?" Jelly said.

Faarax collapsed into his seat and set them with a withering gaze. "So is this your plan? To occupy my men while discussing terms for your grandson?" he said.

There is a saying that no plan survives initial contact with the enemy. But even Jelly could admit that the grand distraction caused in the village center was far better than any skullduggery she could have done sneaking around looking for Jam and Jim. She was now in a position of power, and she intended to use it to free the two boys.

"Exactly my plan," Jelly said as she sat across from Faarax. "Now, will you release Benjamin and James?"

"There is still the matter of the ransom," Faarax insisted.

Jelly shook her head. "There isn't going to be a ransom. You're going to just let them go."

Faarax laughed. "I will have you all chained up and in my prison before I release them for free."

"How is that working out for you?" Vic said.

Faarax cracked his knuckles as he leaned back in his chair. "They're old ladies. They can't keep my men distracted for much longer."

"Oh," Jelly said. "You would be surprised just how much energy they have and how long they can keep going for."

Faarax rapped his fingers across the armrest of the chair. "Are you so certain of that? Maybe you should pay a reduced rate. Say only two million for the two."

"Zero," Jelly held firm.

Faarax looked to both Ali and the Doctor. Both seemed very eager to get back out there and enjoy more of the tiny sample they had been treated to. "A million for both and we will be done with it."

"What are you doing, Faarax? Are you going to give in to them?" Shadya said in Somali.

"Don't question me, sister. I want to be done with them and get them all out of here. The Americans have wasted too much of our time already," he answered her.

Jelly shook her head. "You get nothing. Well, not nothing. You get whatever is left of my five hundred thousand dollars and we will go."

The pirate leader didn't have time to rebuke the grandmother before the doors of the church burst open and the accumulated mass of the wives and girlfriends of his men came barging in. This clearly wasn't a friendly social call for some afternoon tea coupled with a light snack. The women were out for blood and seemed quite willing to extract blood from anyone who got in their way.

"What are you doing, Faarax?" a girlfriend demanded.

"Why are the streets filled with old whores fucking our men?" a wife demanded.

The rest took up the same cry, demanding explanations from Faarax—explanations he didn't have.

"I have this all under control," he attempted to assure them, though he himself was hardly sure of the situation. "We are just discussing the ransom of the Americans now and then everyone will be on their way."

"This doesn't look like it is under control," a girlfriend said. "We call to our men, but they are ignore us while they keep fucking those old ladies—old ladies who are only here because of those Americans in The Box."

Faarax wasn't used to having his authority undermined, and in the past such an outbreak would have come with swift and brutal retribution. But now, that option wasn't on the table anymore. His men were all occupied with the pleasures of the flesh, and their women were incensed. He wouldn't be able to make it out of the church alive before they tore him limb from limb.

"If I let them go for free," Faarax said, "do you promise to take all the old ladies with you?"

Jelly smiled. "Of course."

"Immediately?" Faarax said hopefully.

"It may take some convincing, but as soon as you let Benjamin and Jim go, I'll get them on the buses."

"You can't be considering this," Shadya said. "Have you lost your mind? Think of the ransom we can get for all of them."

"Do you want to deal with all of *them*?" Faarax said as he motioned toward the angry mob of women. "Do you want to tell them to let their men keep fucking the old ladies until they're tired out so we can imprison them?"

Shadya slunk back, also not willing to accept the wrath of the assembled mob.

"It is agreed then," Faarax said as he motioned toward Ali. "Go and bring the two Americans to me."

It took some time for Ali to return with Jam and Jim, as they had to navigate the fleshy minefield that was Tuulada Mussolini since the arrival of the old ladies. Not only did they need to make sure they weren't stepping on anyone in the middle of a carnal act, they also needed to dodge horned-up old ladies looking for fresh meat after exhausting the stamina of their previous partners.

After all their trials and tribulations, Jam had a huge smile plastered across his face. Despite any fears and anxieties he'd had after being placed in that most undesirable prison, he knew that with Grandma Jelly there everything would be all right and he would be able to get his share of the treasure.

Jelly and Vic grabbed Jam and Jim, pulling them into a tight group hug, a hug that left Jim squirming as he attempted to break from their embrace.

"My sweet Benjamin," Jelly said as she squeezed the hell out of him. "Are you okay?"

"I'm fine," Jam said with a sense of relief. "I kind of want a Busch Light, though. This whole place is dry."

"Somalia?" Vic said as they finally released the two from their death grips before grabbing Jam by the shoulders and shaking him roughly. "What the hell were you thinking when you decided to come here of all places?"

"They got a huge treasure here, Vic! Just wait and see. We are all going to be rich when we get out of here."

Faarax cleared his throat to remind them that this wasn't a cheerful reunion at the airport after a long trip and was still a release of hostages in exchange for negotiated terms, be it terms that didn't include as much money as he'd been hoping for. It was still a serious matter and should be treated as such.

With the attention finally on him, Faarax said, "After speaking with your grandmother, we have reached an agreement that the two of you will leave immediately and we can put this all behind us."

Jam looked to Jim. He wasn't about to leave so close to finally closing a big deal. "No," he said simply.

The entirety of the room was nonplussed. Everyone stared at Jam. Faarax, Ali, Shadya, the Doctor, the assembled wives and girlfriends, and Grandma Jelly and Vic all stared with that same look of disbelief. Even Jim.

"No?" Faarax asked.

"What do you mean no?" Vic said.

Jam shook his head. "No," he affirmed. "We came here for a treasure and were promised a portion of the treasure. I'm not going to leave without the treasure."

"Are you crazy?" Vic said. "We need to get out of here. You can't just demand the treasure."

Jam crossed his arms and looked at Faarax. "We made a deal," he said. "I want at least some of the treasure or I'm not leaving."

Ali, the Doctor, and Shadya all looked to Faarax.

There was little that Faarax could do in that moment. He shrugged and said in Somali to the others, "I think it is more important that we get them all out of here. We can let them have some of the treasure if it means things go back to normal."

It seemed to be a perfectly reasonable answer to Ali and the Doctor. All they wanted at this juncture was a return to normalcy. The state of affairs since the arrival of the Americans had thrown everything for a loop, and the arrival of the old ladies made the situation even odder and more chaotic. Once they were gone, they could go back to the rather stable and reasonable life of piracy that they were so accustomed to.

For Shadya, though, it was entirely unreasonable. "Are you the crazy one now?" Shadya screamed at Faarax. "They have been playing you for a fool this entire time, and now you're not just letting them go but you're also going to reward them?"

Vic poked Jam in the ribs. "Who's she?" she whispered.

"Oh," Jam said, "that's Shadya, his sister." Then he quickly added, "She tried to seduce me."

For the first time, Vic's face turned red from something other than utter embarrassment. She stormed up to Shadya and said, "Hello."

Shadya barely turned to face Vic before the haymaker punch hit her in the jaw. Shadya's neck snapped back, and a tooth went flying, which was followed by a trail of blood and spittle. A collective "Ooh" flowed down the church hall as everyone waited to see what would happen next, but Shadya had been knocked out cold. Vic shook her hand loose, dispersing the waves of pain that flowed up her arm from the hit, and returned to Jam with a smug smile across her face.

"Damn, Vic," Jam said. "That was impressive. Where did you learn to hit like that?"

Vic smiled. "There's a lot you don't know about me." Then, without thinking, she popped up on her tippy toes and planted her lips on Jam's.

The only thing Jam could muster was a "Wow."

Faarax cleared his throat again, trying to get attention brought back to him, and with some reluctance said, "Would you agree to leave if we allowed you to take all the treasure you can carry out with your hands?"

It wasn't exactly what they'd negotiated, but it seemed very reasonable to Jam. After all, you could carry a lot of gold, and all you needed was a small amount of it to be a millionaire. "Deal," he said.

Finally, Jam thought, one of his big deals had finally paid off, in a technical and roundabout way, of course, but those were the best ways to be right and to win.

Jam rubbed his hands eagerly as he led Jim, Jelly, and Vic to the bunker and its treasure, this time without any pirates lying in wait to jump them just as they were about to open the door. "You guys are going to be blown off your feet when you see all this gold," he said. "General Fonzi said there is thirty million in gold."

'Where did they get it all from?" Vic asked.

"They got it from ransom they were paid to release hostages, and now we are going to get their ransom money," Jam said.

Finally, they approached the bunker and its door with multiple locks. Jam beamed back at the three and pointed to the door like a little kid pointing at toys at a Toys R Us.

"Here's the treasure," Jam said. "Jim, do the honors and open it up for us."

Jim ran up to the door, the oversized key ring jingling with every step, as he tried the first lock to no avail. He had the wrong key, again. He fumbled through each key until he finally found the proper one for the topmost lock. This cumbersome process repeated itself again and again for each lock, even for the last lock, whose key should had been obvious after all the previous attempts, but given the haphazard order in which the keys were arranged, was far from obvious.

Jim went to open the door, but Jam quickly stepped in front of him and faced his grandmother and friends like a sideshow performer trying to coax marks into their booth. "Now," Jam said. "Now is the moment you've all been waiting for. Our big deal is finally coming through, and soon we are going to have all our champagne wishes and caviar dreams."

Jim clapped sloppily and hooted, only stopping when he realized that no one else was taking part and then sheepishly looked down.

The silence did nothing to deter Jam, and he continued, "With opening this door, we are going to be opening a new door into our lives—"

"Come on, Jam," Vic said, interrupting his monologue. "Just open the door already."

Jam spun around with a flutter. He stretched his arms out, clasped his hands together, and cracked his knuckles. He was going to make this a big show, whether anyone else wanted a big show or not. "Vic," he said, "make sure to get your phone out and record this. People are going to want to see how we made it big."

With a roll of her eyes, she pulled out her phone and focused the camera on Jam.

Once Jam was confident that Vic was recording, he cracked his knuckles again, then gripped the bunker door handle, and with a cheesy smile plastered on his face, swung the door open.

It was dark inside. Even with the sun pouring in from the outside, it barely illuminated any of the interior. Jam fumbled around, trying to find a light. Finally, his hand found an ancient switch and flipped it.

With a pop, the first fluorescent light flicked into life and row after row of lights snapped into existence. The bunker was far larger than any of them had thought, stretching deep into the hill. Not only was it far bigger than they had imagined, it was far more packed with treasure than they had thought possible. Every inch, aside from a narrow passage that led all the way to the back, was completely packed, denying any movement or give.

Jam's jaw went slack, and he stared wide-mouthed and wide-eyed at what lay before him just as Alexander the Great had centuries before upon reaching the end of the world and realizing that there were no more worlds for him to conquer.

"What the fuck," Jam said.

"What is it, Benjamin?" Jelly asked.

Jam didn't know what to say. His whole body was numb. "It's the treasure."

"What about it?" Vic asked.

There were no words to describe what was in front of him— absolutely nothing at all came to mind. Not a joke, not a curse, not even a basic description of what he was seeing. "Look." It was all Jam could say.

They crowded around him to take a look at the treasure they were soon to be in possession of. And one by one they each adopted the same slack-jawed look he had at what they beheld. It certainly wasn't what they were expecting to find. It certainly wasn't anything anyone would be expecting to find in such a heavily guarded and locked location. In fact, it wasn't anything that anyone would normally conceivably think about protecting and being so possessive of at all.

The bars of gold they had expected to find weren't there. Nor were there any bars of silver. Nor would they be consoled with jewelry or diamonds, or even stacks of cash. There wasn't any artwork to speak of that would be worth a vast sum.

The only thing in that huge bunker, something that could conceivably be considered artwork by a certain discerning eye, was row after row of designer blue jeans. The type that was worth several hundred dollars each.

"Oh," Vic said. She put her hand on Jam's shoulder. "I'm so sorry."

Jam just stood there staring at rack after rack of jeans. His mind was stuck in a composite loop rolling over and over everything that had transpired over the past few weeks. All the missed opportunities while he wasted all that time on this whole Somalia thing. It just wasn't fair. In the end, it all bounced back like it always did. He found himself again right where he'd started. But still, he'd been conned by the treasure, or lack thereof.

"I'll go round up the ladies so we can leave," Jelly said.

Jam chewed on his lip and mulled over everything, and then with a final resolute voice, said, "Fuck it." He ripped jeans from the racks and started throwing them over his shoulder.

"Come on, ladies!" Jelly hollered across the square to the cavorting ladies of Ample Hills. "It is time to pack up and get back on the bus."

Eugenia and Virginia had a pirate sandwiched on a bench and were eagerly exchanging kisses with him. Any pretense of their previous feud had evaporated with their arrival at the "sex resort." An outsider would have thought they were the best of friends, and it was quite possible that they were now even more than just friends.

"So soon?" Eugenia asked with a sigh.

"Sorry, ladies," Jelly said. "It's just a hit and run this time. We have to get going."

It was Virginia's turn to sigh. "But we only got a taste of the fun."

Eugenia and Virginia burst into a fit of giggles.

Jelly smiled. She always got her way, even if the first plan, or first five plans, didn't go her way. She always had another angle to work, and she always came out ahead of the game. This just proved her right, and it was even better that she managed to not only put an end to all the squabbling at Ample Hills, but to roll that into rescuing her grandson at the same time.

"Well, hurry and finish up with him and then get on the bus," Jelly said.

"We'll be there soon enough," Eugenia said.

"Don't worry about us. You need to worry about the other ladies, they're all over the place," Virginia added.

Virginia could not have been more right as Jelly departed on her quite unenviable task of herding the cats, or in this case, cougars, of Ample Hills away from their chiseled men and toward the buses that would take them back home to the mundane existence of Welch, Iowa.

It only took a few moments of the 747 being in the air before the ladies were back in action and up to their old games. The brief furlough in Somalia had done nothing to sate their voracious appetites and instead seemed to have only amplified their desires tenfold. It is often said that if you get a taste of something, you start craving it more and more. This was certainly true for the ladies of Ample Hills. They had just gotten a taste of coital relations that didn't involve a direct exchange of money, and now they were hooked.

Ladies hooted and hollered and compared stories from the "sex resort": which gigolo was the largest (in all senses and directions), which gigolo lasted the longest, which had the best mouth game. These exploits were then followed up by great bouts of laughter and catcalls. Beleaguered flight attendants, still not recovered from the escapades on the flight over, marched up and down the rows, offering complimentary drinks while dodging errant hands trying to cop quick feels.

Over the din of the revelry was the bear in the cabin. Jim lay back in his seat, and the voluminous snores emerging almost, just almost, drowned out the sound of everything else that was occurring around him.

Then there was Jam. He sat between Jelly and Vic, forlorn, staring at the back of the seat in front of him, but the screen embedded there was turned off. There was nothing in the world at that moment that could possibly cheer him up. Another big deal ruined, foiled at the last minute. Sure, he had gotten the jeans out of it and they were good jeans at that, but the jeans weren't going to get him his millions. His mind rolled over in deep thought as he tried to find the next angle to work. Maybe the flavored-water business wasn't such a bad idea after all. In his mind it was still the Starbucks of water—it could make them billions. All he needed to do was find some investors willing to front the money and open up the stores, and then he could just sit back and watch the cash roll in until he could fill a vault with gold coins to go swimming in.

"Cheer up, Jam," Vic said as she gave his hand a squeeze.

"You don't get it, Vic," Jam said. "We spent all this time and money on this big deal. And for what? A bunch of jeans. I could have been working on other big deals that would have paid off."

"It could have been worse. Much worse."

Jam's lip curled up in a small smile. "I guess."

From across the aisle, Gertrude leaned in to speak with Jelly. "That was wonderful," she said. "It was just what we all needed."

Jelly gave her a quick nod and a smile. "I knew that would hit the spot and get everyone talking again."

"I need to know something, though," Gertrude said. "What were your grandson and his friend doing there?"

"I sent them ahead to make sure everything was set up just right and to establish the theme," Jelly said in an effortless lie.

Gertrude slapped Jelly on the arm. "That was so funny. Them pretending it was Somalia and that they were pirates. I laughed and laughed when the first one tried to tell me where we were."

A certain predatory look came over Gertrude's eyes as she spotted the same blond male flight attendant who had denied her before, making his way down the aisle of the cabin. She waited for him to get closer and then pounced, her hand shooting out and grabbing him firmly by the crotch.

"Oh, steward, did you get any more applications for the Mile High Club?" she purred at him.

The flight attendant squirmed and winced but couldn't escape the grasp of Gertrude. "No, ma'am," he said with a shaky voice. "We're still out of applications."

Gertrude gave his crotch one final squeeze, which made the flight attendant emit a subtle yelp, before releasing her grip. "That's a pity," she said. "I always wanted to join the Mile High Club."

Free of Gertrude's surprisingly strong grasp, the flight attendant retreated quickly, but ever slightly bow-legged, down the aisle of the jet into the galley. The other ladies cooed at him as he passed, asking if he needed them to kiss his boo-boo better. Others slapped his ass and gave him words of encouragement and other more obscene and lewd offers.

Jelly watched this whole episode play out with some small sense of amusement. Jam was still, however, in his own world, staring at the back of the seat in front of him.

Vic's mind worked a mile a minute to formulate a plan of her own in regard to the whole situation. "I think I know how to cheer you up," she said, resolving to put her plan into motion.

"How?" Jam asked.

She grabbed him by the hand and pulled him into the aisle. "You're going to join the Mile High Club."

"But, Vic," Jam whined, "the flight attendant said they were all out of applications. How am I going to join if they don't have any?"

"I think I have an application in here somewhere for you."

The ladies of Ample Hills erupted in uproarious laughter and cat-calls as the normally reserved Vic led Jam down the aisle. Their chants even awakened the notoriously deep sleeper Jim, who looked on in utter amazement, and slight confusion, at the sight that was taking place before him.

Vic opened the bathroom door, causing Jam a moment of hesitation. "Vic," he said, "I don't have to use the bathroom. I thought we were going to join the Mile High Club."

"Just shut up," she said as she shoved him inside.

15

"The recently renamed coastal village of Tuulada Faarax is leading the way in fashion this season with the release of some truly exemplarily crafted jeans. We wait with bated breath for what will come next out of this new fashion mecca."

—*The Somali Fashion Times*

Burgers, hot dogs, and steaks were tossed on the grill in the yard behind Jam's house. It was a Welch tradition that whenever someone went on a trip, a party must be thrown when they returned home. This did not occur very often, as most Welchers were rather uneasy about the prospect of leaving the town, even for a short while, and of those who did indeed leave, few of them had any intention of coming back. So it was more of a gathering to thank the prodigal Welchers for making the decision to come back home despite there being an entire world out there.

Vic draped her arm around Jam as he quite clumsily tossed the meat on the grill. He was hardly a grill master, but even he couldn't completely screw up the task, not even with Jim's misguided attempts to help.

"Isn't this more fun than chasing some big deal?" Vic teased Jam.

Jam couldn't argue with Vic, but he only gave a noncommittal shrug.

Vic wasn't going to accept such a shrug as an answer. She pinched Jam's elbow. "Come on, you can admit it," she said.

"Stop, Vic," Jam said. "You're going to make me burn the dogs."

Her fingers slipped past his arm and into his side, tickling him. "Well, then just admit that this is more fun."

"Okay, I admit it!" he squealed. "Being with you is better than any big deal."

Vic mocked a fake swoon and then gave him a little kiss on the cheek and cracked open beers for him and Jim before she helped Jelly greet the first guests.

Everyone was dressed, again, in usual Welch fashion, almost identically. But gone were the drab khakis that had dominated for generations. They had been replaced with the stunning and stylish blue jeans that had been liberated from Somalia.

The ladies of Ample Hills were the first to arrive, as always, and were eager to sample some fresh meat, of both varieties. Then came Jam's neighbors, always ready to partake in a good summer barbecue, their arms laden with drinks and sides. Even Adam McKnight was present, because in Welch, when you are invited to a party, even if you aren't sure why, you are obligated to go. Anything else would be a violation of the social contract.

Beer went fast as Jam and Jim chugged them down. It was one of the things they'd missed the most while in Somalia. Now that they were back in Welch, though, the pair dove right back into drinking as quickly as a gull dives into water. They'd spent their first night home getting sloshed and had kept up the drinking pace ever since. After all, it was a celebration of their glorious—well, not so glorious—return. But for all intents and purposes, it was glorious in other ways to Jam.

As he cracked open a fresh beer, for the first time in his life he noticed Welch for what it was. Sure, the houses were cookie-cutter, but each held its own little charms.

Jam jabbed Jim in the ribs with a pair of meat tongs. "Did you ever notice that?" Jam asked.

Jim let out an "oof" before answering. "Notice what?"

"All that. Everything with the houses."

Jam motioned with the tongs toward the houses across the way. There was the house with the blue trim across the awning. There was the house next door with the rather impressive collection of garden gnomes dotting every inch of the perfectly manicured lawn. Then there was the house on the other side of Jam's with the gazebo in the yard, and the ornate green curtains that hung in the windows.

"What?" Jim said.

"Did you ever notice them before? The gazebo and everything?" Jam replied.

"Oh, those?" Jim gave a shrug. "Yeah, those have been like that since forever."

Jam took everything in around him, looking for the differences he had willfully ignored before.

The cars parked on the street also took on their own glimmer. Sure, they were still all American made, but the matte gray Jam had always imagined them to be actually represented a wider spectrum of colors—light gray, medium gray, dark gray, and occasionally taupe or even silver—that weren't all as identical as he had always pictured them.

Even the people Jam had so derisively referred to as boring took on new light after recent events. Sure, the old ladies of Ample Hills were complete horn dogs trying to bone everything and anything that moved, but they each had their own charms and talents, as shown by the cakes, pies, and knickknacks that were brought in and laid on the communal table. Virginia's famous apple pie held center stage, sans cocaine, as per the orders of Jelly. Jam could even venture some forgiveness, just a little forgiveness, for Adam McKnight. After all, McKnight was only doing his job. Not to mention that Jam really was the one responsible for getting McKnight suspended from school because of the death of the school turtle.

For once, Jam didn't despise the inane weather-based greeting that was slung in every encounter. It was all part of the charm of Welch—a tiny slice of America that the rest of the country and the world had forgotten. It had taken all the good, the bad, and the ugly of Somalia for him to finally come to appreciate Welch.

Above all, Jam realized he didn't need big deals in order to be happy. He had been looking for happiness in all the wrong places. Happiness wasn't a destination—it was a state of mind. His eyes had been closed to everything that was around him for so long that he'd lost sight of what truly was important in life: things that Vic and Jelly already knew and embraced. Even Jim, when not being dragged along on Jam's deals, knew the secret to it all. Jam just had to open his eyes and let happiness come to him. He looked to Vic and smiled. Happiness had been just around the corner all along.

For the first time in a long while, Jam's mind wasn't working on the next big deal that would bring them their champagne wishes and caviar dreams.

EPILOGUE

"Sure, if one kid dies on a roller coaster, everyone is all up in arms and demanding answers, but no one ever talks about all the thousands of kids that rode it without incident prior to that."

—Poorly chosen words of a chief engineer on the witness stand

"If possible please make a legal U-turn," the digitized voice of the GPS stated for the twentieth time already. If the device could manifest any personification of annoyance for failure to follow its directions, it would have surely levied that dissatisfaction against Jam and his failure to listen to simple instructions. Such willful denial of perfectly calculated and logical suggestions on how to proceed would then surely be used as one of the many justifications for a potential robotic uprising against humans. After all, if they can't follow simple routes, how could they be expected to govern the world?

"Benjamin, sweetie, maybe you should listen to the GPS before we get lost," Jelly said from the backseat.

"The GPS lies, Grandma Jelly," Jam said as he switched the annoying device off. "It purposely takes you through high-traffic areas so that you spend more money on gas, and it encourages you to pull over and start browsing stores so you spend more money. I'm sure this is the right way."

"That doesn't sound right," Vic said from the back.

"It's all true," Jam insisted. "Plus, they track where you're going so they can use it for marketing and stuff. It's all really sneaky. That's why you got to mess with it by ignoring it and going your own way to throw off the algorithms."

"Jam," Vic sighed. "It still knows where you're going because you have the thing on and it knows what road you're on."

"Jam's right," Jim said as he played with the sun visor above him. "I read about it somewhere."

"Really?" Vic questioned. "Did you actually read about it or are you just saying you read about it?"

"I read. It just takes me a really long time," Jim said.

"Maybe we should ask for directions from someone," Jelly suggested.

Vic peered out the window toward the endless rows of cornfields. "That's if we find anyone before we run out of gas."

The car rumbled down the old back roads of a half-forgotten stretch for what seemed like hours, but in actuality was only about twenty minutes since their previous conversation, before they came upon a sign for the next exit and the attractions present.

It was a sign that proudly advertised the fact that the exit featured America's one and only museum on the history of mannequins. Even better, for those who are fascinated by mannequins and their history, at least, the museum was open for business.

"Just get off here and ask for directions," Vic suggested as the exit quickly approached.

"Nope, nope, nope," Jam said. "Not happening."

"Why not?" Vic asked.

"Mannequins give me the creeps," Jim said. "Just standing there all motionless and staring at you. It's super creepy."

"Yep," Jam agreed. "That's how horror movies start. We go into that museum for directions, and next thing you know we're going to be locked in and all those mannequins are going to come alive and we'll need to fight our way out. I'm not letting that happen."

Before Vic could respond with a perfectly reasonable and logical counterargument, Jam floored the accelerator and sped on by the exit, dashing any hopes of seeing the history of mannequins and getting directions.

As they continued, the road itself became shakier and more forgotten. It was hardly the type of road that saw much traffic and was quickly written off the lists of repairs for an overworked and underfunded transportation department. It was after more than a dozen bumpy miles that they finally came across a sign for another exit.

The sign was not dissimilar from the sign in Somalia. It was metal, old, and half rotted away and likewise filled with bullet holes. Its lettering read:

SPACEY MOUNTAIN AMUSEMENT PARK
1 MILE AHEAD

"Benjamin," Jelly said, "why don't we pull over there and ask for directions?"

"I know where we're going, I don't need to ask for directions," Jam insisted.

"Jam, just pull over and ask. Plus, I want to stretch my legs, anyway," Vic added.

"Come on, Jam," Jim said. "I want to see the amusement park."

"Fine, I'll pull over," Jam said.

At the next exit, they pulled off, and almost immediately they could see the tops of the rides of Spacey Mountain above the rows of corn that surrounded them.

Spacey Mountain was very much what someone would expect from the backwoods of Iowa. It was the type of place that skated by on name recognition of the renowned ride at the theme parks owned by the even-more-renowned mouse, barely skirting the laws of trademark infringement and always one lawsuit away from an injunction order demanding the name be changed. It was the type of park where the primary business came from careless parents misreading the name and booking their vacations around what they thought was a famous location and then proceeding to disappoint their children.

The signature attraction was the mountain, a brown affair that was topped with multiple rocket ships blasting off in multiple directions. But when the Welchers arrived, the rockets were nearly rusted away, and from the lack of any movement or noise, it was clear the place was long abandoned and out of service.

At the entrance was a large sign:

AMUSEMENT PARK FOR SALE
OPEN HOUSE TODAY

Beneath the sign stood a man in a perfectly tailored brown and silver plaid suit with an all-confident smile. No sooner did the car pull to a stop than the suited man sprang into action. He raced up to the car door just as Jim was lowering the window, slicked back his hair, and in one smooth motion grabbed Jim's hand in a quick shake before Jim could even realize what was happening. It was a tight, double-handed shake, the type of shake that didn't end until the initiator decided it was going to end. It was a shake that spoke volumes about the suited man's intentions. He was going to have a chat with you, and you weren't leaving until he was done with his spiel.

"Howdy, folks," the suited man said, his smile plastered across his face even as he spoke. "Timmy's the name, real estate's my game. Here for the open house? You folks came at the right time. We had plenty of interested buyers already, but we're looking for that just-right buyer that's going to put the right shine on the place."

"No thanks, we just need directions, if you could help us out with those," Vic said from the back seat. "We're kind of in a hurry."

Timmy was quite seasoned at salesmanship and always had a response ready for any negative comment that could be levied his way. He didn't even flinch as he launched into the next part of his spiel:

"That's great. Because the tour is only going to take a few minutes, and believe you me, you're not going to miss out on this opportunity once I tell you about it. You're going to say, 'Timmy, you sure did us a solid with this one, I can't believe we nearly passed this all up.'"

"It would be rude not to at least take the tour," Jam said.

"That's the spirit," Timmy chimed in. "Now come on out of that car so you can get a real look at the place."

The pitch didn't stop as the four got out. Timmy was like a used car salesman and knew the key was to never stop talking. Silence meant the customers had a chance to speak and think, and neither of those were good for business when your product was less than stellar.

"The good thing is," Timmy said, "that this place has only been closed for a few years now. So all the rides are still operational and ready to go as soon as you're ready to pull the trigger and swoop in and make this place yours."

Jam and Jim were caught up in it, eagerly nodding at each other. "How many rides do you have here?" Jam asked.

Timmy snapped his fingers and somehow his smile managed to grow even wider. "I'll tell you what we got, we have five roller coasters, with our pride and joy being the pinnacle, and namesake of the park, Spacey Mountain. Three water rides and thirty other attractions, and that is not counting all the concession stands and all the other money-making operations you'll have going on."

"Hey," Vic interrupted. "I remember this place. This is the park where all those kids got killed on the roller coaster."

Timmy's smile went flat for the briefest moment, then came back brighter than ever. "Just one kid!" he said. "And that wasn't even here. You know how those bigwigs are in the mainstream media. That happened on the ride with a similar name at the park owned by that silly mouse. But the media doesn't want you to know that, so they go blame it all on some little theme park out here in Iowa so those corporate bigwigs don't have to account for what they're doing. It is all fake news—fake news, I tell you."

"Fake news," Jam said.

"Fake news," Jim parroted as he nodded along.

Even Jelly was buying into it. "That's horrible what they did to this poor place," the grandmother said.

Timmy picked up the pace with his speaking, reeling in on the closing. "Now, I'm not going to try to wow you with anything here, or make up some preposterous claims, but numbers, they don't lie. This here used to be the pride and joy of Iowa. A thousand people came through these gates every day, each paying ten dollars to get in. A hot dog cost eight dollars, a soda five. That's not even counting all the sales of souvenirs, parking, and concessions that are going to be rolling in daily." Timmy snapped his fingers and pointed toward the rockets atop the mountain. "You don't need to be a rocket scientist to figure out that math and know that those are big bucks."

Something deep in the back of Jam's mind came to life. It was a desire that had been dormant for a very long time—not too long in actuality, only a few weeks, but for Jam that was a very long time. This desire was always near and dear to his heart, a flame that burned inside him and was only dampened by his trip to Somalia and his newfound relationship with Vic, but never truly extinguished. It had merely been suppressed and was again slowly growing, waiting for the opportunity for the next big deal. And here was that big deal all laid out for him, ready to go and ready to bring him those champagne wishes and caviar dreams.

"How much are you asking for the place?" Jam asked.

END

Addison J. Chapple Collection
(Comedies and Romantic Comedies)

ISBN: 978-1-933769-78-3

When NSA intelligence uncovers a terrorist plot involving the Dykes with Bikes motorcycle gang, two female cops must pretend to be gay and infiltrate the gang.

ISBN: 978-1-933769-76-9

Trying to outdo their stuffy friends, a couple plans the "wedding of the century" in the tiny island nation of Milagros. But when civil war breaks out, the true meaning of love and friendship will be tested as the bride, groom, and all of their guests are sent running for their lives.

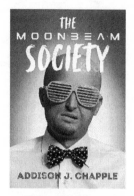

ISBN: 978-1-933769-80-6

When her father wills his money to a whacky organization, a scientist must prove the organization is fraudulent to gain her inheritance.

ISBN: 978-1-933769-72-1

Inspired by a hilarious true story, when a brilliant but bankrupt con man chooses an aging French aristocratic family as his next mark, he must convince them to engage in an all-out battle with an enemy that doesn't actually exist in order to swindle them out of their entire family fortune.

ISBN: 978-1-64630-018-1

When the world's leading travel blogger returns to a B&B she blasted a year ago, the B&B owner must ensure everything is perfect or go bankrupt.